Séance

By
Mike Walsh

Book One
in the *Trilogy of Evil*

Abyss Books
Published by Indigo Sea Press
Winston-Salem

Abyss Books
Indigo Sea Press
302 Ricks Drive
Winston-Salem, NC 27103

First Abyss Books edition published
June, 2016
Abyss Books, Moon Sailor, and all production design
are trademarks of Indigo Sea Press, used under license.

For information regarding bulk purchases of this book,
digital purchase and special discounts, please contact the publisher
at indigoseapress@gmail.com

Cover design by Stacy Castanedo
Manufactured in the United States of America
ISBN 978-1-63066-430-5

To Terri, my other self, who lights up my life.

PART ONE

Chapter 1

Laura Whitney had been blind for almost eight months. The only remedy available to regain her sight in both eyes was a dual corneal transplant. Now, at last, the time for that procedure had come. The reception of the cornea from an anonymous donor was not only a chance to see again but also a way to redeem her life.

Since the terrible damning day when she was robbed of her sight, despairing torment dominated her existence. As an artist, in her mind's eye she had painted hundreds of canvases that could not be fulfilled in reality. But now, finally, a door had opened.

The much-anticipated procedure to replace one of two corneas would take place today. Laura was ready for her new eyes.

Frank, her husband, accompanied her to the New York City office of the ophthalmologist, Dr. Hudson, where the operation was to be performed. She looked so forlorn, he thought, so helpless. He put his arms around her and affectionately hugged her.

"It'll be all right. You'll do fine," he said, keeping a cheeriness in his voice. He kissed her good-bye, loving, longingly.

A nurse came and helped Laura into a wheelchair. Frank watched as she disappeared around a corridor, feeling a sudden wave of anxiety. He shrugged off the thought.

A few hours. Nothing to do but wait and pray. Pray. He had never been strong on religion. But today he prayed. He walked along Fifth Avenue to Saint Patrick's, entered and sat in back of the great cathedral. His thoughts engulfed him and his mind raced with the circumstances that brought Laura and him to this moment....

1

* * *

Eight months before...

Sipping a beer, Frank Whitney watched from the deck of their beach house as Laura set up her portable easel, folding chair and watercolor paraphernalia on the sand. They were on their small parcel of beachfront property on the Peconic Bay at Long Island's east end for a weekend in August. Eighty feet from the shoreline, located on a small peninsula in Southampton, the house backed onto the picturesque bay. Not like the larger, more extravagant, year-round homes in the area, the place had to be shut down for the winter.

Across the bay a menacing summer storm, like an oncoming avalanche, swelled on the horizon and slowly progressed towards them.

"Storm's coming," Frank yelled to Laura.

"I see it," she shouted. "I want to capture a quick watercolor before it arrives."

Laura began to paint as her brush moved over the rough heavy paper in rapid, confident motions. Instead of aroused anxiety about the approaching tempest, Laura felt inspired. An artist perceives, in the same dimension, what the average person rarely sees.

Within an hour the color sketch was finished. She walked to the house, her gear stuffed under her arms. Frank had fallen asleep where he was sitting on the deck, reading a newspaper. She bent down and kissed him gently on the forehead. There is good reason to love it here, she thought. It was the perfect getaway. Frank deserved an occasional break from the damned advertising business in New York City.

Over a cup of coffee, she reminisced that, after seven years of marriage, no children had come from their lovemaking. It wasn't as if they hadn't tried. Frank wanted children as much as she did. And having recently turned thirty-five made her want them all the more.

By the time Frank awoke, Laura had coffee waiting for him. He sipped quietly, smiling at her, his eyes devouring her.

"We're going to be rained out," Frank said to Laura. "Instead of eating here let's head over to the Lobster Pod and have dinner by the bay. Might be a dramatic evening."

"Sounds good to me," she replied.

"I'll call for reservations," he declared.

"I'll shower," she said. "I want to get the beach sand off me."

"Don't forget the paint on your nose."

"My nose?"

"You've got a spot of blue on the tip of your nose," Frank said, a grin on his lips.

"Occupational hazard," she laughed.

In the bathroom, she glanced in the mirror and chuckled. There actually was a spot of ultramarine blue watercolor paint on the tip of her nose. She wet her fingers and wiped off the soluble substance.

She undressed and slid the shower door open. Her overall demeanor was that of a tall, slim woman with an alluring sensuality in her movements. It helped that, at the apartment building where they lived in Manhattan's Eastside, there was a complete gym that she and Frank frequented.

She opened the shower door and stepped into the soothing spray. The sound and spatter of the water muffled any slight sounds in the room. As she soaped up, the cloudy shower door suddenly slid open. Frank stepped into the confined area with her, naked and prepared for frolic.

"Oh, yes!" Laura gushed. "Just what I need."

* * *

A waterside restaurant on the Peconic Bay, The Lobster Pod boasted of magnificent views and grand sunsets. Over drinks, Laura remarked that the storm on the bay would make a striking series of paintings. By six PM the sky had the temper of volcanic activity, overcast with layers of foreboding rain-soaked clouds ready to burst. A shot of lightning dramatically cracked the ceiling of clouds and crashed into the open bay, followed in seconds by the arriving slam of thunder.

"Wow!" Frank said. "Pretty scary."

Laura agreed. "But," she said, "you've got to admit it's beautiful. I hope I can retain these images I see for future paintings."

During dinner they marveled at the ferocity of the storm as it slowly traveled across the bay. By the time they were sipping after-dinner coffee Laura remarked, her voice now brimming with concern, "Frank, I think it's time to get home. The storm is almost on top of us."

"You're right," he said, admitting their fascination had overruled caution. He motioned to the waiter for the check.

"Look," Laura said, pointing to the main dining room. "People have already left. We've been sitting here in our little alcove admiring a storm that's been creeping up on us and not paying attention to what's going on around us."

The thunderstorm was much closer than they had realized. It was now directly overhead.

The waiter approached them. As he reached their table, a bolt of lightning ruptured the sky like a cannon shot and struck with horrendous might. It smacked the building not five feet from where the Whitneys were seated near a window.

The terrible ferocity of the electric bolt blew out the windows surrounding them. Broken glass and fractured wood exploded into the dining room. Frank ducked instinctively. A hunk of flying wood from a shattered window frame struck his shoulder, knocking him to the floor. A large shard of flying glass ripped across the waiter's chest, slicing through his jacket.

Fragments of wood and glass smashed into Laura's face. She threw her hands up to deflect the flying debris. Too late. A hunk of wood hit her in the head breaking her eyeglasses and knocking her unconscious. Both she and Frank were thrown off their seats and catapulted over the table to the floor.

The force of the lightning strike blew tables and chairs across the room. The corner of the building, where the lightning hit, burst into flames. Chaos ruled for a moment — and the storm moved on.

* * *

Laura realized she had returned to reality when she heard a low groan come from within her own throat. Her brain swam in a sea of visions as consciousness returned; the thunderstorm, the impact of the lightning strike, the explosion of fractured glass.

Her head throbbed. She reached to touch her face and felt bandages that covered her eyes and blocked out the light. She

4

realized she was in a bed and tried weakly to sit up. Strong hands on her shoulders restrained her and gently forced her back to the pillow.

"Take it easy, Mrs. Whitney," a soft male voice said. "Don't try to get up just yet."

"What happened?" Laura stammered. "Where am I?"

"Please, Mrs. Whitney. Relax. You're in a hospital."

Suddenly, full awareness returned.

"Frank!" she cried. "Where's Frank?"

"He's all right," the voice reassured her. "He's right here beside you."

"Laura," his wonderful voice filled her ears. She felt his arm touch her as his head settled on her breast. She caressed his face.

"What's wrong, Frank?" she asked. "How badly am I hurt?'

"It's all right, darling," he whispered in an attempt to placate.

She ran her hands over the bandages on her face. They were tight around her eyes.

"Oh God, Frank. It's my eyes, isn't it?"

"Laura, please dear. It's going to be all right." His voice cracked, telling her the worst she suspected might be true.

Something pinched her arm and she felt herself slowly drift back into oblivion,

"What is it?" she cried. "What's happening?"

"Only a sedative, Mrs. Whitney," a deep, fading voice reassured her.

Frank sat by her bed, the sounds of his gentle sobbing muted as the voices around her melded together into garbled tones. She slid over the edge into total blackness.

She was blind. A lightning strike had destroyed her sight in an instant.

The first few days were sheer horror for Laura. In a black, bleak world, she dreaded consciousness. She tried to sink back into the comfort of sleep and oblivion, into a world without thought, with no chance to ponder her dilemma.

She hardly spoke. She felt Frank's presence in the room by the almost imperceptible sound of his breathing. When she awoke she spoke softly.

"Frank, I'm completely blind, aren't I?" she asked, her voice restrained.

"I don't know for sure, Laura," he replied.

She sensed evasion in his voice.

"Why won't you tell me if you know?"

There was hesitation before Frank spoke. "I've been told both corneas were damaged. Your glasses broke and fragments of glass hit your eyes when the lightning struck. The doctors are not sure if it's permanent. We're going to take you to see the best specialists available. We're transferring you to Manhattan immediately."

"How are you?" she asked, shifting the emphasis to him.

He smiled and kissed her hand. "I'm fine. I've only been banged up a bit."

She turned her face toward the sound of his voice. "Kiss me," she said.

He reached over and gently kissed her. She could taste the salty tears on his face.

"You're crying," she said.

"They're tears of thankfulness, Laura," he replied. "You're alive, my darling. You could have been killed."

She kissed the tears away.

* * *

The totality of Laura's situation pressed on her. Her sudden blindness was instantly felt in its damning finality. Had she gone blind over a gradual period of adjustment her attitude might have been different; but to have happened so swiftly was devastating. Her blindness was as dense as the black India ink she had used so often for her drawings.

A sense of loneliness came with blindness. She was deprived of the single resource she needed most, her sight. Laura's entire life had been based on the visual sense. As an artist she learned to think visually. An artist without sight; it could not happen. The odds of losing one's sight in an instant are astounding. The odds of that person being an artist are unimaginable. And to lose the ability to perceive images was overwhelming. If it wasn't for Frank and the realization that she would hurt him severely she felt she could not go on living.

She sat by the window in her hospital room listening to the sounds from the city below; sounds that were an insignificant part in her life now suddenly emerged as her main contact with the outside world. She heard a tugboat tooting out on the river. She imagined the scene in her mind's eye. She could see it develop on canvas; laying in the colors, working swiftly to capture the light, putting in the details as the painting came to life. Never again. Never!

* * *

When Laura was released from the hospital Frank led her to a waiting cab. She lost her sense of bearing while riding through the streets of Manhattan without sight. She knew where their apartment was located in relation to the hospital, but a few turns of the cab in her world of darkness and she was lost.

Frank didn't say much on the trip home. He merely went through the routine of helping her, guiding her.

Laura and Frank lived in a doorman-attended high rise building in Manhattan's east side that had been constructed during the nineteen-fifties. Although there was only one bedroom in their fourteenth floor apartment, the rooms were extremely large. The expansive living room had a wraparound corner window treatment and terrace that exposed them to a magnificent view of the East River and the 59th Street Bridge to the north.

Their furnishings were selected to fit the atmosphere of the location. There was an abundance of numbered prints on the entry foyer and living room walls, Dali, Calder, Lichtenstein, Warhol, along with some excellent photos of New York City. A photographer with whom Laura shared a studio on Twenty-third Street near the Flatiron Building gave these to Frank. Her space there took up the back one-third of a loft in a six-story commercial loft building that was flooded by light from the abundance of windows. It was her private art studio where she created the volume of her paintings.

Frank and Laura met at a New York City advertising agency and had worked together on a number of projects. The image Frank presented at their first meeting was that of a tall, compact six-footer, always dressed in a suit, always with a handful of papers, always on the move. When Frank rose to his present position of vice president Laura decided to end the grind of ad agency life and resume her career as a painter. It didn't hurt that TheArtGallery in Manhattan, which handled her work, was a client of Frank's ad agency. With their combined incomes they easily afforded both the city apartment and the beach house in Southampton.

Laura started across the living room on her own but, after only a few steps, realized she was not going to make it. Even though she knew where the furniture in the apartment was located, it was no easy task to suddenly judge distances by sense alone.

"Sit me down, Frank, please," she said.

Frank helped her to the couch and sat beside her. His arm slipped around her shoulders. "Well, we're home. I've missed you being here," he said.

"Frank," Laura said. "How do you look right now?"

"What do you mean, how do I look?"

"I mean, are you shaven? Do you have a suit on? A tie? Are you wearing jeans?"

"I shaved and slipped into a jacket. No tie."

"Too bad I can't help you with your tie," she complained. "You never could master the knot."

Frank felt uncomfortable for he sensed cynicism in the statement.

"Maybe I should start wearing snap-on bow ties. That might work," he said, trying to lighten things up.

"Don't you see what I'm driving at, Frank? I'll never be able to see you. I can only imagine what you look like. You and I will grow old and I will still have the image of you in my mind as a young man. That's strange, isn't it?"

"Please, Laura..." Frank implored.

"It's my eyes that are dead, not my brain. It's a curse. Sometimes I think it would have been better for that lightning to have killed me."

Frank was beside her now, holding her hand. "Don't talk like that. That's a selfish way to look at this. What would I do without you? How could I go on? You're my life."

Her hand felt for his face and he guided it to her. She kissed him tenderly.

"I know," she said. "And I am sorry. I don't want to hurt you, darling. But the future is so bleak. My world is dark. Funny, isn't it? As an artist I've been censured by critics as having no vision. I guess some of the them were right after all."

Frank chuckled at her humor. "There's always hope," he said. "Remember, doctors have not given up on you entirely. They said there is always the possibility of your sight being restored. These days they do work miracles."

"Is that what it's going to take, Frank, a miracle?"

"We'll beat it, Laura," he assured her. "We'll beat it."

* * *

Frank enrolled Laura in a school for the seeing impaired. The classes were held not far from their apartment and they were lucky enough to get her into an evening session. She subdued her depression by directing her energies in a positive direction. She discovered methods of mobility that she did not know existed.

They began to go out to dinner again. At first Laura was reluctant. She felt very awkward and imagined the stares of people around her. After a few times out she came to terms with this particular discomfort and realized that those people didn't matter to her. She managed her way through the meals and enjoyed the diversion.

* * *

Within months after the accident, eye specialists indicated there was hope for Laura to regain her sight. And then they met Dr. Charles Hudson, an ophthalmologist.

"Mrs. Whitney," the doctor told her, "if you are willing, I am certain we can perform a successful corneal transplant which could very well completely restore your sight."

Laura practically shouted with glee. "Is this true? I heard of this. Can you really do something like that?"

"The procedure is quite common these days," the doctor affirmed. "Corneal transplant is the most successful type in the country. The human body rarely rejects a transplanted cornea. Right now, because there is scar tissue on both of your existing corneas, you will most likely never see completely with both corneas damaged. A transplant on both eyes is the only answer."

9

"Both eyes?" Laura questioned.

"Your injuries to each eye were almost identical. We can operate on both eyes. The Eye Bank gets many donor corneas from recent deaths. You will most likely match one of them. And we have advanced the procedure to laser technology. This system will promote the healing process to occur quicker."

"This is fantastic," Laura exclaimed. "You've made my day. No, by God, you've made my year...my life!"

"Let me know your decision as soon as possible so that I can put you on the list at the Eye Bank. When we are notified of a donor we can set up the operation," the doctor said. "Once you are on the list the procedure will come fast. You'll have to stand by on a daily basis. When you get to the top of the list you will have only a few days to get ready."

"How long once we go on the list?" she asked.

"Three weeks, a month. These things happen fast. The eyes will be taken from someone who just died and we will proceed immediately."

"I say yes. Definitely," Laura said.

On the way home Frank said, "This is great news, Laura. What could be better? How do you feel? Are you up for this?"

"Am I up for it? I can't wait. According to Dr. Hudson they've had great success in these operations. And thousands are done every year. Please let it be true, Give me back my sight. Let me see. Let me paint again."

* * *

Frank and Laura drove to their Southampton house. It was a journey of trepidation for Laura. She hadn't been to the house since the accident. Not able to see her beloved house, the beach and the glorious sunsets over the water was almost unbearable.

With the expectancy of the operation pending in her immediate future she could hardly wait to visit the place. Frank did not have to coax her into going. Now, as their destination drew closer, she developed a sense of misgiving at having come at all.

"I don't know, Frank," she said. "Maybe it was a mistake for me to come now. Maybe we should have waited until after the operation."

10

"Don't be silly. It will do you a world of good to get out on the beach," he responded.

"Well, maybe. But I'm not sure I'm up to visiting. You know people are going to be asking me foolish questions. I feel self-conscious in those situations. Maybe I should have gradually worked up to this."

Frank concentrated on the road ahead. "It'll be all right, Laura," he said.

Without sight Laura didn't realize they were so close to the beach house until Frank turned onto the bumpy road that led directly to the house. The bounces were the same as she remembered them.

"Well, we're here," he said finally.

Frank held the car door open for Laura as she exited and began to walk toward the beach.

"Wait, Laura," Frank called out. "You're not sure of the footing."

"I know every foot of the way," she answered.

Frank insisted. "We have all weekend. Take your time."

"It's all right, Honey," she said. "I know this place inch by inch. I've gone over it a thousand times in my mind."

Laura felt the breeze from the bay fanning the salt air before her. She inHayled the fragrance deeply.

"How does it look, Frank? The water? The beach? How does it look?"

"Just like one of your paintings," he replied.

* * *

Laura lay on the cool sand of their beach, her back resting against Frank's legs. The cool air forced her to pull the sweater tighter around her shoulders.

"Seems like we've done this before," she said.

"Many times," Frank said. "Same girl. Same beach."

"Has the sun set yet, Frank?" she asked.

"Almost. It's a very peaceful sunset. There are very few clouds and the sun is like a red ball."

"Red sun at night, sailor's delight. Red sun in the morning, sailor's warning," she said. "Must be the kind of evening I love to paint."

"Perfect." His hands closed tighter around her shoulders.

"Frank," she said after a few minutes, a change of mood in her voice, "I've been thinking about the operation."

"And?"

"I'm not sure."

"Not sure?"

"Well, all right. I'm frightened."

"There's not much to be frightened of," he said, trying to emote confidence in his voice. "Dr. Hudson is certain there will be no problems."

"I'm still frightened," she insisted. "It's a terrifying thing to have a dead person's corneas planted in your eyes. I don't know how I'm going to react psychologically."

"When you can see and you are painting again, your fears will vanish like the wind."

"And whose eyes will I get? How do we know for sure if my body will accept them? How do I know what new problems I might incur?"

"Corneas, Laura," Frank said. "You will be getting two corneas. The specialists who perform the operation know what they are doing. I'm sure everything will be fine."

"I hope so," Laura said, closing her arms tightly across her chest to ward off the cool air of the evening.

Chapter 2

Vera Lancaster, a medium, who truly believes there is life after death, was determined to make contact with the hereafter.

Her dedicated supporters know she can.

Martha Fuller is one who was certain Vera had accomplished more as a psychic in her forty-one years of life than most could in a thousand years. And, in Martha's mind, Vera had already proved contact.

A true friend since grade school, Martha had been captivated early on by Vera's ability to read students' thoughts. She was convinced that her friend was a cut above the commonplace. Always exciting to be with, there were times when Vera could curl your hair with her psychic acumen. Martha related to Vera because she too possessed some psychic skills. The common bond that existed flowered into a lasting allegiance.

Tonight she was eager to assist in what she considered the most consequential of Vera's efforts. Martha's husband, Bert, did not share her enthusiasm. She sympathized with him but, considering this momentous occasion, too much depended on her being with Vera. She and a third person, Susan Gray, were deemed necessary.

She knew how Bert felt; too much of her time with him was lost to this woman; this fraud, he called her. He let Martha know that their sexual union had slipped from occasional to seldom to rarely. As a result, this middle-aged couple had no children and Bert's bitterness surfaced.

"I don't want you going to this insane palm-reading session tonight," he insisted, his jaw straining at the words.

"It's a séance, Bert," she admonished. "Don't be smug. You know what it is."

"Well, I'm asking you not to go," he said. "No. I'm telling you, once and for all, to give it up."

"Don't be ridiculous. This is the most important séance in my life. All the work we've accomplished has led to this. I can't walk away merely because you disapprove. Vera depends on me and Susan."

"Listen to you...'merely because I disapprove!' What the hell does that say for me? You're my wife. I thought you loved me. I think you're fooling with things that are dangerous. You're in way over your head. This freaky woman has you all screwed up. She's ruining your life. Hell, she already ruined my life."

"Your life is ruined, Bert?" she questioned.

"Yes, Especially my sex life."

"Your sex life. Is that all that counts?"

"No. But you haven't been exactly available."

"But that dirty little barmaid in town has."

Bert Fuller was perplexed. "There's nothing to that. Even if there was, you can't hold that against me. What am I to do?"

What am I to do, indeed, she thought.

Martha finished dressing. Nothing was going to stop her from joining Vera Lancaster tonight. This day was a long time coming. Endless bouts of experimentation led to this crossroad. Vera Lancaster had chosen each woman for her individual psychic strength to assist in her quest. They had experienced the journey with her; were necessary to batter down death's closed door. This could very well be their night of nights; three women ready and willing to challenge the unknown, to prove the afterlife can be reached, that contact with a supreme being was possible.

"I'll tell you what you are to do. Just let me be," Martha responded. She was ready to leave.

As she opened the front door her husband said behind her, "I'm serious, Martha. This is the last straw after a lifetime of this craziness. I won't be here when you get back. I've had it."

Disheartened but determined, Martha turned and said, "Well, just make sure you lock the door when you leave, Bert."

Tonight, Vera's breakthrough séance was to be conducted in the old Victorian house on Lancaster Island off the ragged coast of Maine. The entire island was part of Vera's inheritance as the only surviving heir of the Lancaster family line. Martha Fuller led Susan Gray in preparing the room for the ritual. Together the three prepared the drawing room in the exact fashion Vera described to them.

The room was trimmed in black, including the walls and floors. The startling white of the drapes and an alabaster altar that stood in the center of the large square room contrasted the gloom. On the altar the sign of the pentagram and the magic circle was inscribed on its face.

The women sat at a round table, hands joined, ready to make contact. Vera had briefed the women on the incantations she would chant and urged them to concentrate on willing a spirit to appear. She recited the long list of power names, which were said to summon an entity from a spiritual level.

An hour later, halfway through her chants, her hands suddenly broke from the group as her body stiffened. She ceased her recitation. Her friends watched in awe as a luminescent vaporous substance formed and grew around Vera. Each had seen ectoplasm before and each was braced to expect such an occurrence. But they did not expect to see Vera Lancaster's ramrod-stiff body suddenly rise from her chair a full six feet in the air as if carried by the formless clouds that surrounded her. Vera hung suspended over their heads as the women, their hands now clenched tightly together, watched in awe.

The room began to tremble when a heavy, resonant rumbling reverberated against the walls. The table before them rattled, its legs battering against the floor. Suddenly, the vaporous substance flared out from Vera, encircling her body like a cocoon as the apparition whirled around her in a dizzying display. Its force grew wider as it increased in velocity and noise. The room became a hurricane, the women's hair flying about in all directions. Vera's body, clothed in a white gauzelike robe, hung in the center of the room enveloped in the whirling mist that spun around her in a devastating fury. The women had to press their hands roughly against the table to keep it from pulling completely away from them. They knew without a doubt that their beloved leader had indeed reached something very powerful from beyond the grave.

Martha Fuller knew she would have to speak to the force, to breach the void. She glanced dreadfully at Vera's body, suspended high above them, encircled by the white unearthly cloud. Her leader seemed dazed, out of touch with what was happening to her.

Now thin, spectral flames encircled Vera, as a metamorphosis seemed to be taking place. Vera was physically changing shape before their eyes. The women's faces were contorted into absolute terror. The medium's body twisted in the air until it hung upright, poised over their heads. Vera was enclosed in the grasp of a

15

transparent, demonic shape that now swirled around her suspended body.

"Who are you?" Martha asked of the shape-changing substance, her voice quaking with fear.

The sound that emerged from the vision was hollow and rumbled with a chilling echo, much like a scream.

The force then filled the room, its power now totally devastating. The table flew away from them, crashing against the altar. The women's clasped hands parted, clutching at their own throats, in fear of their lives. Susan Gray was thrown against the wall with an awesome force that left her lying in a distorted, limp heap. Martha Fuller scrambled to the door and grappled with the knob. She fainted, the sound of a terrifying fury ringing in her ears.

The vaporous cloud slowly morphed into a shape that vaguely resembled a human. It glided across the room, stopped, turned its dark head back to the devastation in the room. The luminescent face cracked a devious smile while its red, serpentine eyes gleamed.

A demon, temporarily isolated in the abyss of the netherworld after an interval of decades, found a door that had opened for it and was able to join humanity once more. The misty form dissolved through the closed door and was gone in an instant

Vera Lancaster's body lay prostrate beside the limp forms of her cohorts. Her adored visage suddenly glowed, revealing an angelic luster as she joined the minions of dead.

* * *

Selected vital organs were separated from the medium's body according to her wishes and distributed to waiting recipients throughout the country. Vera Lancaster's corneas would soon find their place as the new vehicle of sight for a needy recipient.

Chapter 3

The operation took less than two hours. Laura opted for local anesthetics and therefore was conscious. Her face was completely cleansed and covered with layers of white sterile cloth. Dr. Hudson viewed the procedure through a high-powered microscope as he performed the microsurgery. He sliced out a circular section of damaged cornea with the laser. He then carefully lifted the damaged cornea away from the body of the eye.

Dr. Hudson then cut a circular piece from a donor cornea measured to the exact same dimensions as Laura's bad cornea. This circular "cookie" was fitted precisely into the opening where the removed piece had been and was stitched into place with a super-thin thread.

After completion of the procedure a pad and a rigid plastic shield was then fitted over the eye to protect it from injury. Laura was given instructions. She was to return to Dr. Hudson's office the next day to have the patches removed for an examination. Within two weeks she would go through the same procedure for the second eye.

* * *

After both procedures were completed Frank escorted Laura to have the bandages removed. Laura braced for the occasion. Dr. Hudson informed them that the operation went to perfection.

"Don't open your eyes quickly," he warned her. "Let them adjust to the light for a good few moments."

Laura kept the lids closed and waited.

"Do you sense a difference?" the doctor asked.

"There seems to be a haze. Red. Like a dim red haze of light," she said.

Finally the doctor said, "All right, now. Slowly. Open your eyes. Remember, slowly."

She let the lids open, quivering, straining to move slowly, squinting as she tried to control their movement. Then they were open fully. Nothing. Dull haziness. Black. Oh, No!

"Can you see anything?" the doctor asked.

"No!" Laura exclaimed. "No. Nothing."

"Give it a few moments, Mrs. Whitney." He threw a thin ray of light from a flashlight into the dark room.

"Oh, yes. Something," Laura said. "I see something. A dim light. Over there to the right."

He slowly passed the light across her eyes.

"It's moving to the left, now. Yes. I can make out a light."

"You're going to be all right, Mrs. Whitney. The operation appears to have been successful."

Flashes of light. No more darkness. Blurred images coming into focus. People. People standing in front of her. She heard them talking. But now she saw them. Two doctors. A nurse.

"How do you feel, Mrs. Whitney?" Dr. Hudson asked.

"Dr. Hudson," Laura said. "So...that's what you look like."

Laura could not control the tears that filled her eyes. Thank God, she silently cried. Thank God.

"There is an added benefit involved," Dr. Hudson said. "Your eyesight has improved. For the present you will have to wear contact lens but soon you won't have to wear eyeglasses anymore."

Laura was overjoyed. She had worn eyeglasses most of her life.

In the months to come she would be facing many rules set by the doctor. Laura was informed to limit her painting to very little at first, not to strain her eyes. She had to follow rigid instructions during a period of adjustment, which was about three weeks. She was told to avoid strong sunlight, wear dark sunglasses, avoid strain to the eyes with long periods of reading, no heavy lifting, no rubbing the eyes. She was to faithfully use medication prescribed to her and report any prolonged pain or change in her vision immediately to Dr. Hudson.

Chapter 4

After eight desolate months Laura Whitney's enthusiasm for life returned. Her exuberance abounded. Frank was affected by it immediately. He too loved life now more than ever because of Laura's constant rejoicing.

On a clear bright day Laura and Frank walked through the city. Only a few billowy white clouds brushed the expanse of blue sky. Laura saw burgeoning color everywhere, in storefronts, automobiles, clothing, buildings, billboards, children. The sights and sounds of the city became complete when embodied once again in physical form. It was total. It was overwhelming. An endless variety of scenes for her to capture on canvas; subjects she had largely ignored. Her concept of her environment broadened tenfold. Her paintings would be destined to capture life on new terms. She would no longer be confined to merely repeating the same scenes from a thousand angles. She saw new life all around her. Colors teemed everywhere like she had never seen before. There was grandeur to this new world, a saturation of hue and form that flourished with a splendor that took her breath away. Wherever she looked, there for her to see, to love, consume; to capture on canvas forever.

She painted scenes she had never considered before; a fruit stand on Second Avenue, a street at night buried in snow, people sitting on the stoop of a tenement house, people coming out of the subway in the rain, quaint corner restaurants, a woman arranging flowers at a street shop. She found an abundance of new everyday situations. In the past Laura had painted scenes from a limited frame of reference. Her landscapes and seascapes had always been simple scenes of escape. Before, where she had painted flawless idyllic scenes, she was now producing bold compositions with powerful bursts of color and verve. Her paintings exploded with power and richness previously contrary to her style.

And Laura became inspired.

She began a painting of Times Square at night in the loose, colorful, painterly style she had recently adapted. The painting was teeming with energy, vibrant with splashes of color capturing the dynamism of the area. As she worked on the composition she decided to add snow to the painting and make it a winter scene. The deluge of color against a snow-laden setting would enhance the variety of color. The yellow taxicab and red sedan dominating the foreground now contrasted against a field of ultramarine blues of the snow on the ground. From the wide expansive foreground the tire tracks in the snow led the eye to a vanishing point in the explosion of color across the top half of the painting.

Still not enough, Laura decided. Once the painting had dried a bit she laced it with hundreds of blurred strokes of white paint indicating the wildly blowing snowflakes. Finally she felt she had captured the essence of a Broadway snowstorm.

She had outdone herself, she thought. Her efforts succeeded in creating what she considered her best painting ever.

Frank saw the difference in her work. Her ability to produce near masterpieces astounded him. He firmly believed that where once she had been a good artist, she was now on her way to becoming great. Her paintings thrived with life. People, whom she had avoided in her work, now dominated her canvases. Her tight style loosened and she painted in broader, more spontaneous bursts of color. Her forms were not as labored as they had been. Her work appeared bold and painterly, the texture, shape and color filling out the body of the composition where once she had relied on an adherence to great detail. Laura's world was totally dominated by the wonder of work. The contrast between the depression during her blindness, and the vibrancy and optimism she now exhibited was astounding. Frank was elated for her, but he could barely keep pace with her seemingly unbounded energy.

And her sexual drive returned.

Life became normal again. They easily fell into a daily routine that not only satisfied them but also kept them both eager to attack each new day with increased verve.

They drove to the beach house with a renewed excitement that Laura thought might not recur. When they arrived at the house she stepped inside, threw her hands in the air, looked around in every direction and cried, "Welcome back into my life, house."

The hint of summer was in the air. The trees had begun to bloom and the birds sang their welcome to her. She hastened, barefooted, down onto the beach and spun joyously into the water, splashing and kicking at the small waves in a gleeful, unrestrained dance of bliss.

She and Frank made love. It was one of many times in recent weeks during which they had devoured each other with alarming lust. Laura faded into a heavy sleep that night, secure and content with Frank's presence by her side.

It was the night of the first vision.

* * *

She plummeted into the abyss, a continuous uncanny darkness. She could see nothing, blackness surrounding her, an intense, hostile presence. She felt fear and foreboding.

A dim light appeared, draped in a pale mist. A large room. Black walls. Dim shapes in the foggy light. Three women, their hands clasped, sitting around a table. They seemed mesmerized. Laura looked directly into their terrified faces. Eyes filled with fright.

The light threw pulsating, vague shadows across their forms. The women screamed. Hands parted as a fury devoured the room. The suspended table crashed to the floor. Chairs overturned. One woman flew against the wall. Another cowered in a corner of the room. A white mist encircled one woman lifting her into the air.

Laura was trapped in her own mind. She could only scream. Louder! Louder!

Her eyes opened. She was sitting up in bed, her body drenched in perspiration, Frank holding her by the shoulders.

"Laura! What's going on?" he cried. "What is it? You were screaming in your sleep."

Her eyes blazed with terror. She was staring beyond him.

"Laura, wake up!"

"A nightmare," she managed to say, coming back to consciousness. "Bad."

"All right, Honey," Frank soothed. "Calm down. Take it easy." He guided her gently back to the pillow. He wiped the perspiration from her brow.

"It's all right," he said.

"It was frightening," she stammered. "Women screaming. They

were terrified. I was with them. It was horrific."

"Just a dream," he reassured her.

"But the vision. It was so very real."

"They always are."

"Damn," she swore. "I haven't had one like that since I was a kid. I can still see those women crying out in fear. I don't know what they were afraid of."

"I'll get something to calm you," he said.

"No. Don't leave me just now."

He sat on the edge of the bed with her. He comforted her while she slowly calmed. Eventually she dropped back into sleep. As she slipped over the edge her body shook again as if loath to face the terror that still might lurk in the blackness of sleep. He watched for a while and, when he was certain she was resting peacefully, he turned off the lights and climbed in next to her.

Chapter 5

On a warm June afternoon Laura Whitney and her childhood friend, Jennifer Douglas, had their first lunch together since Laura's operation. They met at a small "tony" restaurant on the east side of midtown Manhattan. Laura waited for Jenny in front of the brownstone in which the restaurant was located. Jenny looked perfect as she emerged from the cab she took from Penn Station. For as long as Laura knew her Jenny always had a tight, trim body. She still had it. She looked wonderful in tan slacks, white blouse and jacket over her shoulder. Laura threw her arms around her friend.

"Oh, Jenny, darling," she cried, sincere emotion straining her voice. "It's so good to really see you again."

"The same, Laura," Jenny beamed. "How are you feeling?"

"Just fine. Absolutely."

They got a table in the garden at the rear of the building and ordered pèna coladas.

"Have you been painting?" Jenny asked as they sipped their drinks.

"Yes, very much so. I've been turning out work at a greater rate than before the accident. I've done over a dozen new works already."

"That's just wonderful. Wonderful. I see you gave up your eyeglasses. Are you using contacts? I remember you never liked them."

"My eyesight has improved. I don't need glasses anymore. I now have twenty-twenty eyesight."

"I can't believe this. I assume this was a result of the operation."

"And Jenny, I see composition so much greater now than I ever did. I see perspective in my mind almost three-dimensional. I see a scene I want to paint and it's like taking a photograph. I can close my eyes and I remember it completely. And I see the colors so vibrantly. It's remarkable."

"Whose corneas did you get? Was that person an artist?"

"I have no idea. The doctor and The Eye Bank people keep the identity of the donor a secret. I guess that's the right thing to do. So I don't know whose corneas I got. Whoever it was has given me a power I never had before. It's like wishing for super eyes from God in a prayer and getting exactly what you asked for."

"Super eyes. How marvelous for you," Jenny said sincerely.

"What I mean," Laura continued, "is that the person whose corneas I got had excellent eyesight. Also a tremendous ability to see scenes as structured paintings. He or she might have been an artist but I guess I'll never know." She smiled at her friend. "Thank you so much for your concern," she said. "How about you? You're looking great. How're the kids and Ralph?"

"Kids are fine. Danny's in Little League and Leslie's a soccer kid. They're all healthy. Ralph is busy as hell. He's always working, especially around tax time."

"Sounds like Frank. Advertising business. It shows no mercy. The demands never change."

"Have you thought of going back into advertising?" Jenny asked.

"I don't think so. Painting is everything to me. I've always wanted to devote my life to painting. Now, more than ever. My new eyesight exposes so many scenes to me that I had never seen before. And my paintings have been selling. It's absolutely miraculous."

"I'm so happy for you."

"I see things...I don't know...things I'd never seen before."

"Such as?"

"It's hard to explain. Images. I can look at something I want to paint and my mind goes wild. I see images as I've never seen them before. It's like my mind turns my vision on. When I see something that might make a good painting, I mentally run through it as if I were painting it on the spot. It's amazing. There is something magical suddenly. I know exactly what the finished product will be. I can see it finished. But I see it develop, quickly stroke by stroke."

"Sure sounds like super eyes to me!"

"Yes." Laura did not tell her friend of her bout with dreams nor the fact that she was beginning to see things that frightened her as well. She shrugged off the occasions as an overactive imagination;

yet she had never experienced such happenings before her operation.

"Appears like only good things can come of the operation," Jenny said, a beaming smile punctuating her admiration for her friend.

Laura lifted her glass and clinked it against Jenny's. "I'll drink to that."

* * *

Jenny Douglas lived in the town of Northcove. Located on the north shore of Nassau County on Long Island, it was an upscale community of over-priced homes, good schools and close transportation. Jenny grew up in Nassau County and knew exactly where she wanted to live. Her children, she vowed, would go to the Northcove schools when their turn came.

Jenny met Ralph Douglas at the corporation for which they both worked in Manhattan. Ralph always told the fabricated humorous story of how they met. At the office, he maintained, he was walking past her desk when she put out her foot and tripped him. He fell to his knees and looked up at her. Seeing him kneeling in front of her, she immediately said, "Yes, I do," as if assuming he was ready to propose marriage to her. To Jenny's affable chagrin, Ralph constantly told this story to anyone who had not heard it. The trouble was some people actually believed the incident that never happened.

On the trip home from their luncheon Jenny walked cross-town to Penn Station. It was a delightful day and she had plenty of time to make the train and beat the children home from school. As she waited for a light on the corner of Madison and Thirty-sixth Street her eyes fell upon a man on the opposite corner. He was tall, a little over six feet, slim but with broad shoulders. He wore a black suit. His shirt was black. At first she thought he was a priest but realized there was no white collar. There was no white anywhere on his clothing. Even his hair was black.

His face was startlingly handsome; sparkling white teeth showed under his winning smile. But it was his unblinking eyes that locked on her and made it almost impossible to turn away. Even as the light changed and he walked past her, she turned her head to follow his gaze.

How familiar he seems, she thought. Do I know him? But he looked right at me and kept on going. If I know him then surely he knows me and would have stopped to say hello. I guess not.

Later, in Penn station, she boarded the two-ten train to Northcove. Perfect timing. She would get to town with plenty of time to drive to the bus stop and pick up Leslie and Danny. Luckily, both children went to the same grade school and got off at the same bus stop, only a few blocks from their house. Actually, they could walk home but she had the car at the station and decided to pick them up on this particularly lovely day.

At Penn Station she chose a window seat in the car that she boarded. It aligned with the platform on which passengers assembled. She absently stared out the window watching the activity around her. She sensed someone on the platform moving close to her window. She turned to her left and was suddenly startled; she was staring into the face of the man she had seen on Madison Avenue. He was leaning over, looking directly at her. Separated by the window, there was no more than a foot of space between them. His thin lips cracked into a sinister grin. Jenny jumped back, shocked by the sudden appearance of this mysterious figure. His grin broke into a broad smile and he moved away. He disappeared quickly into the moving throng leaving behind a woman puzzled by the sudden sense of dread that swept through her body.

* * *

Jenny made it to the school bus stop fifteen minutes early. While she sat in the car, waiting for the kids, she thought about the mysterious man who appeared in the railroad car window. Who was he? And why did he follow her? Did he follow her? A chill of fear made her shiver. Just some nutcase, she resolved. I'll probably never see him again.

Her two children got off the bus, holding hands as they walked away. Leslie was two years older than Danny and she played older sister very well. Danny was in first grade and his bigger sister was in third. How she loved them, she thought, watching them react to seeing her. They broke hands and raced to her.

She rolled down the window of the SUV. "Surprise," she shouted.

The kids piled in the back, throwing their backpacks across the seats.

"What's going on, Ma?" Leslie said. "Why are you here?"

"Nothing's going on. Can't a mother pick up her children when she feels like it?"

"Yeah. I guess so."

"How about we stop at MacDonald's for some shakes and fries?" Jenny offered.

"All right," voiced Danny's approval.

Chapter 6

Johnnie Limbo never knew his real name. Somewhere, in his bitter early childhood, he had been dubbed with the nickname "Johnnie Limbo" and it stuck. All he knew, growing up in a rough New York City neighborhood, was that he had been called Limbo by his peers. He wasn't even sure of the surname Johnnie. His ethnicity could have been of any white European lineage, Italian, Spanish, English, and Irish. He was a mutt and it was hard to tell his origins.

Johnnie was part of a street gang in the Bronx. His group was known as The Devils. The gang was a mix; white, black, Hispanic.

Johnnie was an orphan who grew up in orphanages run by Catholic nuns. By the time he was fifteen, Johnnie skipped out of the institutions that tried to direct him to a decent life and opted to street gangs and a life of crime.

Johnnie fought his way into The Devils. He was a tough kid and proved his mettle in many street fights. The members sold drugs, committed numerous robberies, careful enough to break into homes out of their territory. Their turf was sacrosanct in their beliefs.

Nonetheless, as careful as the gang members thought they were, almost all spent some time incarcerated. All except Johnnie. He had no record. Now, though, at age thirty-three, Johnnie was being held in The Manhattan House of Detention in lower Manhattan on charges of manslaughter to which he was soon to stand trial. He had killed a man in a barroom fight over a woman whose name he didn't even remember.

Nothing, Johnnie thought, was as displeasing as any time spent in a lockup in the Downtown Lockup in the early hours after midnight. He was in an isolated cell awaiting his destiny; awake, lying on his bunk when the vision of a strange man dressed in black appeared outside the bars. Strange, Johnnie thought that a civilian was allowed back here at such an hour. The man was hardly noticeable, clad entirely in black. Even his unblinking eyes had no normal color; they were the strangest eyes he had ever seen, almost yellow like a wolf's eyes but changing color in various degrees of light.

"Hurry," the man said. "Let's go. I'm taking you out of here."

"Who the hell are you?" Johnnie questioned. "You some kind of freak lawyer?"

"I am your salvation, John," the voice in the dark answered. "Come out. The cell in unlocked."

Johnnie Limbo got to his feet and approached the cell door. He touched it and it swung open.

"Is this some kind of fuckin' joke?" he stammered. "Who the hell are you?"

"Come with me, John, to a new life," the strange man said.

Johnnie did not argue when good fortune presented itself. Whoever this guy was, he was going with him. He threw on his clothes, slipped into his shoes and joined his benefactor outside his cell. Together they marched boldly through the corridors of The Tombs, passing guards and personnel who paid no attention to them. It was as if they were invisible.

"What is going on?" Johnnie whispered to the man beside him. "How come they don't see us?"

"We are ahead of their perception of us as reality," the man said.

Johnnie had no idea what he was hearing but he smiled at the concept even if he didn't understand what was happening.

Outside his strange benefactor explained to Johnnie Limbo.

"From now on you are mine," the mysterious man in black said.

"What are you talking about? Yours? You gay or something?"

"Hardly." The enigmatic one smiled. "I will take care of you, splendidly. Food, drink, women, riches. You'll never have to steal again."

"What are you talking about?"

"Your choice is simple. Work with me or go back to jail," the stranger commanded.

"Hey," said Johnnie. "Just wait a damn minute. Who the hell do you think you are?"

"Watch carefully," said the mysterious man in black. He smiled wryly and pointed a finger at Johnnie.

In an instant Johnnie was back in his jail cell, sitting on a bunk amidst a group of incarcerated subhuman men.

"Damn!" Johnnie swore. "What the hell is going on?" He got up, pushed his way to the cell bars. He grasped the bars and cried out to no one in sight, "All right! Whoever you are. I'll go along with what you say. I get the message. Get me the fuck out of here."

The amazed prisoners watched Johnnie appear in their midst and disappear just as quickly.

Johnnie stood once again on the street next to his savior.

"Get the point?" the man in black asked him.

Johnnie Limbo decided not to question this strange person again.

"My name is Elymas," said the stranger. "That's all you need to know."

Chapter 7

Laura felt the need to paint more than ever before. By the end of June she wanted to remain at the beach house for the rest of the summer. Frank would come only on weekends as he had for every summer. He would commute to New York City on Monday mornings and out to Southampton on Thursday evenings. At first he wouldn't hear of establishing their former routine.

"It's too soon after the operation," he implored. "You haven't fully recuperated. Besides, this was only our first weekend at the house. Why can't you give it more time?"

"I'll be fine," she insisted. "I'll bury myself in work. I have all I need to paint. Besides, you'll be gone for only four days a week."

"What about the strain on your eyes?" Frank asked.

"I've been painting already for over a month," she countered. "I'll be careful. I won't strain my eyes. I know when to call it quits."

Finally Frank gave in. But he insisted that Charlotte Danfield, the wife of a client who lived nearby, drop by to check on her. She agreed.

"Four days," Frank said. He thought for a moment. "I guess it'll work."

"We'll make it work, Frank."

* * *

Laura set up her easel on the beach and began a new canvas. She had always wanted to do an oil of the house but had continually found some reason to postpone its creation. Now she felt the importance of the effort for a personal motive. In the past she had avoided projects that took her away from producing paintings that would sell. This painting was for her and Frank only. It would never be sold. It would hang in their Manhattan apartment and would serve as a reminder of the Hampton house when they were not there.

It was eight in the morning when she started the painting. She decided to let him rest. She made a pot of coffee and took a cup down to the water's edge. She sipped it as she sketched in the outline of her composition.

What a pleasure, she thought. She could live here the rest of her life. But she knew that was impossible. Frank could never commute such a long distance. His working hours demanded that he be close to Manhattan. And, to maintain their life style, financial demands must be satisfied.

Their beach house was similar in size and shape to others along the winding strip of beach, modest in size but large enough to accommodate weekend guests. The house exterior had a shell of shake shingles and possessed the weathered look that was almost inevitable with structures built along the water. It belonged on that beach, she mused, in that environment. She wondered how empty the land would look without the house where it was. As her painting developed, the house and surrounding landscape complemented each other. It fit. And so did she.

Time passes quickly for the artist. Laura became so intensely absorbed in work that hours raced by without awareness of their flight. Time seemed to condense. Laura realized the time when Frank called to her from the deck.

"It's eleven o'clock," he said. "Let's go for a drive and have a light lunch."

"I don't think so, honey," she called back. "I want to continue this painting I started."

Frank walked down the beach and stopped beside her. He stood silently contemplating her work for a moment before he spoke.

"Laura," he smiled, obviously elated, "you've finally started it. The house. Great. How long will it take to finish?"

"I guess a few days. I want to stay with it. I don't want to break the mood. I can get a good bite into it today. The light is good. No clouds. I want to make the most of it."

"Did you have anything to eat yet?"

"No. I just had some coffee."

"All right then," Frank told her. "I'll whip us up a batch of scrambled eggs and sausages. I'll call you when it's ready and you can take a break."

"You got a deal," she replied.

She smiled, her eyes staying on the painting, while her hand moved the brush from the palette to the area of sky on which she was working.

"Looks good already," Frank said.

"You're sweet to say so. But it's got a way to go."

Frank walked back up the beach to the house as Laura continued the task at hand. The colors that served as the subtle underlying mood of the piece were almost completed. These areas were done in bold, sweeping strokes and would be later painted over with details. To the layman, the painting looked rudimentary and clumsy at this stage of its development. But Laura easily visualized how final attempt would look when she finished the details. She paused and studied the overall effect thus far.

She felt the presence of someone behind her. Instantly she thought Frank was there looking over her shoulder. But she had been looking in the direction of the house for as long as she had been working and she did not see him come out. She suddenly felt the touch of a hand on her shoulder, thinking one of her neighbors might have been walking on the beach and had silently slipped up beside her.

She turned.

Laura jumped up with a start from her folding canvas chair. She knocked over her painting stand and the materials fell to the sand around her. A sudden chill came over her.

There was no one there.

What the hell, she swore. Someone touched me! I felt it!

Yet when she looked around there was no one on the beach within at least a couple hundred yards of her. The neighbors to the east were putting a small boat in the water. They were closest to her, but they could have never touched her and yet cover the distance back in the time it took her to turn around. This was impossible, she thought.

She glanced at the house. Some motion on the deck attracted her attention. Was it Frank? No! A misty shape, almost transparent, like a shadow, a phantom, passed across the front of the house and faded around the corner. It could have been Frank, but the figure was light, ethereal, feminine. It seemed to fade away. Were her new eyes playing tricks? It had to be that and nothing more.

But she felt fearful. Something happened that she didn't understand. First the terrible nightmare, now this.

Laura gathered her spilled paints and propped up the work stand. She looked at her painting. She thought that some paintings brought to mind situations that existed at the time she painted it. She could remember some specific details that had occurred at the time a painting was executed. Most were forgotten. But she knew she would remember the feeling of that phantom hand touching her shoulder whenever she saw this specific painting again.

Her thoughts were interrupted as Frank called from the house that lunch was ready.

* * *

Ralph Douglas rose at six AM as he did every morning. He showered, shaved and was almost fully dressed when his daughter, Leslie, knocked on the bedroom door. He opened it to see his puzzled children, half dressed for school, standing there.

"What's going on?" he questioned. "You guys are going to be late. Where's Mommy?"

"We don't know, Daddy," the child answered. "She's not in the house."

"What do you mean she's not in the house? Of course she is. Did you look in the basement? Maybe she's doing some laundry."

"We looked, Daddy. She's not there."

"Maybe she's outside somewhere, talking to someone."

"No, Daddy. We can't find her anywhere."

Douglas checked the upstairs rooms calling out her name. She was not there. He scoured the entire first floor and the basement. Nothing. Finally, the garage. Perhaps she got in one of the two cars to go somewhere and was taken ill. He entered the garage from the family room. The garage door was down and Jenny's car was still there. He checked inside the car. Not there. He went outside the house. His station car, which he left in the driveway, was gone. What was going on? She had apparently gotten up early and driven off.

Now he was getting worried. Why would she go somewhere this early without letting him know?

He spotted a neighbor across the street picking up a newspaper in her driveway.

"Sheila," he yelled. "Have you seen Jenny at all this morning?"

"No," came the answer. "Anything wrong?"

"No." Not yet, he thought.

He went to the backyard. Damn, he thought. He'd forgotten about the in-ground pool. Suppose she had fallen in. Jenny was not a good swimmer. A cramp could have done her in. But she would never abandon the children for a swim this time of day. He was relieved when he found nothing in the pool. He opened the door to the small pool shed, which contained no more than a shower, a room for changing and some shelves with towels and pool paraphernalia. She was not there either.

Gone.

* * *

At Southampton Laura got a strange phone call from Ralph Douglas at about eleven AM.

"Laura, this is Ralph. Do you know where Jenny is?"

"Why...at home. Isn't she?"

"No. That's why I'm calling you. You're her best friend. I thought perhaps you might know something. Did she say anything to you to indicate she was going somewhere or doing something we didn't know about?"

"No, Ralph. Nothing. I haven't talked to Jenny since we had lunch together. She never mentioned anything about going anywhere. What is wrong?" A sudden, terrible wave of consternation overcame her.

"Jenny is gone. My car is gone. It wasn't in the driveway this morning. I've called the police but all they can do is put out a call to watch for her. She's not a missing person yet."

"What happened, Ralph?"

"The kids came to me this morning. Early. I was getting ready to leave for work. They wanted to know where Jenny was. I looked everywhere. She wasn't in the house. Apparently she got up early and drove off. No word why. No note. Not a thing to let me know if there was something wrong. If you can remember anything she might have said when she talked to you. Anything, Laura. It might help."

"Of course. But I remember a general conversation about you, the kids. Nothing unusual. Let's see, she talked about adding a

Mike Walsh

fourth bedroom to the house. Asked about my work, my operation. Not much else. Now you've got me worried."

"I'll call you later and let you know what's going on. I may be overreacting. It's just not like her to go off like this."

"Keep in touch, Ralph. If she calls me I'll let you know."

When Laura hung up the phone she thought, why would Jenny leave Ralph and the kids? She loved them too much for any motive...a lover, career. Her family life outweighed everything else. She would never leave her family for any reason. What the hell was going on?

* * *

Jenny Douglas did not return. Two weeks after her disappearance Jenny was considered a missing person. Her car was found at the Northcove, Long Island railroad station. Apparently she drove to the station and boarded a train to either the east end of Long Island or Penn Station in Manhattan. No reason for her departure was established. It was considered that Jenny abruptly abandoned her family.

Chapter 8

It was one of those parties you go to but wonder all evening why you bothered to come in the first place. In Laura's case she knew why. The man who threw the annual affair was an important client of Frank's advertising firm. Not showing up, especially since they lived only a few miles apart, could be problematic for Frank.

Frank pulled into the massive circular driveway at the Danfield's Southampton waterfront mansion. A parking attendant took their SUV. The mid-July annual holiday festivity at the Danfield's was scheduled this year as usual. They invited a number of special guests to mark the occasion. Every year since Frank acquired Fred Danfield as a client he had come to the gathering.

"A lot of cars already here. We're not the early birds this time," Frank commented as they approached the house.

"Good," Laura said. "I hate being first."

Laura never ceased to be amazed at the size and grandeur of the Danfield's summer home. Its enormity was overpowering. She thought that her beach house could fit into the Danfield's garage. Although the home was considered year-round, the Danfields rarely used it in winter. The house was situated on four acres of prime oceanfront property on top of a bluff that afforded a magnificent view of the Atlantic Ocean from almost any room. It was one of the true luxuries of wealth.

Frank took Laura by the arm and they walked slowly to the entrance. The weather was perfect, hardly a cloud in the sky. Charlotte Danfield was waiting to greet them. She looked exactly as Laura had last seen her. A fashion model in her youth, Charlotte Danfield was still strikingly attractive, tall and statuesque in an original summer dress. She approached Laura with arms open, smiling broadly.

"Laura, darling," she cried, "I'm so elated for you. You look just wonderful. Beyond words."

"Thank you, Charlotte," Laura said, feeling uncomfortable as the woman hugged her.

"I'm so glad to see you again," Charlotte Danfield sounded sincere. "Frank told us about the operation. We're all so happy for you. It's the most marvelous thing to happen, that a talented person like you should be given back your sight. Your gift is too great to have been stifled so soon in life."

Laura smiled awkwardly. "Thank you. I appreciate my eyes now more than anyone could ever know."

"Oh, of course. Certainly you must," was the response. "Have you been able to work?"

"Yes," Laura said.

"Her paintings are better now than ever," Frank interjected.

"That's absolutely marvelous." Charlotte Danfield would not be silenced. "Have you experienced any major problems adjusting to your new sight?"

"No. None, really," Laura said, touching the rim of her sunglasses. "Except for these, of course."

"But they shouldn't present any problem. Should they?"

"No. I merely have to wear them during my adjustment period."

"I'm sure that everything will work out just fine," Charlotte Danfield said cheerfully.

"I hope so," Laura said, knowing the course of conversation for the evening would be much the same. Perhaps, she thought, once they've all gotten past the questions and the good lucks, maybe it'll be all right.

Fred Danfield came and stood beside his wife, taking her right hand in his.

"Laura," he said. "It's so good of you to come. Frank informed me of your good fortune."

"Thank you, Mr. Danfield," she said.

"You're taking good care of her, I presume?" he said to Frank.

Frank nodded, smiling meekly. He squeezed Laura's hand and directed her into the house. She followed his lead. People spoke to her; some put their arms around her shoulders to emphasize their feelings.

The interior of the house fulfilled the promise offered by the exterior. It was enormous, featuring a seashore quality embellished with nautical trappings in the great room, which, Laura thought, must have been a pleasure procuring. This year the massive room was decorated in the most scrupulous detail; lobster pods, harpoons, oars mounted above the fireplace. The oversized bar was fashioned with sections of an old deck hatch cover with the brass handgrips still intact. One of Laura's larger oil paintings of surf breaking on a rocky shore adorned a south wall. Frank persuaded her to offer it as a gift to ameliorate his relationship with the Danfields. Laura agreed but Charlotte Danfield wouldn't hear of it. She insisted on paying Laura for the eight-foot painting.

Because they were ahead of the main assemblage of guests, Danfield's wife was able to collar Laura and parade her before some of her latest finds in the art world. She respected Laura's opinion because of her growing reputation and she jumped at the opportunity of having caught Laura alone. Although she was a paradigm of sartorial eloquence, Mrs. Danfield's tastes in art ran to a high of mediocrity. She was a young grandmother in her early fifties who had married an ambitious man driven to make many millions as an importer of foreign steel.

Within a half hour Laura was relieved of her burden as the party began to populate and her hostess was forced to abandon her. The explosion of people was a treat to her eyes; the conglomeration of color inspired her. She thought what a great painting this scenario might make if it was done in a loose style, accentuating the medley of colors emanating from the casual summer attire. She became separated from Frank and was obliged to mingle as people arrived. She tried not to get herself trapped with any one group for too long. She listened to shallow discussions on the economy, politics, philosophy, religion, art and decided that she had learned nothing new.

"There you are, Laura darling," a high-pitched voice called to her from a group gathered around the bartender. It was one of the women from the ad agency, a recently hired account executive who worked on an undergarment client.

"Hello..." Laura stumbled over the name.

"Millie Sanders. I work with Frank on the SoftSilk account," the girl said.

"Yes, of course." Laura remembered her name once she identified herself. "How are you?"

"Oh, I'm just fine. But how are you feeling?" Millie bubbled.

"I hear the operation was a success."

"I'm doing all right. Still adjusting."

"That's just so marvelous. It's so amazing the things they can do these days," the girl continued. "Blind one day and able to see the next. You never know what's going to happen."

"I guess," Laura said, trying to be polite.

"Where is your marvelous husband?" Millie asked.

"Circulating."

Millie deposited her empty glass on the tray of a passing waiter and helped herself to a fresh one. She took a long gulp and sighed measurably.

"Listen, Laura, I had this simply marvy idea for a full color campaign on the SoftSilk ads and I wanted to talk to you about it."

Laura noticed that Millie Sanders was now holding an almost empty glass and was looking around for another passing waiter.

"What was your idea, Millie?" Laura braced herself.

"Oh, it's so perfect. But I'll need your consent to use some of your paintings as background settings for some new ads."

"My paintings?" Laura was puzzled.

"Yes. I was having lunch uptown last week, and I happened to be walking by the TheArtGallery. I went in to admire your work and got this fantastic idea buzzing around in my head about using some of your paintings."

"I don't see how my paintings could help a women's garment manufacturer," Laura said. "I paint outdoor scenes. Realistic stuff. I really fail to get the connection."

"But that's the beauty of the campaign," Millie Sanders was adamant. "Picture a SoftSilk product on a full length model silhouetted against a full page color background of one of your paintings."

Laura conjured up visions of a large bra breaking across a seascape.

"I'll have to think about it," she said, but had already made up her mind against the idea.

"Let's have lunch in town soon," Millie said. "I'd like to begin layouts and I want to decide which paintings would be best."

The idea of lunch in the city prompted Laura to think of Jenny Douglas. Where was she? The last she heard from Ralph there was still no word of her whereabouts.

40

"I'll call you," Laura said, knowing she would not call. Millie Sanders vanished in the sea of color chasing another waiter.

Laura looked for Frank and found him with four men, among them Fred Danfield, the host, a tall, elegant man, distinguished by white hair cropped short. Frank spotted Laura across the room and smiled at her. Eventually the men drifted away or were joined by others who hastened them off to meet friends. Laura found herself alone with Frank for the first time since they had arrived.

"By the way," Laura said, "did that Sanders girl from your office mention that she wanted to use some of my paintings in an ad campaign for SoftSilk?"

"I heard something about it," Frank said. "But I haven't seen anything she's worked up yet."

"Why didn't you mention it to me before?"

"I figured you'd get a good laugh. I didn't want to spoil it for you."

"What do you mean, a good laugh?" Laura pouted. "How do you know it would be such a bad idea without giving it a chance? I should have accepted the assignment," she kidded. "Then what would you do?"

"I think I would still have rejected it. I don't want your work exploited."

"I'm glad to see you're looking out for my interests," she chuckled. "What do you say we go home and screw," she said to him.

"You say the sweetest things."

"I mean it. Come on."

"Give me a little more time," he said. "We haven't been here that long. They would notice we were missing."

"So what."

"The 'so what' is that I'm working right now."

"Quit. We'll live on the beach and go clamming."

"What'll we do in the winter?"

"We'll screw all winter."

Frank smiled and kissed her on the forehead.

"Screwball," he said. "No pun intended."

Fred Danfield came suddenly to them and brought a small group with him. Laura felt uncomfortable as a few people gathered in a cluster around her. It wasn't the closeness of the people, though, that disturbed Laura. It seemed to be more the appearance of some vague dynamism in the group.

"Roger," Danfield said to a man to his right. "Step over here, will you. I'd like you to meet the Whitneys. Frank and Laura...allow me to introduce...Roger Evans."

"How do you do?" the man said. He reached out his hand and took Laura's. A tremor went through her body that left her feeling slightly disoriented. He had transmitted energy between them.

He was a tall, thin, casually dressed man, khaki summer slacks, plain short sleeve polo shirt, brown hair just starting to show signs of gray. His piercing dark eyes held hers fast.

Laura let go of his hand and said, "Glad to meet you," but wondered if she really was.

"Roger is our guest for the weekend," Charlotte Danfield interjected. "We're going to see if we can coax him into a performance. Roger is quite talented."

"What is it you do, Mr. Evans?" Laura asked. She had to know.

"I'm a mentalist. Or spiritualist, if you will?"

Somehow, Laura knew.

Chapter 9

At first Roger Evans was agreeable to indulge in the entertainment offered at the Danfields' summer party but once he joined the crowd in the large den a feeling of reticence overcame him. There was someone or something in the gathering that conveyed a sense of concern to him. When he was introduced to the Whitneys he knew the sensation he felt originated with Laura Whitney. What was it? Danger? What did this woman represent? Who was she? There was something about her that transcended comprehension.

She definitely presented a challenge to Roger Evans. It seemed to him that Laura Whitney was an enigma. Strong psychic disturbances emanated from her. The moment Evans touched her hand he felt magnetism, a psychic presence he could not deny. She was exactly the type of subject he had once welcomed as part of his past involvement with psychic experimentation.

But Evans had drifted away from such ventures. He drank too much these days, a result of guilt. Where once he had been actively immersed in intense paranormal experiments Evans now approached each new phenomenon he encountered with the utmost trepidation. These days he never wandered beyond the realm of simple mind reading.

"Ladies and gentlemen," Fred Danfield announced to his guests, "can I have your attention, please? Gather in a little closer. It's time for some entertainment."

Roger Evans joined Danfield on the first two steps of the sweeping staircase that led to the sleeping quarters.

"Allow me to introduce a friend of mine," he said to the assemblage. "This is Roger Evans. Roger was not invited here tonight to perform but I managed to talk him into doing a bit of business to amuse you."

The comment raised a mild ripple of approval as people gathered closer around Evans. A small table had been set up in front of him that contained only a black kerchief.

"I am a mentalist," Evans informed the spectators. "I hope

43

everyone here is at least vaguely familiar with the term." He lifted the kerchief from the table and fondled it while he talked. "I do not perform magic tricks. What I do does not involved magic or tricks."

He walked to the front of the table. "Since I normally work with an assistant I am going to ask for a volunteer to help me tonight." He motioned to Danfield. "Fred, would you be so kind as to contribute your services?" The crowd applauded as Danfield stepped forward.

"All right, Fred. Thank you. You're not as pretty as the girl I normally work with, but, for the house rates you'll do. Now, can we have some volunteers from the audience? I would like to collect some personal objects from about a half dozen people. Watches, cigarette lighters, jewelry. Which, Fred guarantees, will be returned."

The remark drew a round of mild laughter. Evans had Danfield blindfold him with the black kerchief and he turned his back to the group. As Danfield passed through the crowd more objects were held out to him than Evans would have time to experiment with. But Danfield had his eye on Frank from the moment he moved into the group. He gathered a handful of items and stepped before Frank who was standing next to Laura.

"Okay, Frank," Danfield said, "give me something to use."

"Here," Laura said, removing her watch. "Let him try this." She handed the watch to Danfield. She felt somehow compelled to give Roger Evans something belonging to her.

The items were laid on the table in front of Evans. He spoke to Danfield loud enough for everyone to hear with his back still turned. "Do you have enough?" he asked.

"Yes. I think so."

"Good. Now if you will be good enough to place one of the items in my right hand."

Danfield did so.

Evans turned and faced the audience. He held a woman's bracelet above his head in his right hand while his left hand gently touched his forehead.

"I get the initials J.F. A woman. Blonde." He paused a moment for effect. "Will Jane, no Janet F. please stand."

A murmur of low gasps buzzed through the crowd as Janet Farley stood up.

"Is this your watch Mrs. F.?" He handed it to Danfield, who passed it to the woman.

"Yes, it is," came the answer. Applause.

Danfield handed Evans the next item, a key chain. Evans held it, again above his head for effect, and rubbed his temple.

"I get the impression that the owner of this key chain is concerned over a recent business decision. Without getting too involved I will say that you need not worry. You have made the right choice by merging your firm."

The audience again responded with a round of applause. The owner of the chain had let everyone know it was his when Evans first raised it over his head. The people in the group knew of the man's recent partnership and were astounded that Evans could pick up the fact so easily from merely touching an item that belonged to that person.

"By the way, Mr. W., it is the best move you will make in a long time," Evans said. Ted Waller raised his drink to salute Evans and said aloud "Thank you."

Evans was next handed a pendant. He held it aloft.

"Mrs. G.B. I get the message that you are concerned about a member of your family who is ill. Do the initials J.M. mean anything to you?"

A woman in back who was standing near Laura and Frank spoke up. "Yes," she said. "Yes. That would be my mother."

"I would be foolish to tell you everything will be all right. The operation will succeed. But have faith. And trust in a greater power."

Evans placed the item in Danfield's hands and received, in turn Laura's watch. He fondled it with both hands for a moment and then, like the others, held it high over his head. His left hand rested on his temple. He did not speak for a long moment. When he finally did there was a noticeable tremor in his voice.

"Are you...?" he stammered. "Are you...Vera Lancaster?"

Laura's hand clutched Frank's as a sudden chill overcame her. She sensed something was wrong. Evans was not behaving in the same confident manner with which he had handled the others.

"I see...I see..." Evan's body began to shake. His left hand, which had been touching his temple, now covered his entire brow. His right hand wavered over his head like a tree branch caught in a storm.

"Who's there...?" he cried. "Are you Laura?" He was becoming louder, obviously physically bothered, his voice edged with fear. "What do you want...? What...?" He ripped the blindfold from his eyes. They were wide open and blazing with raw, naked terror as he stared directly at Laura. His legs wavered and he fell forward, crashing across the table and bringing it to the floor with him.

* * *

Danfield and a small cluster of people, including a doctor who lived down the beach, were gathered around Evans who sat in an armchair in an upstairs bedroom. Fred Danfield spoke to Evans when he had regained his senses.

"What happened?" Danfield said. "You called out two names; Laura and Vera something. It seemed as if you were shocked by what you saw."

"I don't know what happened," Evans told Fred Danfield when he had regained his senses. "When I handled the watch, I had a vision."

"What was the vision?" Danfield asked.

"Women in a dark room," Evans said. "They were gathered in a circle at a table. I remember only that I felt threatened. I don't know why."

"You called her name, Roger," Danfield said. "You asked if she was Laura. Then you passed out and fell across the table. It seemed as if you had seen something and were shocked by what you saw."

"I don't know what it was specifically," Evans said, the fear in his eyes having considerably subsided. "A vision. Eyes. I saw a pair of eyes. Bright eyes and people in the darkness."

Laura stood just outside the bedroom door with Frank beside her. She held his hand all the while. Laura's hand stiffened when Evans mentioned that he had a vision of eyes.

"Here is Laura Whitney," Danfield told Evans. "She's the woman whose watch you held. She's concerned about you. You called out to her."

Danfield beckoned Laura and Frank to join him. They moved to Danfield and stood beside him where he sat. Laura waited for someone to speak.

46

Danfield broke the silence. "See now," he said, his voice consoling. "Nothing in the world to be upset about. Just a simple case of nerves and an overreaction to a fine performance."

Laura forced a strained smile. Her heart was pounding while she fought to appear calm. She had to know what Evans thought his vision of eyes and a sense of threat meant. It apparently related only to her.

"Mr. Evans," she said, "I know this is not the time, but I must know what you think your vision meant. I recently had an eye operation and the coincidence is too startling for me to let it go without asking. I couldn't help overhearing what you said about brilliant eyes in a dark room. What can it mean? Why were you terrified? And who is Vera Lancaster?"

Evans was still perplexed. "Mrs. Whitney," he said, "please believe me when I tell you that I have no idea what this means. I never heard that name before. I received an impression from you immediately when we were first introduced. Once I blanked my mind out I was handed your watch and I reacted strongly. The vision could mean anything."

"But you seemed terrified." Laura said. "Surely a feeling so strong has to mean something to you."

"I can't explain it," Evans said. "Perhaps you have doubts about your operation?"

Laura could feel people in the group around Evans staring at her.

"I have doubts, of course," she said. "Yes. Do you think you sensed my fear of the future?"

"It's possible, Mrs. Whitney," Evans responded, wanting to end this conversation immediately. "It's the only explanation I can think of that makes sense. And I have no idea who the woman is that you mentioned."

"Vera Lancaster," Laura said. "That's the name you used. Who is she?"

"I don't remember anything else," he said.

But he did remember. Evans had no answer. There was no reason to reveal he had a flashing vision of his own death. He was not suicidal but the vision seemed to impart the concept of suicide. It wasn't until he handled Laura's watch that the scene rocked his consciousness. He saw himself falling from a height, a thick purple cord wrapped around his neck, his body jolting to a devastating halt as the cord snapped taught, killing him. He saw his body dangling at the end of the cord, dead.

* * *

Later, at their own home, Laura resumed the questions, which still bothered her about Evans' performance.

"I don't buy what that man Evans offered as an explanation about what happened tonight, Frank," she said.

"Sounded logical to me," he answered.

"Logical, I'm not sure. But he didn't tell us what he meant when he asked if it was me during his vision. Also, he cried out 'Are you Vera Lancaster?' Who is she? And why did he see a pair of eyes in a dark room? Is it possible...do I have her corneas?"

"Evans is an actor, Laura," Frank offered. "He plays a game for his audience. What he did tonight was for effect. It's probably the kind of thing he works into every performance to scare the suckers."

"No, Frank. I don't think so. He sounded genuinely involved. He was getting sensations from me. He must have a true ability to sense things. I am convinced of that. Look how he was able to connect the right people to each object."

"For crying out loud, it was nothing more than a trick." Frank sounded irritated.

"There might be a degree of trickery involved," she insisted. "But I'm sure he has some mental ability. ESP. Clairvoyance. I'm not sure of the correct terms. But he saw something about me that scared the hell out of him. Suppose there is something dangerous about having the transplants that we don't know about or hadn't thought about. It's a new world I've entered, one that I never thought about before. I don't know if I've had enough time to accept it."

"Please, honey," Frank offered. "Don't make anything supernatural out of mere tricks. He probably had it rigged with Fred Danfield who to collect items from. He knew the names and situations in advance. He should never have upset you like this." He came to her and put his arm around her shoulder. "Think only of the positive. You're able to see again. You're able to paint."

"I'm only concerned, Frank," she said, "that something might be wrong."

That night in bed as Frank slept, Laura lay awake. In her mind she tried to conjure for herself the image Evans had seen. Two eyes, gleaming out of the blackness around them. She tried in vain to derive meaning from his outburst. Finally, after hours of frustration, she fell into a fitful and restless sleep.

* * *

The next day, Sunday, Laura and Frank were invited to dinner at the Danfield's. Laura, was, at first, reluctant to return only a day after the incident with Roger Evans, but she told Frank to say yes. She decided that she would like to see Evans again. Perhaps, by now, he could answer the questions still bothering her.

Charlotte Danfield greeted them and brought them to the patio behind the Danfield house. They followed her to a wall at the west end of the immense stone patio. No other guests were here today. Thank God, Laura thought. She was not in the mood to get involved with a crowd. From their position they were afforded a magnificent panoramic view of the Atlantic Ocean and the two hundred yards of gleaming white beach leading to it. Laura sipped a martini with Charlotte Danfield and Frank.

"Where's Fred?" Frank asked.

"He's down on the beach," Charlotte Danfield said. "I'll get him." She descended the long flight of steps to the beach. Below they could see Fred Danfield near the water's edge speaking to another man.

"Is that Roger Evans with Fred?" Laura asked.

"It sure looks like him," Frank said.

Charlotte and Fred Danfield spoke to one another briefly and both started back up to the house. Evans turned away from them and stood with his back to the house facing out to the sea. Laura wondered why he wasn't returning with the Danfields. She was certain he was aware of her presence. Then she thought maybe he doesn't want to see me.

The Danfields came onto the patio. Fred walked quickly to Laura and he threw his arms around her.

"Was that Roger Evans?" Laura asked.

Mike Walsh

"Yes," Danfield answered. "Roger is staying with us for a few days."

"Why didn't he come up to the house?" Laura asked.

"He felt he would be interfering with our dinner. He preferred not to come up."

"A shame," Laura said. "I wanted to talk to him. I still have unanswered questions to ask."

"I don't know if I'm ready for any more of that psychic business," Frank interjected trying to send a message to Laura to curtail her scrutiny.

Laura suddenly broke away from them, so abruptly Frank found himself unable to rationalize her action to the Danfields. She walked briskly down the steps to the solitary figure below.

"I'm sorry," Frank apologized to the Danfields. "I don't know what's come over her. She is never rude."

"It's alright, Frank," Chrlotte said. "After what she's been through nothing will ever be the same again."

As Laura drew closer to Evans she could see that he was kneeling on the beach, writing something in the sand with a stick. As she came up to him he turned, saw her coming and got to his feet. He suddenly walked rapidly down the beach away from her.

Laura came to where Evans had been kneeling and looked down at what he had written in the sand.

A name carved there in large capital letters that sent a wave of chills through her body.

It said simply, JENNY DOUGLAS.

Laura looked up at Evans' form vanishing down the curve of the white beach, his path marked by the footprints he left in the wet sand.

Why did he write Jenny Douglas' name in the sand? What did he know about Jenny?

* * *

On the way home Frank finally spoke to Laura after a restrained evening. He was cross with her for her abruptness and his impetuosity showed.

"Why did you walk off like that?" he queried.

"I felt compelled to see Evans. It was vital."

50

"So what happened?"

"Frank, when I got to him he had written a name in the sand."

"What name."

"He wrote...Jenny Douglas."

"Jenny's name?"

"Yes. What in the hell does he know about Jenny? She's still missing. How could he know that?"

"I don't get it," Frank said, his tone relaxing.

"I don't either. How did he connect Jenny to me? Could he have meant he knows where Jenny is?"

"That sounds possible."

"Have you mentioned Jenny's name and disappearance to Danfield?"

"No. Never."

"Then Evans has to be psychic. Yesterday he mentioned the vision he had experienced. It was basically identical to the dream I had."

"You really do believe that, don't you?" Frank was not as resolved as Laura.

"Yes. He feels things. Knows things. And is afraid of something about me."

"Oh, for God's sake, be serious."

"I am serious, Frank." Laura became pensive. "I'm beginning to think it has something to do with the operation. The eyes. And who is Vera Lancaster? Did I get her corneas?"

Frank had no answer for her the rest of the way home.

* * *

That night Laura had a second vision. In her subconscious she saw clearly. It was as if she were wide-awake. She sat up in bed, a sense of presence in the room other than her and Frank. The room was engulfed in darkness with only the palest moonlight coming through the bottom of the shades. Laura's eyes roamed the room.

As her eyes adjusted to the blackness she began to see things. A chair, the corner of a bureau, the end of the bed. But there in the inky blackness of the far corner of the room something flickered.

Two unblinking blood-red serpentine eyes stared at her out of the dark.

Mike Walsh

She stifled a scream.

Wake up Frank, she thought. Quickly. She reached over and nudged him. He didn't move. Harder. His heavy breathing continued. Was this a dream?

A dark liquid shape moved and blended with the shadows. She felt her skin crawl with the chill of apprehension. The shape became more definable. A man cloaked entirely in black stepped forward, his right hand extended to Laura, beckoning her.

A dimmed vision unfolded to her. She was watching Jenny Douglas drive away from her house in the early morning and drive to the Northcove railroad station. She called to her, but seemed to have no voice. Jenny left the car in the station parking area and boarded a train heading for New York City.

Suddenly she was jolted into consciousness in her own bed.

Chapter 10

Laura and Frank awoke at five AM. In order for Frank to arrive at his office in Manhattan by approximately nine o'clock it was necessary for him to catch a train at about six AM. Before her accident she and Frank talked about someday giving up New York City and moving to the Hamptons permanently. But she knew that dream could not be realized for many years to come. Both would have to abandon careers in Manhattan. Besides, their current house was not heated, just a fireplace for chilly nights. It was situated in a summer community during which all water was shut off for the winter.

After a brief breakfast she drove him to the station. There were only a few other couples parked there this early, like them, waiting for the train.

"I'll see you Friday evening," he said. "I'll call you before I leave and let you know what train I'll be on."

"I'm gonna miss you," Laura said. "Four days is a long time."

"Laura," Frank said. "I'm still not sure about you staying alone for four days. Are you sure you'll be all right?"

"Certainly. Now don't you worry," she replied. "I'll be fine. And we have plenty of neighbors along the beach. It's not as if I was isolated."

He reached over and kissed her, a lot more passionately then a mere good-bye kiss.

"You're sure you don't want to come back to the house with me right now?" Laura asked when they finally broke. "That kiss held a lot of promise."

"Don't make leaving any harder for me then it already is," Frank said. "I've got a lot of work piling up. I can't take any more time off."

"Why are you imagining things?" Laura quipped, impishly.

For the slightest instant she thought Frank was going to tell her to drive back to the house, but as he started to speak they heard the wail of the incoming westbound train.

"Interrupted by the efficient punctuality of the Long Island

Railroad," Frank muttered flippantly.

He kissed her again, not quite as passionately.

"I will miss you too," he said.

She watched him board and waited until the train was completely out of sight before she started the SUV and pulled away. As she drove towards home she thought again of the incident with Roger Evans. She was convinced that Evans had not fully disclosed the truth of what was troubling him.

When she got back to the house dawn was just breaking over the horizon. She walked to the beach and looked back towards the house. The light of the rising sun was behind it and the building was enfolded in shadow. It possessed an unreal quality that matched her mood.

She suddenly felt cold. She closed her arms around her body and walked to the house.

Something unexplainable had happened to her this weekend, she decided. Am I a conveyor of some psychic force? Could I have become a catalyst of tragedy? Perhaps that was why Evans had this sense of apprehension. What did Evans know about Jenny Douglas? Why had he scrawled her name in the sand? Strange events were multiplying. What was that awful sensation of that hand reaching out and touching me on the shoulder? And the vision of Jenny driving away?

Could our house be haunted, she thought. Some force here that Evans saw through me; a ghost in our house?

Laura had never given much thought to the supernatural. Occasionally she might read an occult novel. She had heard about houses that were supposedly haunted, about poltergeists, ghosts and such, but she had always treated these subjects as merely the fantasy of someone's imagination. She regarded the appearance of ghosts as so much absurdity invented by creative people to sell books or movies. Through these vehicles a ghost always appeared dressed in clothing of the period in which he or she died. Laura considered the foolishness of this condition. Where did the clothing come from? Did the ghost stop at a "ghost store" to pick up "ghost garments?" It seemed so ridiculous to her. And if the body was interred and subject to massive decay, how could it resume a corporeal condition when it appeared as a ghost?

She heated the coffee and sat in the porch sipping it. After a while she went upstairs to the sleeping level where she kept some reading material that she had accumulated over the last few years. She looked through the magazines and books but found nothing that satisfied her curiosity. She decided to drive into Southampton village and buy whatever she could find on supernatural occurrences. Besides, it gave her an excuse to pick up some art supplies that she needed.

She waited until nine o'clock to make sure the stores were open. She parked in the heart of town and walked through the village. Although she lived closer to the town of Sag Harbor she enjoyed walking through Southampton. She loved the village. She was prompted to buy a house near town but finding their cottage on the Peconic Bay fulfilled her desire and was a lot less expensive.

She walked to the art supply store where she bought her painting materials. She selected a batch of oil paints, some new filbert brushes, a supply of primed, rolled canvases and a load of wood stretcher bars. She loaded everything into the back of the parked SUV and continued empty-handed along the street.

She bought a few reference books about the occult in a local bookstore and went into a diner. There, she sat in a table at the rear and had her third coffee of the day. She began reading a book on parapsychology. It briefly touched on such phenomena as psychic forces, ESP, clairvoyance, apparitions, mediums, channeling. Within minutes she became totally absorbed in the text.

A hand suddenly touched her on the left shoulder. She jumped with such a start that she almost upset the table and its contents.

"My dear!" Charlotte Danfield said. "I didn't mean to startle you so. I'm sorry."

Charlotte sat down opposite her.

"Oh, Mrs. Danfield," Laura said, slightly ashamed. "I'm the one who should apologize. I was reading and forgot for the moment where I was. Time and place seemed to have disappeared."

The waitress came over and began wiping up the spilled coffee. Laura ordered another and one for Charlotte Danfield.

"I'm glad I ran into you, Mrs. Danfield," Laura said. "I was going to call you later today."

"Don't you think it's time we dropped the Mrs. Danfield?" Charlotte Danfield said. "Call me Charlotte, please." She began thumbing through the paperbacks on the table. She frowned inquisitively and asked, "Isn't this a little out of the ordinary reading material for an artist?"

"Probably. But I was curious about extraordinary things that have been happening lately," Laura said. "I wanted to talk to you. I have to know more about Roger Evans. Have you any idea why he was reluctant to see me Sunday?"

"I don't know what came over him," Charlotte replied. "He didn't return to the house until after you and Frank had left. He wouldn't talk to me about the way he acted. But Roger has been known to become a bit withdrawn at times. You'll have to forgive him. He has had a tough time of it for the last few years."

"What do you mean?" Laura asked.

"Oh, I'm sorry. Of course you wouldn't know." Charlotte was apologetic, her tone setting a somber mood. "Roger had a terrible experience involving his wife."

"What happened?"

"Well, there was a time in Roger's life when his involvement with psychic experimentation was his entire endeavor. A ghost buster, so to speak. He operated sometimes with two men who live in Manhattan, a priest and a parapsychologist. But he probed most occult occurrences with his partner, his wife, Audrey. Together they worked as a team."

Charlotte Danfield took a sip of coffee and continued. "His use of Audrey as an associate in a particular experiment about two years ago resulted in permanent mental damage to her. Roger had attempted a procedure using his wife and a woman who supposedly had been possessed by the spirit of a person known dead. Roger had talked Audrey into the experiment and he presided over a double hypnosis. From what I understand he had hypnotized both women.

"Roger couldn't bring his wife out of her deep trance but the hexed woman survived the ordeal, freed of her nightmare. In one sense, he had succeeded. Roger's wife, though, has been institutionalized since then, lost in her own secret world."

"I'm so sorry to hear that." Laura was sincere, yet thought there had been immediacy in Evans' actions at Charlotte Danfield's house that transcended a long existing trauma. "But I feel that what happened at your house goes beyond his wife's situation. I believe he saw something in a vision that involved both of us, him and me."

"Whatever Roger saw or felt must have a root cause," Charlotte said. "He is known as a man of integrity. You're not suggesting that he faked all this for effect, are you?"

"No. Of course not. It puzzles me, though, why he wouldn't even speak to me on the beach. I was never completely satisfied with our first meeting and his brief explanation about what had happened. I believe he's frightened of something and it has to do with me."

"Frightened of you? I find that hard to believe."

"Charlotte," Laura said. "Do you remember what I told you when I tried to talk to Roger Evans on the beach?"

"About what, specifically?"

"Evans had printed the name 'Jenny Douglas' in large capital letters in the sand."

"Oh, yes, of course. You mentioned that. Do you know whom he meant?"

"Yes. She is a personal friend. And I wondered why he had written her name. There was no way he could have known I had a childhood friend named Jenny Douglas? I mean, you hadn't mentioned it to him in passing, had you?"

"No, I never mentioned it, I'm sure. I don't even know the name."

"Did Fred ever?"

"No. I'm willing to bet he hadn't. We hadn't seen Roger for six months before this past weekend."

"I can't figure it out," Laura said. "I don't know why he printed her name. But here's the strangest thing...Jenny disappeared. She went missing and left two children and her husband."

"Lord, no!" Charlotte Danfield was genuinely surprised. "I'm so sorry. How did it happen?"

"We don't know."

Charlotte Danfield sipped her coffee. "Are you suggesting there is some bizarre connection between Roger and your friend's disappearance?" she asked.

"I'm not sure. But why did he write her name? I can't put a name to it, but something is happening. He was disturbed the first time we met."

"Roger is psychic. He sees things," Charlotte said.

Mike Walsh

"You're saying he can predict things?"

"Well, yes. He does possess some ability."

"What sort of ability?" Laura questioned.

"He can foresee future events. Clairvoyant, I guess you'd call it. Extra sensory perception. I'm not sure of the specific terms. He really can read minds. Many times he does in his act. I know that he gets messages when he handles objects."

"But there was something about me which jolted him."

"With a personality like Roger who can tell what it was? He might have been playing a game the night he first met you. He might even be playacting now. He won't tell us anything. But I wouldn't try to make anything supernatural out of it, Laura."

"I would still like to talk to him," Laura said.

"Roger has returned to New York. He left early this morning."

Damn, Laura silently swore. He was probably on the same train as Frank.

"Laura, I wish you wouldn't take any of this seriously. I think you are taking a simple theatrical performance and building it into something mysterious which just isn't the case."

How could you know? Laura thought. How could you know about the hand on the beach touching me, the terrible vision seeing those women in trouble, a dream about an ominous figure showing me Jenny leaving her family? What did Evans mean by writing her name in the sand? Was all this a connection to Evans' apprehension?

"I must talk to Evans, Charlotte," she said, forcefully.

"I guess you must," Charlotte Danfield agreed. "I would probably react the same if I were in a similar situation."

"Is there number where I can reach him in New York?"

"Sure," Charlotte said. Digging through her handbag, she produced a small telephone book. "Actually, he is listed in the phone book." She found the number and Laura wrote it down on a blank page in one of the paperback books.

"Thank you, Charlotte," she said. "I must ask one more favor of you."

"Surely, Laura. What is that?"

"Don't mention this conversation to anyone, please."

58

Chapter 11

Frank Whitney worked the speed bag, establishing a forceful rhythm with both gloved fists that sounded like rolling thunder. He was good at it. He liked to work the bag whenever he went for a boxing workout at a gym on the lower eastside of Manhattan. His boxing ability was established in college where he won the middleweight college championship two years running. These days he was more in the light-heavyweight class.

Boxing seemed natural to him. It was a perfect method of pushing the body to extremes and keeping his prowess for defense at a maximum potential. Not that he had ever really needed a good physical defense in his adult life. He just couldn't break the habit. Through exercise as a requirement, he discovered the boxing ring and he stayed on course.

Generally there was always an acquaintance in the gym who would go a few rounds with him in the ring. Today was different. No one he knew showed up. So he worked the big bag and the speed bag.

A man about his size, in boxing regalia, approached him. He knew this man by sight. He was a professional boxer seen constantly at the gym. He was also a contender for the cruiserweight championship. His name was Buddy Nelson.

"Say, pal," Nelson asked Frank. "I seen you around the gym. I like your style."

"Well thank you," Frank said. "I consider that quite a compliment coming from you, Buddy."

"It's okay," said Nelson. "How'd ya' like to go a few rounds with me, a little warm up."

"I'm not exactly in your class, Buddy," Frank said.

"Hey, I'll go easy."

"I'd love to," Frank said. "If you think I'll give you enough competition."

"Don't worry. You look better than most of the turkeys I work out with."

The two men climbed into the ring. The owner of the

gymnasium entered to serve as referee. Workers at the gym dubbed as corner men for the two adversaries.

"Three three-minutes rounds," the referee said. "Agreed?"

Both fighters nodded.

The bell rang and the men squared off. Nelson was left-handed, a southpaw. He led with an extended right hand, measuring Frank for the quick jabs that were to come. Watch for that lightning right jab, Frank told himself. And Nelson's power was in his left hand. He was known for his strong left cross.

Frank was right-handed. He led with his left. The men jabbed, feeling each other out for the first minute of the first round. Frank kept his foot motion moving to the outside of Nelson's right foot, stepping away from the threatening left hand.

Nelson smiled, acknowledging that Frank was doing the right thing. Suddenly Nelson stepped into Frank's defense, unleashed two quick right jabs and followed with a left uppercut that caught Frank just on the tip of his jaw. His reflexes backed him just out of range of the full force of the blow. But it was a good shot. It threw him off balance.

Frank now knew the reality of this short fight. Nelson was out to put Frank down.

Frank regained his stance and resumed boxing as he parried Nelson's onslaught at the end of the first round. His corner man splashed water on him, as he took the mouthpiece from his mouth.

"Watch out, Frank," the gymnasium employee warned him. "This guy is looking to take you out. Keep your distance. Jab. Jab. Don't get in close. That's where he'll nail ya'"

Frank nodded. The mouthpiece back in place, the bell sounded for round two. The opponents moved to the center of the ring and touched gloves. Nelson let loose a quick overhand roundhouse left that Frank partially blocked. But the blow bounced along the top of his head, dizzied him and put him to the canvas. He got groggily to his feet and took an eight count. The referee wiped Frank's gloves on his shirt and stepped aside as Nelson closed on Frank once again.

Damn, Frank thought, I'm getting the shit kicked out of me. For the remainder of the round he stayed out of range and boxed as best he could. Nelson constantly took the aggressive lead, driving Frank back. And just before the close of the second round Frank caught Nelson off balance. He let go with a double left jab that distracted Nelson just enough to throw in a forceful straight right with the power of his body behind it. It caught Buddy Nelson right on the button and dropped him to his knees as the bell rang.

Now an interested crowd formed around the ring for the final round. Men, working out, stopped their activities and gathered for the show.

"That guy put Nelson down," one said.

"Who the hell is he?"

"Damn, did you see that right hand?"

Everyone wanted to see the third round. The two men approached each other as the bell rang. Frank expected Nelson to come out charging, asserting he could wipe up the floor with this upstart, to prove that the knockdown was a fluke, an accident. But he didn't. Nelson boxed, jabbed and kept Frank at a distance for the entire round, getting in a few good shots, which Frank would remember for the rest of the week. Frank realized he had been totally out-boxed in the final round.

As the bell rang at the end Buddy Nelson came to Frank and put his left arm around his shoulders.

"Damn good fight," he said in Frank's ear. To the men gathered around the ring, he held Frank's right arm in the air and shouted "How about this guy? Whatta ya' think?"

The men around the ring applauded Frank. As he left the ring some clapped him on the back, some muttered praise as he headed for the showers.

Back at the advertising agency word spread about what Frank had managed. The mouse under his right eye that lasted all week was his badge of honor that the rumor was validated as fact.

* * *

The sun was bright in an almost cloudless sky for the remainder of the day. Laura took advantage of the good weather and worked on her painting of the beach house. She had to set up her easel approximately in the same location in the previous sitting. Position was necessary for the proper composition. She found that she was uncomfortable all day. She realized that she was glancing back over her shoulder too many times and her head twitched inadvertently to her left. Nonetheless, the painting was progressing well. Within two days she had over half the work done. She had begun to add detail, and, by using photos she was painting Frank into the scene. She positioned him on the deck, just coming out of the doors.

As the light faded she packed up her materials and was halfway to the house when the phone rang. It was difficult to run on the sand with her arms full but Laura managed to it before it stopped ringing. She was pleased to hear Frank's voice.

"So how's my girl?" he asked cheerfully.

"I'm fine. How are you?" she responded, her voice perky. "Where are you calling from?"

"Ultimate Massage Emporium. Where else?"

"Are you still at the office?"

"Caught in the act. Yes. I had plenty to catch up. Believe it or not, on the SoftSilk account. It's so damn lonely in the apartment without you, I figured I'd put in a little extra time here and get ahead of it."

"Did you have dinner yet? You know it's almost eight-thirty."

"No, I haven't," Frank said. "But I'll stop for a bite as soon as I leave here."

"And when will that be?" Laura knew he would not eat properly.

"Laura, you do so sound like the doting wife."

"Don't I though," she quipped.

Frank laughed. "How's the painting coming?"

"Just great. I was working on your face when you called."

"How do I look?"

"The added touch of putting you in the painting makes it a veritable masterpiece," she kidded.

"Dammit," Frank said. "I love you and I miss you already."

"I miss you too," she said.

"Why don't you come into the city for a few days?" Frank suggested. "We'll do the town. We haven't been out for a long while. We can spend a few days in town and you can go back to the Hamptons on Monday."

"While you work in the office each night until nine or ten. What do I do in the meantime?"

"If you come in I promise I won't work a minute past six. Then

62

we'll have the weekend free."

"I'll bet."

"Come on. How about it? Hit a couple of great restaurants. See a show. We'll have fun."

Laura pondered a moment. She wanted to get into Manhattan. She wanted to speak to Roger Evans. She had intended to phone him, but she knew that wouldn't be satisfactory. She wanted to see him in person, to feel his reaction to her questions.

"All right," she consented. "You talked me into it."

"Great," Frank's voice rang out. "When can I expect you?"

"I'll tell you what," she said. "I'm way ahead on this painting. I'll work on it tonight and tomorrow. I'll meet you at your office tomorrow around six o'clock and we'll go out for dinner."

"Sounds great. I'll make reservations for us. Want to see a show? What would you like?"

"How about the Ultimate Massage Emporium? Don't they have a floor show?"

"Touché," Frank laughed. "Just dinner then. And afterwards we can hit a few nightspots. Okay?"

"You've got a date. See you tomorrow," Laura said. "And Frank, I want you to leave there in ten minutes and get something to eat."

"I promise," he said.

* * *

Laura hung up the phone and found Roger Evans' number. She dialed it and waited while it rang many times. She was about to hang up when someone finally answered at the other end.

"Yes?" the soft voice said.

"Roger Evans?" Laura asked.

"Yes. This is Evans. Who is this?"

"Mr. Evans," Laura tried to keep the edge out of her voice. She didn't want to scare him off again. "This is Laura Whitney. We met at the Danfields..."

"I know who you are," he answered quickly. "What do you want?"

"Mr. Evans, is it possible to see you, talk to you? I'll be in Manhattan tomorrow."

"Mrs. Whitney, I'm leaving on an extended trip in a few days. I've got to get prepared. I can't spare the time. Besides, we really have nothing to say to each other."

"I think we do," she insisted. "Please, Mr. Evans, I won't take much of your time."

"Mrs. Whitney, I implore you," Evans blurted out. "I can't help you. I don't know what you want of me."

"I need to know the truth," Laura said. "I believe you know more about me than you've admitted. Something has been happening to me in the last few weeks. I can't put my finger on what it is specifically. Unnatural things."

She told him about the dreams, the hand touching her, the name, Vera Lancaster, and, of course, Evans' strange reaction to her when he first met her.

After a long silence Evans sighed and said, "I sympathize with your situation, Mrs. Whitney, but I don't know what I can do to help you."

"Just talk to me, please. Perhaps together we might find a common link to our thoughts. Give me just a half hour of your time. That's all I ask."

Again the long silent pause, as if Evans fought a bitter battle with his conscience.

"All right," he said finally. "Tomorrow." He gave her his address.

* * *

Laura caught an early train. She made it into Penn Station by twelve-thirty and took a cab to the address Roger Evans had given her. He lived on the fourth floor of a small apartment building on the east side not far from where she and Frank lived. She found his name and rang the bell below it. She announced herself to Evans and he buzzed her in. He was waiting for her on the landing by the elevator. He escorted her to his apartment and closed the door behind her.

"May I get you something to drink?" he asked.

"Coffee would be fine if you have it made."

Within a minute they were seated opposite each other over a glass-topped coffee table, Evans on a large chair and Laura in a sofa that practically enveloped her. The apartment was done in an ordinary motif, the walls painted white, with a few colorful prints hung in the living room. The eclectic decoration seemed to fit the lean man who dressed in jeans and sweatshirt.

Laura sipped the coffee and stared at him. He seemed reserved, nervous. "I'm grateful you decided to see me before you left." she said

"Mrs. Whitney," he said, "I told you I'm going on a tour that will take me away from New York for at least two, maybe three months. If you hadn't called last night; you sounded forlorn, I would have left without giving it a thought. But I felt I owed you at least that much. Sometimes exaggerating what you don't know can be far worse than the truth."

"Why did you write that name in the sand on the beach Sunday?" Laura asked.

"I wasn't aware that I had written anything with meaning. Perhaps I was subconsciously doodling."

"You wrote the name Jenny Douglas in the sand. What could that name mean to you?"

"Nothing. I have no idea why I wrote it."

"That is the name of my friend. Did you know that she has been missing from her family?"

"No. I'm sorry. I had no idea," Evans said. "I'm clairvoyant. Not exceptionally so, but enough to get along. I can see things at times. But I'm not always right."

"Tell me, Mr. Evans, what is happening between us? What is it you know about me? What is there about me that you seem to fear?"

"Mrs. Whitney," Evans said flatly, "do you know anything at all about ESP?"

"Only the little I've read."

"Have you ever heard the term metagnomic?"

"I'm not sure. It's vague to me."

"It means that someone possesses supranormal awareness," Evans said. "Some people have this ability; to see things others don't see; to read people's thoughts, to foresee future events. It is quite evident to some that they possess this faculty. And there are many who have the ability but haven't the slightest idea they do."

Evans took a sip of the coffee in front of him. Laura noticed he was less nervous now. He talked more freely, much more at ease than when she first entered the apartment.

Laura finished her coffee. Evans got up and took the cup. "Here," he said "let me freshen that for you."

He went to the kitchen and returned in a moment with a fresh cup.

"Mrs. Whitney," he said, "did you know that you have the capability of psychic experience?"

Laura was startled. She put the cup down for fear of noticing how much her hand suddenly shook.

"Me? Psychic?" She was extremely skeptical.

"Yes. But I don't know to what degree you have developed."

"Are you certain?"

"Yes. I'm certain. I felt strong psychic disturbances the moment I met you at the Danfields"

"This really is difficult to believe," Laura said.

"Then you never knew about it?"

"No. Never. I hadn't the slightest idea that I could be psychic. I've never had any indication that I was."

"You must have had some idea you were able to pick up ideas or events before they happened in your lifetime."

"Never. I tell you I've never even thought about it."

"Well, believe me, Mrs. Whitney, you are metagnomic. You may not be aware of it but you are."

"Did you react so strongly to me the first night we met because you believe I have some psychic inclination?" Laura asked.

"No. When I first met you I felt magnetism, a bond. When I held your watch and made contact with you, something reached me. I actually went into a trance."

"What did you see?"

"A room. Women around a table clutching hands. A séance. Death. I saw a collapse. She seemed to be overwhelmed by some vague, misty, cloud-like force. It was a substance that appeared forcefully and trashed the room and everyone in it. The woman conducting the séance lost consciousness. She appeared to have died."

Laura felt fear clutch at her throat.

"This was my nightmare. The same vision I had," she said. "You've just described it. You said it was a séance. Are you sure?"

"Yes. It was a séance," Evans said. "Something astonishing happened, something unnatural. I can't pin it down. I believe what I experienced might somehow be connected to you."

"How could a séance be connected to me? I never attended one."

"You said you had the same vision that I described. There obviously is a connection."

Of course, it's obvious, Laura thought, there must be a connection.

"Mrs. Whitney, has anything changed in your life recently? Something that might dramatically affect your mental faculty?"

"Yes," Laura replied, ready to list the reasons for her session here with Evans. "My nightmare visions. My friend vanishing."

"No. That's not what I mean," Evans insisted. "I mean something that changed your life; physically, psychologically."

His statement was an instant eye-opener for Laura.

"Of course," she said. "Yes. A while ago I was hurt in a freak accident. I was blinded. And recently I had a corneal transplant in both eyes. Is it possible...?"

"There you go!" Evans interrupted. "That might be the cause of your disturbance."

"You're not implying that my operation gave me...an awareness of psychic phenomena?" Laura was incredulous.

"I'm only searching for answers," Evans responded. "Anything else you can think of that was a drastic change in your life?"

"No," Laura said. "No, dammit. If this is true...then whose corneas did I inherit? Was it Vera Lancaster, the woman whose name you called out?"

"I don't know."

"It could have been," Laura insisted. "You said you saw a séance. Was she a...what are they called, a channelor?"

"A medium."

"Was she a medium?"

"Yes. Vera Lancaster is a medium."

"You know her?" Laura asked, her voice quaking.

"I know of her."

"What does she have to do with me?"

"Mrs. Whitney, I haven't the faintest idea."

Laura sat back into the cushioned sofa. She was more puzzled now than she was before. Evans noticed her concern.

"Be careful, Mrs. Whitney," he said. "In the near future. I sense danger."

"What danger?"

"Death. It is nearby. It stalks us. I saw my own body, hanging from the end of a rope."

"And what did you see about me? What should I fear?"

"I'm not sure. But at the séance, Vera Lancaster, the medium...it seemed as if she had made contact with..."

"With what, Mr. Evans?"

"A spirit. She might have broken through. But if she did, we don't know if the spirit was benevolent or..."

"Or what?"

"...a demon, a being of complete evil."

Chapter 12

Laura decided to walk back to her apartment. It was only about ten blocks from Evans' place. Along the way she intended to pick up a few basic items at a local grocery store. While crossing Lexington Avenue and Forty-eight Street, amidst the moving people, a familiar face suddenly flashed in the crush. She turned back to the spot where the face appeared and there it was again, for an instant, like a blinking beacon in a sea of bodies. And then it was gone.

There was no doubt she had just seen Jenny Douglas walking among the pedestrians.

She ran across Lexington Avenue at an angle she calculated would intercept her friend. When she got to the sidewalk she spotted Jenny ahead of her by half a block. Remember what she is wearing, she told herself. Tan jacket, brown slacks and her obvious blonde hair.

She kept her eyes on Jenny who was moving uptown. Her friend seemed to be with a man who walked next to her. At first Laura wasn't sure but she noticed he would extend his hand to her waist or shoulder along the way. They crossed street after street in the upper East Side. Then they suddenly turned left on one of the cross streets and cut across Madison Avenue. Laura kept them in sight and watched the two climb the front stairs of a large, elegant house. The man with her took a key from his pocket and let them in the front door.

Laura climbed the stairs after them and stood before a double set of massive oak doors. She rang the bell. The blond haired man who was with Jenny, appeared at the door.

"Yes," he said. "Can I help you?"

"I'd like to speak to Jennifer Douglas please."

"Who?"

"Jennifer Douglas."

"There's no one here by that name," the man said.

"I saw her enter here a few minutes ago with you. Blond, slim, thirty-five years old," Laura said.

"No one here like that. Are you sure you have the right house?"

Another man came suddenly from behind the person at the door. He was dressed entirely in black. His chiseled handsome face cracked a smile. Laura felt a sudden rush of apprehension in his presence that made her tremble. Her first instinct was to run, to get away from him as quickly as she could. His stark, staring eyes bore into her like knives. The eyes seemed to change color as they locked onto her.

Dear God! She shuddered. What the hell is happening? Cold fear gripped her, sending icy shocks through her body. Who was this person? Her entire being cried out to leave, as if he were trying to persuade her by mental suggestion. But she knew the truth. She knew Jenny had entered this building. Laura fumed.

"I believe you've come to the wrong address," the man in black said, wryly smiling.

"I don't think so," Laura answered. "I followed my friend here with this man." She pointed to Johnnie Limbo.

"Sorry to disappoint you," the man in black said.

"May I come in and look for myself?" Laura asked, wondering if she had the courage to carry out her request. Her mind told her this was not a place for her to linger.

"Why no, Laura," came the answer, "you may not."

And the front door slammed shut. He called me Laura, she thought. He knows my name.

* * *

Laura dialed information on her cell phone and got the phone number of the police station nearest to the address Jenny had entered.

"What can we do for you ma'am?" The police operator asked.

"A friend of mine was reported as a missing person a few weeks ago," She gave Jenny's name and address and her own name and address. She was connected to a detective who introduced himself as Detective Flynn.

She repeated the information about Jenny as a missing person.

"I saw her today," she added. "On a street in Manhattan."

"Where is she now?" Flynn asked.

She gave the officer the address. "I followed her. I rang the bell and the people there would not let me in. They denied that Jenny was in the house. But I saw her go in. And here's the strange thing, officer, the owner of the house called me by my first name. I've never laid eyes on him, ever, and he knew my first name."

"You're absolutely sure?"

"Absolutely," she affirmed.

"Okay. We'll meet you at the house."

Laura was told to wait on the corner nearest the house in question. A squad car pulled up at four-thirty. Laura was getting worried that she would run out of time to meet Frank this evening at their apartment.

"Mrs. Whitney," the detective said, emerging from the car. "I'm Tom Flynn. I checked your story and Jennifer Douglas is considered a missing person. Let's get to the house."

The squad car double-parked in front of the house. Flynn met Laura with two uniformed officers. All four climbed the steps while Detective Flynn rang the doorbell. The same man answered the door.

"Yes?" he asked casually.

"We have a warrant to search the house," Flynn said. He held the paper in his right hand. The man in black came and stood beside the man in the doorway.

"What is the problem, officers?" he asked. His voice resonated in Laura's ears, bouncing around in her brain like a bell-ringing clapper.

"Mrs. Whitney, here, claims that she saw a friend of hers, a missing person, enter this house this afternoon," Flynn informed them.

"This person," the man in black said, pointing to Laura, "came here earlier with that story. But no one entered this house today."

"Can I ask your name, sir?" Detective Flynn said.

"Certainly. My name is Saylem," Elymas said, using an anagram of his real name.

"That's it? Saylem. One name?"

"That's correct."

"Do you own this house?" Flynn asked.

"Yes. As a matter of fact, I do."

Flynn held up the warrant. "We'd like to search the house if you don't mind."

"No, I don't mind. Certainly. Come in."

As they entered Laura said, "And how did you know my name?"

"I'm sorry," the man in black said. "I don't follow."

"You called me Laura when I was here earlier. How did you know my name? I've never met you."

"I think you are mistaken once again, Miss...."

"Whitney," Laura said, thinking he probably knew that too.

"Well, Miss Whitney," Elymas said smugly, "I never used your name."

Laura frowned. Liar, she thought. What have you done to Jenny? Who are you and what is going on?

The police officers entered the house. The two great front doors led to an entry hall. Two interior doors opened to a massive foyer. In front of them was a tremendous winding staircase that ascended to upper floors and encircled a three-tiered crystal chandelier. What an impressive house, Laura thought. Who was this man and what did he have to do with Jenny? And why did she feel so terribly uncomfortable around him?

The officers dispersed throughout the house while Laura stayed downstairs. While sitting and waiting, Laura noticed that there were places on the walls where paintings had obviously hung. There were picture-hangers in many spots along the walls of the great hall. Yet there were only a few minor landscapes remaining. Where were the missing paintings?

Laura wandered to a closed room that was probably, she thought, a parlor. She looked around to see if anyone was nearby. Convinced she was alone, she swung the doors open. A long, narrow room spread before her. Again, the walls held many hangers, but few pictures. She thought either these people were in the process of moving in or moving out. It puzzled her.

Laura went back to the foyer and sat down. It took almost an hour but, when the officers reassembled, they informed Laura that Jenny was not in the house.

"She is here," she insisted. "I saw her come in here, I tell you."

"You must have been mistaken," Detective Flynn said.

"Can't you do something?" Laura pleaded.

"Not at this time, I'm afraid," said Flynn.

"I can't let this go," Laura said. "I know my friend came in here. Her family is worried to death about her. The fact that you can't find her doesn't mean that she isn't here. She might be held prisoner. She might be kidnapped."

"Then what was she doing walking around on the streets when you saw her?" asked Flynn.

"You found no one else in the house," Laura responded. "Yet the woman I followed went in. Whether she was Jennifer or not, where is she?"

"Perhaps you were mistaken about which house you picked out."

"I don't buy that. Something's wrong here and I'm going to find out what it is."

"Suit yourself, Miss Whitney," Flynn said. "But I'd say you just made a mistake."

What had happened to Jenny? Why did this diabolical person come out of nowhere and abduct Jenny? Could her best friend have had a lover that she had kept a secret and had suddenly given up her family for him? No. Laura did not believe that. Not for an instant. There was something of pure evil occurring here; something she was going to have to unravel herself. She was determined to get to the bottom of this mystery,

As the police left and Laura walked away, she glanced back at the house from across the street. Something at the corner of the roof caught her attention. She thought she saw a shape move; a slight movement. But it couldn't have been so. There was no one on the roof. Only the grotesque shape of a gargoyle looked down. It had not been there before. Could she have been mistaken about this? Was she mistaken about Jenny? Could she have only thought it was Jenny she had seen?

* * *

Back in her apartment she searched through her personal telephone directory for Ralph Douglas's work number. Douglas's secretary put her through.

"Laura," Ralph Douglas said. "Have you heard anything?"

"I'm in New York City, Ralph. I think I may have found Jenny..."

"What? Are you serious?" Ralph Douglas's excitement

exploded. "Where? When?"

"Well, let me explain," Laura said, her voice calm. "I saw a woman whom I was certain was Jenny. I followed her."

"You actually saw Jenny? In New York?"

"A woman I believed was Jenny. It was on Lexington Avenue. I saw her from a distance of a couple of blocks. I mean everything about her was Jenny. Hair, build, and the way she moved. God, I know Jenny so well. It had to be her."

"Did you talk to her?"

"No. She was too far ahead of me to stop her before she went into a large house."

"Where is this house?" Douglas asked.

"East Side, uptown. Anyhow, I saw her go into the building. I rang the bell and the people there wouldn't help me. They denied anyone came into the house. But I saw her go in. They are obviously hiding something. So I went to the police."

"God damn, Laura. Good for you. What happened?"

"They got a search warrant. I went back there with a police escort. They found nothing. The thing is I saw a woman enter the building. Whether it was Jenny or not, the police found no woman in the house. I saw a woman enter. Why did the police not find that woman no matter who she was? I don't think they believe me, Ralph."

Douglas became excited again. "You're saying they're not going to follow up on this?"

"They might. I don't know."

"Laura," Douglas asked. "Are you convinced it was Jenny you saw?"

Laura hesitated only a moment, and then said. "Yes."

"Give me the address. I'll get a private investigator to follow up."

Laura relayed the information to him. "I hope I'm right, Ralph. I hope it was Jenny I saw. If it was there's a mystery going on in that house."

"I'll find out. What police station was it?"

Laura gave the station number and Tom Flynn's name.

"And, Laura, thanks," Douglas said. "You've done more than the police have been able to do."

"She's my friend, Ralph. Keep in touch. Let me know what you find out."

Laura quickly ran through the mail and read the most pressing. She called Frank at his office at five-fifteen. The voice on the other end was brusque.

"Whitney," Frank said.

"Frank, it's me," Laura said.

"Laura," Frank responded joyously. "Where are you?"

"I'm home."

"At the apartment?"

"Yep. I just got in and I'm about to take a shower," she smiled at the thought of the image of her Frank would undoubtedly conjure at the moment. "I'll expect you in about an hour for a romp in the sheets"

"I'll be there," Frank said, his voice telling her there was a smile on his face. "How's the painting of the house coming?"

"It's almost finished. I should wrap it up this weekend. See you later." Then she added, "You won't forget?"

"Fat chance."

When she hung up she showered, relishing in the warm water rushing over her body, soothing, relaxing. And yet she could not fully relax. The dilemma of Jenny Douglas haunted her. What in the name of heaven had happened to her friend?

As she dried herself in front of the bathroom mirror a sudden movement behind her startled her. It was reflected in the mirror, a fleeting, vague motion, a woman's image, gossamer-like, ethereal. She gasped, catching her breath as a chill of fear came over her. She spun around. The door was closed. No one had entered. There was no one there.

God dammit! she swore. Not again. Ghosts appearing behind me, touching me. What's going on?

She wrapped the towel around her and entered the bedroom. Nerves, she thought, only nerves. Calm down. My new eyes playing tricks. Could have been anything. A cloud passing over the sun, cutting off the rays coming into the bathroom window. My damned imagination. That talk with Evans didn't help. Forget it. Don't make anything supernatural out of this.

Despite her apprehension over the day's events, the disturbing conversation with Roger Evans, and the sight of Jenny on the streets of Manhattan, Laura had committed to an evening of sexual pleasure with Frank. He would be looking forward to a romp. She could tell him of her activities afterward. But her mind raced with the occurrences of the day. It was hard to shake images of what she had witnessed.

She dug out a scanty black lace outfit she had bought at Victoria's Secret. Frank had seen it when passing a window display and encouraged her to buy it.

"No. You buy it for me," she said at the time.

"I'd feel a little awkward buying it," he had replied.

Having fun with his shyness, Laura insisted he go in and make the purchase. He did, while she waited outside. Through the store window she could see how uncomfortable he was with the sales lady. When he came out of the store she asked if he got the right size.

"Of course," he had responded. "I merely pointed you out when she asked me your size."

She stretched out on the bed, waiting for Frank to come home. Her mind wandered and she saw, in her rumination, the movement in the bathroom mirror again. The same sudden moment of fear she had felt overcame her. She shook her head and brought herself out of it immediately. But the thoughts persisted.

It was a marvelous romp—for Frank. Frank was consumed with an urge that had been misplaced lately in their harried lives. She wished it would go as well for her. Her confused mind provoked her to "fake it" for the first time in their married life.

Afterwards Laura told Frank about seeing Jenny Douglas on Lexington Avenue.

"You're kidding me!" he exclaimed.

"I swear, Frank, it was Jenny."

"What did she have to say? Why did she walk out on Ralph?"

"She did not walk out on Ralph." Laura was adamant. "I never got to talk to her. She got away from me and went into a house." She told him about the episode with the police and the people in the house, especially the strange man who apparently owns it.

"Sounds odd to me," Frank said. "The police have got to follow this up."

"I left the information with Ralph. He's going to pursue it."

"All of this must have taken hours," Frank said. "What time did you get here?"

"I came in earlier," she said, realizing she would have to explain how she had spent the day. She decided to tell him of her visit with Roger Evans.

"You remember Roger Evans," she said, "the mentalist we met at the Danfields."

"How could I forget?"

"I went to see him today."

Frank showed his disappointment with a frown. "Was this before or after seeing Jenny?" he asked.

"Before."

"Why would you possibly want to see him?" he asked.

"I had to get him out of my system. I wanted to know exactly what troubled him about me."

"What did you learn?" Frank asked. Laura could tell merely by his tone of voice and rigid expression that he was agitated.

"Well, for one thing, I believe now that I must have inherited that woman's corneas. The one he described in his vision. He said her name...Vera Lancaster."

"This sounds a little far-fetched to me," Frank said.

"Far-fetched or not," Laura continued, "I think he's solved a piece of the puzzle for me. If I did get her corneas it makes sense that I'm having visions. She was a medium, a spiritualist."

"Laura, honey," Frank said, attempting to thwart Laura's obsession with mysterious connections to this unknown woman, "you can't believe that the corneas from someone's eyes carry with them spiritual possession. Is that what you're saying?"

"Something like that," she said. "I'm not sure what, but I believe Vera Lancaster's corneas are in my eyes now and I believe there's something wrong."

"What could be wrong? You have better eyesight now than you had before. You don't need eyeglasses anymore."

"I found out that she died at a séance. I assume she was an organ donor and that other people also received parts of her body. I received her corneas."

"Fine, I'll go along with you so far. But you contend that those corneas carried with them a window to this woman's soul. You seem to imply that part of her still lives in you and that part retains the visions you are seeing."

"Yes. Something like that," Laura said, then asserted, "Exactly."

"Therefore," Frank said, "if other donor parts of her body went to other people these persons might also be affected by spirits."

"Possibly," Laura uttered, "but I only know what's happening to me."

Chapter 13

Laura had completed over a dozen paintings since adjusting to her new corneas. She kept two favorites for herself and had shipped the rest to Vernon Hayle's TheArtGallery on upper Madison Avenue.

Vernon Hayle, an elegant, meticulously groomed, slightly built man who proudly proclaimed his homosexuality, knew exactly which art sold and had a gifted eye for selecting rising new artists. He made a large profit for each of the ten years since he had formed his gallery. He was enthusiastic about new talent and never refrained from showing his ardor.

Laura hadn't seen him since her operation, although she had spoken to him many times on the phone. He had been to see her at the hospital immediately after her accident and he gave in to tears when he saw her eyes in bandages. Such a senseless loss. Laura was one of his favorite artists whose work steadily sold. The end of such talent was pointless.

She received Vernon's phone call just after her love session with Frank. She was elated at the sound of Vernon's voice. She valued his unwavering loyalty. He had encouraged her vigorously at the sight of her very first painting.

"Laura, my darling," he said, his voice ringing with enthusiasm, "the new work is no less than brilliant. How are you?"

"I'm just fine, Vernon. How are you?"

"The same, Laura. The same. My life doesn't change much. But you, God, you have changed. The crate arrived this morning and I was absolutely beside myself when I opened it. It's a new you. A complete new dimension. A side of you I didn't know was possible. I simply cannot describe to you in mere words how I feel. If I had ten artists like you to represent I'd be a rich man."

"I thought you already were a rich man," Laura quipped.

Vernon chuckled at the remark. "Can I buy you and Frank dinner tonight? How is Frank by the way? Does he own the ad agency yet?"

Laura had to hold back her laughter. "Not quite," she said. She turned to Frank. "Vernon Hayle. He wants to take us to dinner tonight. What do you say?"

"Fine with me," Frank said.

"Frank says yes," she told Vernon.

"Great. Shall we say Marie's around eight?"

"That's fine."

"Laura, my dear," Vernon added. "I can't wait to see you."

* * *

Marie's was a marvelous, intimate Italian restaurant on the East Side, not far from their apartment. Frank and Laura walked to their rendezvous, taking advantage of the clear warm night.

Vernon was waiting for them at the bar. He could hardly contain himself when he saw Laura enter. He hugged and kissed her. Frank felt slightly uncomfortable at his cheeky affection for his wife, but he shook Vernon's hand, restraining his feelings. He knew how much Vernon had influenced Laura's artistic life and how highly she thought of his judgment.

They were seated immediately in a dimly lit corner table and Vernon spoke after the waiter took their orders.

"Laura," Vernon said. "You are inspired, my dear. Your work actually smacks of genius."

"Oh, come now, Vernon," Laura said, smiling slightly, actually flattered. "You're getting carried away with the compliments."

"Not at all. I mean it. Your latest paintings are truly magnificent. You are becoming one of our great painters. Mark my words."

Laura blushed. Frank quietly sipped his drink. He agreed with Vernon. But he, of course, was prejudiced.

"I'm going to buy one of the paintings from the latest batch for my collection," Vernon said.

"Oh, Vernon, that's marvelous. Which one?" Laura was genuinely excited.

"The 'Broadway Snow Storm.' I simply fell in love with it the moment I saw it. You were absolutely inspired when you did that one."

"I loved doing it," Laura said. "I'm proud that you will be its owner."

"I brought a check. It merely wants the amount to be filled in. How much shall I make it out for?"

"Vernon, you know better than I what it would be worth," Laura admitted. "Anything you say."

"Laura, any amount I pay you today for that painting will be like stealing it. Some day it will be worth a fortune. No matter what I give you I'm going to feel guilty." He paused, his pen poised over the check. "Shall we say twenty-five thousand?"

"That's a bit much, Vernon. It's only a small painting," Laura said.

"Twenty-five it is," Vernon insisted. "And believe me, it's a small price for that work. I promise you this, Laura; it will stay with me till I go to my grave. I shall never sell it."

Laura was sincerely touched. She knew Vernon purchased paintings for his own collection on a speculative basis, buying cheaply when little-known artists were willing to give up their work for a small price and selling the work when a name had been established. Vernon knew what to buy and when.

"Thank you, Vernon. I'm truly honored that you want my painting. This means more to me than selling the whole lot."

Vernon smiled. Laura smiled. Frank smiled. It was a perfect evening.

Until Laura slept that night. Another vision came to shatter her tranquility and peace of mind.

She was in an apartment that seemed familiar. But it was dreamlike. Yes, it was a dream, another vision of which she was cognizant. She had been here before. When? And why was she here now? This was not at all like the dreams that repeated themselves, visions of Vera Lancaster, and the room where the séance was held. She felt no fear, yet she was aware of impending alarm. She moved silently through the rooms until she saw a man on the terrace outside a sliding glass door.

It was Roger Evans.

He seemed to be in a state of panic. Something terrified him. His fear seemed life threatening.

She watched as he backed against the terrace railing. Was he performing some magic trick? But no. He held his hands before his face partially hiding the panic and fear that Laura saw clearly.

Laura screamed silently and awoke from the dream.

Mike Walsh

* * *

Roger Evans knew, because of his self-admitted cowardice, that he would be useless to Laura Whitney. But his former colleagues, Gerry Stuart, a Catholic priest and Carl Spendler, a parapsychologist, were the right people to try to resolve her problem.

The trio had participated in many supernatural procedures. These were memories he once cherished; the three men sharing the quest for knowledge. As a team they were indispensable, each complementing the other on the tasks they incurred.

But the ordeal involving Evans' wife stifled his ventures into the occult and ended the team's total endeavors. The episode changed his life forever and left him a defeated man.

Since his wife's confinement, Evans had seen either man only for brief intervals during which they, as good friends, attempted to bring some little joy back into his life. Stuart and Spendler were still involved as a team in psychic research of the supranormal. Their enthusiasm seemed never to dim. Evans believed, even today, they were probably pursuing something, somewhere, that related to the unnatural. He felt that Laura's situation was typical of the diet on which they fed. She seemed possessed by a spirit with dubious intent.

He e-mailed a letter to Father Gerald Stuart telling him about Laura Whitney. Evans' hope was that Stuart and Carl Spendler might contact Laura. Spendler had been mentor to both men and he was the man to whom both aspired. In his letter to Gerry Stuart he wrote the phone number Laura Whitney had given him.

He was still packing his suitcases at two in the morning. He had consumed too much liquor to think clearly and knew he needed sleep. His flight was departing at eight AM. He managed to get one suitcase finished while the other lay open on his bed when he heard a noise in the apartment. He was in the bedroom and the slight movement, like the whisper of a breeze, came from the living room.

Evans straightened up from his chore and turned toward the other room. It had turned noticeably darker in there, as if the light bulb had been extinguished. He moved toward the doorway, curiosity urging him on. And then he stopped.

A dreadful alarm, like a jolt to the heart, overtook him. His apprehension over the past few weeks was now a sudden reality. There was something sinister in the next room. He felt it.

He could not face what he suspected was there. He sensed it had come to harm him. He must escape. But fear overwhelmed him. It froze his body and weakened his ability to move.

What in the name of God was it?

His heart pounded in his chest so violently he swore he could hear it. He sobered quickly, fighting the fuzziness in his brain. The terrace, he thought. His only escape route. There, he might climb to one of the adjoining terraces. He had to get out of his apartment. Whatever was in the next room was not normal, not human.

He threw open the hanging drapes, struggling with the cord. He got the sliding glass doors open and stumbled onto the small balcony. He slid the door shut behind him. His body seemed to move slowly; a grinding, rusted motor that refused to work.

He turned and looked back, like Lot's wife staring into the face of doom. Darkness enveloped the bedroom. A mist danced in the air like a dark Pollock drip-painting coming to life. At its center was a changing shape; the form of a man, yet not a man. It quivered, its form changing in an instant. It flinched and grew taller, bending and curving. Its features were murky, grotesque.

As the shape floated to the closed glass door it penetrated the solid surface, gliding through it as if it were liquid.

Horror froze Evans.

Suddenly the drapery cord flew through the air and wrapped itself around Evans' throat. It tightened quickly, choking the life out of him. As he struggled desperately to free himself he was inevitably forced by an inhuman strength, edging him over the balcony.

His brain cried out as he realized he was going to die. The cord wrapped itself around the railing of the balcony. Evans was living out the vision he had seen of his own death. He tried to cry out for help, but he had no voice. The cord had cut it off.

As he fell over the edge, the form took shape in the mist. Evans saw the face of death staring at him. It was an attractive, slender man in a black suit with serpent-like colorless eyes. Not at all what he expected death to be.

He plummeted into space. His neck snapped like the sound of a gunshot. The body swung, a pendulum ticking away meaningless time.

* * *

Laura learned of Roger Evans' death in the newspaper. It was an article buried inside that she might very well have missed had it not been for the large headline...

"MENTALIST FOUND DEAD

"Early this morning a man was found dead, hanging from the balcony of his fourth story apartment by a neighbor in the Beacon Hill section of Manhattan. Roger Evans, a magician and performing mentalist, was an apparent suicide. Although no suicide note was discovered the police have ruled out foul play..."

Laura nearly fainted as she read the story. She grabbed the arm of a chair to steady herself. Good God! Evans dead! Suicide! Her latest dream had been of Evans. She had witnessed him cowering in fear on the terrace of his apartment. Once again she had foreseen a death. The impact hit her with an awakening jolt.

She wandered around the apartment in a half daze. Finally she called Frank at work and told him about Evans' death.

"I can't believe what's been happening. He warned me that he had visions of his own death. By hanging. Why would he kill himself?"

"Please calm down, Laura," Frank consoled her. "You're making this sound like it's your fault. It's not."

"Frank." she cried. "Don't you understand? I went to see him the other day."

"So what? You didn't kill him."

"The paper says it looks like suicide. But why would he kill himself? What is going on?"

"That man wasn't all there to begin with," Frank said. "He seemed strange to me from the start. Why should you concern yourself whether or not he committed suicide?"

"He must have died because of me. Don't you see? He was terrified."

"Laura, please, you're sounding ridiculous," Frank replied, his voice externalizing the frustration he felt. "Why would he agree to see you and calmly talk to you if he was terrified? Look, I'll be right home and we can discuss this then. But don't upset yourself and don't assume any guilt because of a deranged man's reasoning."

"But I can't push aside the coincidence. Why should he die right after he saw me?" She began to cry. "And that terrible nightmare. I can't stand it anymore."

"Stay calm, Laura. I'll be right there."

Within thirty minutes Frank was home. He spent the afternoon calming her and reassuring her she need not accept the burden of guilt for motivations she could not possibly know.

Chapter 14

Vernon Hayle hung Laura's painting, "Broadway Snowstorm", in a place of honor in his gallery. It was now his favorite and became the centerpiece in the large open room where his best pieces were displayed. Laura was on her way to the top, he thought as he moved among the few patrons spilling in on this rainy day. Her work dominated the room with more than half the paintings assigned there—he had considered giving up the entire space for her—but, he decided, not yet. He would let her grow in stature first.

As he moved among the onlookers he noticed a distinctive man standing in front of Laura's "Broadway Snowstorm" oil painting. He was dressed in a black raincoat, black Fedora, black suit; an Armani, thought Vernon. Semi-long black hair hung outside the perimeter of the hat, covering his neck but not quite touching his shoulders.

Vernon could not make out the man's face; he was viewing him from the rear, but he was ready to bet he was as attractive from the front. There was something odd about his manner though. He was not merely staring at the painting; he was physically addressing it by movement. It was the strangest thing, thought Vernon. The stranger's hands were held in such a way as to imitate the act of painting the picture. His left hand appeared to hold an invisible palette while the right mimicked the motions of wielding an invisible brush. He dabbed the non-instrument at the non-palette over and over, ever so gently, appearing to touch where paint would have been and transferring it to the canvas. Yet he never touched the painting. He stood at least six feet away from it.

Curiosity guided Vernon. He drew closer, quietly, so as not to alert the person of his presence. As he approached from the left side of his target, the man turned slightly so that most of his face was exposed to Vernon's view. Vernon's breath drew in sharply. The remarkable beauty of the profile startled him. He became exhilarated as he moved closer, watching the stranger paint an imaginary canvas before him while his eyes were closed all the time.

He did not see Vernon approach him.

"Hello," said Vernon. "May I help you?"

"Pardon," said the stranger, turning his full countenance to Vernon who thrilled at the sight of the strikingly beautiful person.

"I am the proprietor of this gallery," Vernon said. "Can I be of assistance in any way?"

"Not, I think, at the moment," the exquisite visitor remarked. Vernon had to lure him into conversation. He could not let this person exit his life as swiftly as he had entered it.

"I see you admire Laura Whitney's Broadway oil," Vernon offered. "It's my favorite."

"Yes," the man answered. "Mine too. I know it well."

Now this was odd, thought Vernon. How could he know this painting well? It has been only two places, here and Laura's studio. Could he know Laura? Was Vernon's luck going to hold up?

"Are you a friend of Laura Whitney?" Vernon asked.

"I don't think so."

Vernon could not respond to this nebulous statement "My name is Vernon Hayle," he said, handing a calling card to the visitor.

"Saylem," the imposing man said. "Happy to make your acquaintance."

The Victorian English this person used enchanted him. Vernon had to look up at him. Saylem was at least three inches taller. Looking into his eyes was a strange and exhilarating experience for Vernon. They seemed to change color, as if they reflected the colors surrounding him.

"Only Saylem?" Vernon questioned. "No first name?"

"Saylem will suffice," came the answer.

"I couldn't help noticing how your hands were moving," Vernon said, keeping the conversation moving. "Sort of like the motions of a painter. Are you an artist?"

"Not that you might think."

"But you seemed to be mimicking the motions of a painter."

"Yes, I was. I was mentally painting this picture. I know every stroke, every nuance by heart."

"I hate to pursue it, but you must know Laura."

The man smiled. "I'm sorry if I gave you the wrong impression. No, I don't really know Laura. I merely admire her work."

He is marvelous, Vernon thought, trying to avoid staring. He wondered what sex would be like with a man who exhilarated him so. He'd never experienced such sweet sensations so quickly before. How do I prolong this conversation and strike a relationship? "Would you like to meet Laura?" he asked.

"That's not necessary," his visitor said. "But I would like to get to know you better."

Vernon almost fainted.

* * *

As a young man Vernon Hayle had aspirations of one day becoming a first rate artist. But the deterrent to that ambition that beset him from childhood was a second rate talent. He set standards, early on, for the quality work he sought to produce but could never personally achieve. By the time he had finished college he realized he was not going to become the artist he thought was in him.

Inherited wealth could not give him what was in his heart but it did provide the next best thing. Vernon would not abandon his love of art. Therefore, he found the quality he sought in other artists. He opened his first gallery at the age of twenty-six. By thirty he was a consummate success and owned three galleries; one each in Paris, New York and Los Angeles.

His life became satisfactory. The galleries provided him with a substantial income that he did not need. The Hayle family came from old money going back hundreds of years. There were houses in New England, Florida, Bermuda, and Europe. The apartments alone in upscale Manhattan owned by each of the three siblings of the Hayles presently had a combined value of somewhere around one hundred million dollars, a small portion of the surviving estate.

Vernon's life improved also when he met, and took as a lover, a young man named Charles Collins, a person without status, money or credentials. But, the lack of standing was made up tenfold in physical beauty and a desire to please. Charles demanded attention as a tradeoff for his commitment.

Vernon installed Charles in a Greenwich Village apartment in a brownstone that Vernon bought as an investment. Charles, also an aspiring artist, was totally dependent upon the good graces of Vernon Hayle. Within months Charles was madly in love with Vernon. He doted on every action, gesture, and word from Vernon. Vernon was his champion. Vernon called the shots. Vernon was completely, unequivocally in charge of their relationship and the direction it took. Charles could add to the equation only sincere and all-abiding ardor.

Vernon called Charles with the taunting image of Saylem searing his imagination, his voice permeated with apology.

"About tonight, Charles. I don't think I can make dinner."

"Why not?" Charles asked immediately, the query edged with chagrin. "I had something special planned."

"I've got some business that may keep me late tonight. I can't spend the time at dinner."

Charles was disappointed. They had a routine almost every night. He asked Vernon to make a selection for dinner out; they rarely ate at home. And most of the time Vernon left the decision to Charles. But Vernon negated tonight's selection by his announcement.

"That's okay," Charles responded eagerly. "After dinner I'll go back to the gallery with you."

"No. That's not just the problem. I'm checking out the work of a new artist. I may not be back 'til midnight or so."

"Why don't I join you?" Charles would not be slighted.

"No. I must do this alone. The subject is on Long Island. I'll call the car and have Jeffrey drive me. Why must you insist on spending so much time with me tonight? I have commitments. You know that."

Charles responded coyly. "It's not that important I guess. Only that it's our anniversary."

"What? Oh, I'm so sorry, Charles," Vernon said remorsefully. "I've been so preoccupied lately. I didn't mean to trivialize the occasion. It's two years, yes."

Charles beamed. "You know it is. Of course."

"Look. I'll make it up to you. Dinner tonight, but we'll do something special on the weekend."

"The Hamptons?"

"Perhaps."

"What had you planned?" Vernon asked.

"Waterfront Club on the East River."

"All right. What time?"

"Seven."

"I'll meet you there," Vernon agreed with the choice. Waterfront Club was one of his favorite spots. "But I've got to leave at nine."

"All right. That's all right," Charles said, happily. "I understand."

After the conversation with Charles, Vernon called the number on the card that Saylem (Elymas) had handed him. He came on after two rings. "Yes?"

"Hello, it's Vernon Hayle. We met at my place, TheArtGallery. Do you recall?" Vernon tried to keep the excitement out of his voice.

"Certainly," the exciting voice resonated with promise. "How could I not remember you? Shall we meet for drinks later this evening?"

"Why yes," Vernon was genuinely surprised. "I was thinking the same thing."

"Shall we say nine-thirty at The Clubhouse Hotel?"

"Excellent choice."

* * *

"What's wrong, Vernon?" questioned Charles Collins. He was concerned that suddenly Vernon seemed miles away from the marvelous waterfront restaurant. "You seem preoccupied all through the meal. Is something troubling you."

"There is so much more to life than satisfying our picayune pleasures, Charles. Things don't always go smoothly, you know."

"Are you displeased with me?" Charles fretted. "Is that what you're trying to say?"

"Please, Charles, don't blame yourself. My peccadilloes are mine, purely mine. How I feel right now shouldn't involve you. I'm only human. I make mistakes and have problems like anyone else."

"But what is it you're feeling? You know how much I love you. Maybe I can help. There's nothing to make you feel better than good sex."

Now Vernon was perplexed. "Charles, sex is not the answer to everything. Are you trying to claim me as a possession?"

"No, Vernon. I'm not being possessive. I just sense that you're not yourself suddenly and I want to help..."

Vernon was obviously irritated. "Finish up here," he rankled. "I've got to run." Vernon checked his watch. "Damn, look at the time. I want you to head on home. Thank you very much for making the reservations tonight and thank you for remembering our beginning."

"You're welcome Vernon," Charles said, then coyly added, "I love you."

Vernon called his chauffeur, Jeff, on his cell phone. "I'm ready," he told him. "Pick me up in about fifteen minutes."

He paid the check and together they walked to the entrance.

"You get a cab home. I'll probably see you later. But, just in case I'm really late, don't wait up for me."

"All right Vernon. Whatever you say."

Charles got a cab before Vernon's limo showed up. One street later, which lead directly from the restaurant, Charles told the driver to pull over. He waited until Vernon's black Mercedes drove past the cab and he urged the driver to follow it. The limo did not head for The Midtown Tunnel and to Long Island, where Vernon implied he would be going. Instead it headed west, across town, to Forty-fourth Street and stopped at the Clubhouse.

What the hell is going on? Charles wondered. Is he planning something for our anniversary? Perhaps I should go home and wait for his phone call.

Instead he paid the cab driver and waited across the street for Vernon to come out. It took two hours. When Vernon exited the hotel entrance he was escorted by an extremely attractive man dressed completely in black; his hair was as black as his suit. Charles turned his back to them and watched their reflections in a store window. Vernon's limo was waiting for them. Before Charles could wave down a taxi the limo was long gone.

Damn, he cursed. Vernon has taken another lover.

* * *

After two Old Fashions with Charles at The Waterfront Club and two B & B's here with Saylem, Vernon was loose enough to tango.

"Where would you like to go?" Saylem said as their cocktail hour wound down.

It had certainly been an eventful time for Vernon. He had found a new, fantastic soul mate in one day. Is this what a "whirlwind romance" felt like, he thought? Or is it just a fling for Saylem? Is this enigmatic man one of those people who uses you for pleasure and abandons you as quickly as a blink of an eye? The thought made him reflect on Saylem's eyes. They were strikingly unique. The pale gray of the pupil seemed liquid. Transparent. When he looked directly at you he didn't blink. He drew you into them like vessels needing to be filled. His eyebrows were so perfect they could have been painted on, every hair distinct.

Saylem had begun immediately with a conversation Vernon would not have expected so soon. If fact, he had never experienced such rare outspoken frankness.

"Do you currently have a lover?" Saylem asked.

"Why...yes," answered Vernon.

"You realize you'll have to dismiss him immediately."

"I...I don't understand."

"Of course you do." When he spoke, Saylem emitted an aspect of confidence beyond reproach. "Those are my terms," he affirmed. "I will allow no other way."

"I'm to be your lover?" Vernon asked.

"Was there any question?"

"Well...no."

"Good. Then pay the bill and let's get out of here," Saylem said haughtily as he rose from his chair.

This can't be happening thought Vernon. I wished for it and I got it. But can I handle this domineering, puzzling person? The Mercedes waited outside at the curb. As they entered the back seat Vernon thought he saw Charles Collins on the other side of the street lurking in a storefront. Couldn't be, he told himself. Charles went home. Then the person in question turned fully around. It was Charles. The little shit has followed me here. Damn it. He'll learn he can't squeeze me like this.

"Where to?" the chauffeur asked.

"Uptown, Jeff," Vernon Hayle said proudly.

* * *

The sex was not what Vernon expected. It was savage. Saylem was taller, outweighed Vernon by twenty pounds of muscle. He roughly manhandled Vernon, crashing him to the bed and turning him over on his stomach like a rag doll. He stripped off his pants and flung them to the floor.

"Wait!" Vernon said. "Wait. Don't you want to shower first?"

Saylem didn't answer. His strong hands pinned Vernon to the bed. One hand under his chin, pulling back his head, the other between his shoulder blades, pressing him down.

"At least let me lubricate. And you should wear a condom." Vernon pleaded.

Saylem answered by ramming into Vernon, hurting him and thrilling him, taking him to a place of pleasure he had never been before.

"Oh, Jesus!" Vernon cried out in pain and ecstasy.

"Jesus? No. I don't think so," said Saylem calmly.

* * *

The next morning Charles Collins confronted Jeff, Vernon Hayle's chauffeur.

"Where did you end up last night? Where did you deliver Vernon?" he asked.

"Long night," Jeff said. "Why weren't you along?"

"I had things to do," Charles lied.

"So did Mr. Hayle. I guess I got in around midnight. Then he dismissed me."

"Anybody with him?"

"You didn't know? I thought at first it was going to be a threesome," Jeff said. Then realized something adverse was going on here. "I'd rather not get involved," he said.

Charles reached in his pocket and pulled out a fifty-dollar bill he'd put there just in case.

"Come on, Jeff," he said, reaching the bill out to the chauffeur. "You know me. This will never go past me."

"Mr. Collins," Jeff said. "I could lose my job."

"He'll never find out. I guarantee it."

Jeff pondered a moment, and then said, "If this gets back to him, I'll hang you out to dry along with me."

"Fair enough," Charles said. "Now give. Did he have that guy with him? The one he met at The Clubhouse."

"Yeah. He did.'

"Where did they go?"

"To Mr. Hayle's apartment."

"Did he stay all night?"

"I don't know for sure. I went home. But when he dismisses me for the night it means I don't have to drive the guy home. It's the same with you."

The bastard slept in my bed, Charles swore.

"Did you get his name?"

"I think he called him Saylem at one point. The last name is your guess as good as mine."

"Thanks, Jeff. I appreciate this."

"Fine. Just remember what I said. If I swing, we both swing."

"Agreed." Charles said.

Chapter 15

Father Gerald Stuart had finished hearing confessionals. He drew the heavy drape and closed the confessional door. There were only a few people left in the church.

It seemed to him there were more sins committed lately than any time he could remember since he had become a priest. Signs of the times? He reflected, though, that the nature of the sins was low on the bar. The evil that people acknowledged, he thought, paled in comparison to the true evil in the world.

Since his first year in the seminary Father Stuart was a student of the occult. Tales of demonic or spiritual possession had always intrigued him. They consumed his interest as a source to prove that evil exists as a physical force in all mankind. Gerry Stuart believed the devil manifested his presence in humanity in many forms. To prove, beyond any doubt, that such manifestations did exist would be a monumental accomplishment. Documented evidence of spirit possession was irrefutable proof of not only the spirituality of man but also the physicality of Satan.

Gerry Stuart spent many working hours responding to reported cases of spirit possession that might have been better utilized in his young years as a curate. He learned. He researched. He entered into associations with people involved in the investigation of occult occurrences and psychic phenomena. It was at one such instance that he first met Roger Evans. He had responded to a supposed case of spirit possession in a rural town in northern Pennsylvania. The publicity from the press had brought enough psychic researchers and ghost hunters to flaunt the event.

Roger Evans approached such phenomena with almost the same restraint that Gerry Stuart exhibited. Because of this, they found admiration for one another that otherwise might not have occurred. They worked together on a few situations and ultimately joined forces with a man to whom both developed unfaltering praise, their mentor, Carl Spendler, a full-time parapsychologist.

Spendler had spent his life combing the far-off cities of the world, tracking the most outlandish tales of demonic possession.

His experience proved invaluable to both Gerry and Evans, who found under his tutelage, that they had a great deal to learn. Spendler taught them to dismiss fakes without wasting time and effort.

Spendler was ten years older than either one, and, it seemed to Gerry Stuart, those extra ten years of exposure was invaluable in their relationship. He taught them by his experience and they learned from it. When they were united they were a good team.

The e-mail letter from Roger Evans came at a time when Gerry welcomed the distraction.

Gerry had been immersed in parish work in the last year and had meant to contact Roger Evans more times than he could remember. He saw Carl Spendler often enough and mentioned that they should get together on another fishing trip. The last one seemed to have done wonders for Evans. His depression had been completely abandoned that particular day. Now, as he read the message from Evans, he felt somehow guilty.

He eagerly opened the file and devoured the long message.

Gerry,

I've come across a situation that you and Carl might find interesting enough to pursue. A woman named Laura Whitney has recently developed psychic qualities. Not that there is anything earth shattering in this alone. The thing of it is, I first met her at a gathering in Southampton and was severely jolted by the impressions I received from her... a séance in which a woman died, a terrifying image of my own death, of all things, by hanging. And here's the strange part of all this, while I was in a slight trance I apparently uttered Vera Lancaster's name...you remember her, the medium. She might have been the woman I saw in the séance who apparently died.

You know how I feel about these matters ever since Audrey's tragedy. I don't know where this might lead but I just can't face anything like this anymore. I don't have the courage. At any rate, I've since met this woman twice and I get the feeling of impending disaster each time. I don't know what exactly has me believing she might be a victim of some mystical force. I met her the second time and received an impression of impending calamity.

I know from the past that these things can only get worse. I couldn't swear to anything as severe as possession, but there is definitely some foreign influence that is trying to make her life unbearable.

If you are interested enough to at least talk to her I am listing her phone number here for you. By the way, she came to me for help today. I would love to get involved but I just don't have the heart or the time for it any more. Chances are, by the time you receive this letter I won't be around. Very best to Carl.

Your friend,
Roger

P.S. I still think of our great fishing trip.

Gerry reread the e-mail letter. Why should Roger get impressions of his own death? And what did the image of the séance mean? And that line, "I won't be around." What was the significance of those words? Was he going somewhere?

Gerry felt an urgency to talk to Evans. He felt sorry that he had not taken a stronger role as a friend in Evans' life. He searched through his phone book for Roger Evans' number and dialed. The phone rang only twice when he heard a brusque male voice, not Roger's, on the other end.

"Yes?" the voice said.

"Roger?" Gerry questioned.

"No. Can I help you?"

"Is Roger there. I'd like to speak to him please."

"Who is calling him?"

"My name is Gerry Stuart," Gerry said, impatience starting to edge his tone.

"What can I do for you?" the voice asked.

"I'm looking for Roger Evans. I'm an old friend of his," Gerry was perplexed. "Say, what is this? Is Roger there or not?"

"Mr. Stuart..." Detective Hodges started to say.

"Father Gerald Stuart," Gerry corrected him. "I'm a Catholic priest."

"I'm sorry, Father," the police officer said. "My name is Hodges. I'm a police detective. I suppose there is no other way to break this to you. Roger Evans was found dead yesterday."

Gerry stared in utter disbelief at the receiver, numbed by the words the detective had uttered.

"Father Stuart, Father..." the detective's voice snapped him out of his bewilderment. "Are you still there?"

Gerry put the phone back to his ear. "Yes. I'm still here. What in the name of God happened to him?"

"We're not sure yet but it looks like he took his own life. I'm sorry to have to be the one to inform you this way."

"Damn. I can't believe this. Roger dead," Gerry said, sadness in his voice. "Suicide?" he questioned

"That's what it seems. Is there anything I can help you with?" detective Hodges asked.

"I was calling Roger because I received an e-mail letter from him. I think now that perhaps I ought to show it to you."

"Is it relative to his death?" Detective Hodges asked.

"It might be."

"All right, Father. Are you in town?"

"Yes."

"How long would it take you to get over to Evans' apartment?"

"I'd say about a half hour."

"Fine. I'll wait for you here then."

Gerry printed two copies of Evans' letter, tucked them in his coat pocket and caught a cab to Evans' apartment. From where his parish was located on the West Side of Manhattan to Evans' place it was a short ride through Central Park. He glanced around as the cab wound through the park, taking particular notice of the joggers along the way. He thought of Carl Spendler, who was a devoted runner. He knew it was too late in the morning to spot him; Spendler was an early runner. How could he tell Carl of Roger Evans' death? He would have to, though. Carl needed to know.

Gerry got to the apartment and was admitted by a uniformed policeman.

"I'm Father Stuart," he said. "I was to meet a Detective Hodges."

"Let him in," a voice called from inside the apartment.

A large man, whose clothes didn't quite contain the huge frame they were expected to enclose, confronted Gerry. His hand smothered Gerry's as he clasped it and pumped.

"I'm Tom Hodges, Father," he said. "I'm glad to meet you."

"How are you?" Gerry said mechanically, his eyes

uncontrollably searching the living room.

"The body is gone," Hodges said, reading Gerry's eye movement. "We're checking for signs of foul play, but it doesn't look that way at all. More like a simple case of suicide."

"It's hard to believe Roger would kill himself," Gerry said.

"It happens," Hodges said. "Every day of the week. Believe me."

"How did he die?" Gerry asked Detective Hodges.

"You sure you want to hear this?"

"Yes."

"Apparently he wrapped a drapery cord around the terrace railing, tied it around his neck and leaped over."

"My God," Gerry exclaimed. "Why?"

Hodges ushered Gerry to a sofa and sat opposite him on a straight-backed chair.

"We don't know why," Hodges said. "I thought perhaps you might help us. You mentioned a letter, Father."

Gerry handed Hodges a printout of Evans' e-mail and waited while the detective quickly read through it.

"This seems to confirm it. He doesn't give a reason but he says here at the end that he won't be around. Looks like suicide to me. But we don't have all the facts yet. Do you know anything at all about this woman he mentioned, Laura Whitney?"

"Nothing. This letter is the first I'd heard of her."

"Well, we'll talk to her. Tell me, Father, have you known Evans long?"

"About twelve years."

"Did you know him well?"

"Fairly well. We were close at one time. We worked on projects together. Research on psychic incidents. But I must confess, I haven't been close to Roger in the last few years."

"Do you know anything about his mental condition?" Hodges fished for facts. "Was there any reason why he might take his own life?"

"The only thing I might put my finger on was a tragedy in Evans' life a few years back," Gerry said, observing that Hodges was taking notes. "His wife suffered a severe mental breakdown. Roger loved her very much. It threw him into a depressed state for a while."

"Thank you. We'll check that," Hodges said. "By the way, did you know Evans was scheduled to leave for Europe the morning he died?"

"No. I didn't," Gerry Stuart said. Then he added, "Could that be what he meant about not being around?"

"Could be. We'll know eventually. Just strikes me as strange that he would begin to pack his suitcases, have his ticket paid for, then change his mind and kill himself. But then again, who knows what goes through a person's mind when he decides to end it all? I've seen far stranger things than this."

"If only I'd read my incoming e-mail sooner," Gerry said. "It might have made all the difference. Perhaps I could have prevented his death by talking to him."

"Perhaps, Father," Hodges said. "But don't blame yourself. If he'd planned to end his life nothing could have stopped him. You might have been lucky enough to stall the act. But in the end he would have found a way to kill himself no matter what."

"If it comes to that I suppose you're right," Gerry sighed.

"Of course, Father. Can you give me a phone number or an address where I can reach you in the event I might need you?"

"Certainly," Gerry said. He gave Hodges one of his cards.

When he stepped back into the street, he thought immediately again of Carl Spendler, knowing that he should call him right away, but in his soul he wanted to prolong the confrontation for as long as he possibly could.

PART TWO

Chapter 16

Carl Spendler pumped hard, forcing the rhythm, his body strained and tired from the grueling hour he had run at a sustained, accelerated pace through the winding trails of Central Park. His legs ached with the steady pounding they had taken, but he knew it was what he needed and he would inflict even more pain before he called it quits. He sucked the air in deeply, feeling it inflate his lungs. It felt good. It wasn't like that when he first started these early morning runs. Then he couldn't sustain a quarter mile without gasping for breath. Now, six years later, it was a different story.

He started his runs every morning at six AM, when his schedule would allow, and was usually in a shower in his nearby townhouse by seven. It was, he felt, a good habit to have finally acquired.

He was a tall man, standing six foot one, but a shock of speckled grey hair and his lean appearance exaggerated his height.

Often, he wondered, as he followed the same path every morning, what was the possibility of being mugged this early in the day? He took notice that he had seen, on occasion, characters whose presence at those times was questionable. He wondered what he would do, how he would react, if confronted by molesters. Would he try to outrun them? Would he put up a struggle? He carried nothing with him except his apartment keys. Perhaps that was the reason he never had been mugged. Was it that muggers were aware that a jogger could outrun them or that joggers didn't carry money?

Spendler supposed that by now he was a familiar sight to the people of the neighborhood who were up and about at this hour. He invaded the streets, bursting out of the park, his presence vigorously dominating the activity of the hour. He didn't recognize many of the people he passed but he was convinced they were the same early risers who saw him every morning.

As he swung past the expansive apartment house across from the park exit he noticed, as usual, the woman in the second floor apartment, standing in full view in the living room window, staring down at him. She was there every morning as he ran. She was always in the same red robe, her form strikingly contrasted from the surrounding shaded windows like a lighted beacon in a storm. Was she really watching him, he wondered? Did she watch him exclusively? Or was he no more than a familiar object moving through a sea of motion to which she gave only her fleeting interest? It puzzled him.

She acknowledged his presence by her unrelenting stare, her dark piercing eyes probing him. But she never nodded recognition. He had seen her in the neighborhood, shopping. Always that intense stare. What were those penetrating eyes saying to him? Could she be alluding to the possibility of secret, sexual favors? Was there promise masked by that deep look, or was Spendler's middle-age imagination running as wildly as his hammering pulse?

This morning he decided to test her mettle. He raised his right hand and, looking up, directly into those piercing eyes, he waved to her, his mouth breaking into a broad smile. There was no response from that somber face in the window; only the immediate closing of the window curtains indicated a reaction to Spendler's harmless overture. Well, he thought, at least now he knew she might be no more than a busybody.

He let himself into his brownstone house, a full block west of the park, and, tossing his running togs into the bathroom hamper, he plunged immediately into a cold shower. While he washed, he mentally reviewed the content of the speech he was to give before an NYU class this morning. An old friend who taught a course on parapsychology had invited him to deliver some opening comments. It was not his wont to speak before classes that he himself did not conduct. But, this was for a friend, and not for profit.

Spendler had been considering introducing a new element of conjecture into this morning's talk. Since parapsychology was a study of abnormal occurrences, those beyond the limits of psychology, Spendler reckoned he might give the class pause. He intended to blame all supernatural phenomena on the power of the mind. It was an approach not given much credence but which he believed might very well be the key to many of the mysteries that passed for supernatural occurrences.

He came out of the shower, toweling himself as he stepped into the bedroom. As he dressed, his sight fell on the photo of his daughter that rested on his dresser. Her blue eyes and bright blonde hair were difficult not to notice. Now she was his entire family; all that remained of a twenty-four year marriage. The inevitable divorce should have occurred long before but Sheila, his wife, wanted their daughter to graduate college before she had to cope with the trauma of a broken home. He agreed with her and actually commended her for sticking it out for so long.

He knew he was difficult to live with. Throughout the years his efforts and time were given over to the pursuit of occult matters. It had been a trying experience for a woman who had never truly sympathized with his odd interests. Sheila would have been happier with a house in the suburbs, married to a nine-to-five commuter; he knew that all along. She should never have been tied to a man who spent months at a time in Egypt, the Far East, wherever the game dictated, but damn little time at home.

Sheila never wanted to understand what his work meant to him. She had no concept of its purpose. His daughter, Karen, did though. Beautiful Karen, his joy. She was attuned to her father's work even as a child. She saw him as a gifted person who might one day uncover major breakthroughs to mankind's ultimate understanding of itself. Her mother never saw Spendler's calling in life as quite so important. She viewed him as a modern day witch-hunter and opportunist who capitalized on the superstitious masses, thriving on the hope that there might be an answer to the unexplainable.

He had published books on psychic phenomena, spiritualism, channeling, paranormal psychology and mediums that had gone into multiple printings. His name was fairly well known in circles of occult studies as a purveyor of knowledge, who doggedly hounded an occurrence until it was exposed as either truth or fantasy. He found truth to be the vast minority.

Spendler made a living from royalties on his books, lectures, and articles in magazines, occasional guest appearances on radio

Mike Walsh

or TV and fees for ghost hunting. He earned enough from these various activities to continue the lifestyle he had maintained for so long without any worries about change. It was a stable market and a continued source of income.

But Spendler was beginning to doubt. He worried about the changes in his attitude in recent years. Unlike his wife's skepticism his doubts were founded on a lifetime of toil that produced little, if any, answers to the riddles that plagued him throughout his life. Spendler believed in the spirit, the supernatural and in actual psychic occurrences. He had seen too many unexplained episodes in his lifetime to doubt; yet he did.

* * *

Spendler stood before an audience of students as he referred to his notes on the lectern before him. The seats in the college classroom were all filled. He was surprised but pleased. He hadn't expected this kind of crowd at an extemporaneous occurrence. Perhaps, he thought, his reputation did precede him.

He started the session with a quotation that summed up his dissertation.

"There is a line from Milton which states 'The mind is its own place, and, in itself, can make a heaven of hell and a hell of heaven'.

"I refer to it for one reason," he continued. "It is to draw your attention to the fact that parapsychology is a science of the mind and cannot be measured in the same terms as our physical sciences. It deals with phenomena relating to the mind or personality that go beyond the measures of normal psychology. The prefix 'para', in fact, is a Greek word meaning 'beyond.' And yet it is the mind itself that creates the conditions that are beyond the mind. No mind, no psychic phenomena.

"It is akin to the old adage about the tree falling in the forest. If there is no ear to hear, does it really make a sound? Hence, if there is no mind to perceive, can there really be a psychic occurrence? Without the human mind in the equation what would psychic phenomena be? Merely the passing of an ill wind across a barren desert? Or would such phenomena exist at all?

"In our ignorance we brand what we do not understand as

abnormal or supernatural. Unnatural? Under what conditions? What we consider normal today was considered outright supernatural one hundred years ago. Who knows what the future will bring? Future discoveries about the abilities of the mind will undoubtedly far exceed even our wildest dreams. Our descendants may very well treat telepathy, extrasensory perception, clairvoyance as everyday matters of fact. The abnormal of today will be tomorrow's normal. What we continue to discover about the extra senses of the human mind have existed in mankind since the beginning of time. The abilities have always been there. We all possess the material to be psychic. It is merely a matter of development and application.

"Down through the ages the special few who have applied their extrasensory powers did so cautiously. The seers and prophets were regarded as abnormal, to be persecuted, despised. Psychic phenomena were given a back seat in the cultured civilizations of the world.

"Today, the study of psychic phenomena is no longer ignored. There exists, like the more exact sciences, a basis for such studies. It will be a long time before many occurrences will be accepted as fact. For man, because of his ability to reason, is doubly plagued by his ability to question and to doubt.

"Man has always rejected as superstition what he could not measure in terms of pure scientific reality. But he is capable of far greater feats than were ever considered possible.

"Many believe there is a positive nexus between the thought waves in all humans; that people who have already tuned in on these waves are our 'sensitives'. If the spiritual level of man is one with the spiritual body of the universe then perhaps man is a finite part of the spirit of God, if you will.

"If man is a fragment of universal thought, then there is no limit to the capabilities of the mind. Psychic phenomena, as we call them, are therefore nothing more than portions of total thought. What we term the unknown may very well be truth.

"In the realm of the unknown there is far, far more that we do not know than that which we have learned so far. It is the wise man who approaches life with an open mind. The parapsychologist tries to uncover the truth. In dealing with the sensitive who claims to have made contact with souls of the departed, the

105

parapsychologist attempts to establish basis for proof. If, indeed, the soul of man transcends physical death, then that soul must be linked to the concept of a spiritual universe that also must exist. The body dies, the spirit lives on, reunited with its original source.

"Just what is that spiritual world? We may never know. We have only the vaguest concept. Does it consist merely of departed souls? Or is it an embodiment of the forces that control good and evil in all mankind? What is really 'out there'?

"The medium who claims contact with the departed uses an ability of the mind to elicit information from his or her subject. In the documented cases of ghostlike appearances in séances, energy transmitted by a medium may take the form of ectoplasm and appear to form an apparition, but actual proof of life after death, no.

"We are creatures of the mind. We are dominated by the mind. And yet we have no idea of the full range of its capabilities. What lies beyond, what phenomena that may exist, may very well exist because of the mind. We make our own heaven and our own hell...and may God help us...I thank you."

As applause from the class erupted Carl Spendler stepped away from the lectern and turned to the professor who stood to the left side of the room near the door. The professor stepped forward and shook Spendler's hand.

"Thank you, Dr. Spendler," he said, his head turned fully to the class. "I'm sure we have all been enlightened by Dr. Spendler's remarks here today." He turned to Spendler and said softly "Thanks, Carl. Good thoughts. What do I follow with?"

Spendler smiled. "I'm sure you'll think of something, Peter," he said. He turned fully to the class. "It was my pleasure," he said to the students.

He knew he had covered so little of such a broad subject that it could take a hundred short talks like this to merely scratch the surface. He hoped though that he had piqued their interest enough to want to know more.

When he returned to his apartment he checked his answering machine and found three calls. Two were routine but the third cheered him. It was from Father Gerry Stuart. He immediately dialed Gerry's number.

"Hello," the voice answered.

"Gerry, you old son of a gun, how the hell are you?"

"Carl. It's you."

"In the flesh," Spendler said. "I couldn't have been more pleased to hear from you. What's up?"

"I'm afraid it's not good news, Carl," Gerry said.

"Sounds serious."

"It is. I don't know how to break this to you," Gerry said, his pause accentuating his reluctance to continue.

"Well, what is it?"

"It's Roger Evans, Carl. He's dead."

Spendler was stunned by the revelation. After a moment he found his voice. "When? How did it happen?"

"Yesterday. It was on the news. Apparently he committed suicide."

"What?" Spendler was astonished. "That's crazy. I can't accept that."

"That's how it looks to the police."

"For God's sake," Spendler exclaimed. "What a terrible shame. What a waste."

"Can I see you, Carl?" Gerry Stuart asked. "There's something I'd like to talk to you about concerning Roger."

"Sure. Anytime."

"How about hopping over to the parish."

"Sure. What is it about Roger you want to tell me?" Spendler asked, his curiosity vexed.

"Well, it's not so much Roger as an e-mail I got from him. A woman whom he believes might be possessed came to him recently. Looks like she might have been there on the day he died. The e-mail is dated Wednesday. I'm going to forward it to you and then we'll talk."

* * *

"What do you think, Carl?" Gerry Stuart asked Carl Spendler at Father Gerry's quarters that afternoon.

"About Roger's death or the woman?"

"All right, both."

"It's hard to tell from this message that Roger meant to kill himself. You said he was booked for a European tour and was half

packed, ready to leave. Suicide seems out of the question. You
don't think this Whitney woman had anything to do with his death,
do you?"

"I doubt it. For one thing, the police say there is no evidence of
a struggle and I doubt that anyone could have wrapped a rope
around his neck and thrown him over the terrace railing without
signs of a struggle."

"Good lord," Spendler exclaimed. "Is that how he died?"

"Yes. Hanging from the terrace."

"I think solving the mystery of Roger's death should have to
remain in more qualified hands than ours," Spendler offered.
"We'll have to let the police worry about that."

"And the Whitney woman?" Gerry queried.

"I think it might be worthwhile for us to at least talk to her."

"You're right," Gerry said. He picked up the phone and dialed
the number Roger had given him. A woman answered.

"Ms. Whitney?" Gerry asked.

"Yes?"

"My name is Stuart. Father Gerald Stuart. I'm a friend of Roger
Evans." Gerry swore he heard her choke on her breath for an
instant. "I wonder if it would be possible to speak with you about
him?"

Laura didn't respond immediately. Gerry wondered why the
long decision to answer.

"Ms. Whitney," he prodded.

"Yes," Laura answered. "I'm sorry, Father...?"

"Stuart. Father Gerry Stuart."

"I'm sorry. Yes, I suppose it would be all right. I'm afraid I
can't help you much. I didn't know Roger Evans that well. And I
can tell you absolutely nothing about his death."

Was Gerry mistaken or did he detect sobs?

"Actually it is Roger's relationship to you that I would like to
speak to you about."

"His relationship to me?" Laura was perplexed. "I don't
understand. We had no relationship. I only met him a few times
and briefly at that."

"I think it would be better if we came to see you instead of
discussing this matter over the phone," Gerry said. "Would this
evening be all right?"

"Yes, I suppose so. That's all right. You said we, Father. Is there someone else involved?"

"Yes. I'm bringing a man named Carl Spendler with me. He and I were closely associated with Roger Evans at one time."

Chapter 17

The receptionist at Frank Whitney's advertising agency buzzed him in his office.

"Mr. Danfield is here to see you," she announced.

"Send him right in," Frank said.

Fred Danfield was ushered into his corner office by Frank's private secretary.

"Fred," Frank said cheerfully, rising from his desk and shaking Danfield's extended hand. "To what do I owe this visit?"

"It's not business," Danfield said. "I just want to talk to you."

"Have a seat, Fred," Frank offered. "Would you like something to drink? Coffee."

"Sure. Whatever you have," Danfield said.

Frank informed his secretary and she returned instantly with a cup of black, decaf coffee, exactly how Danfield drank it. He was one of Frank Whitney's major clients and Frank made it a point to know all Danfield's habits.

"What can I do for you?" Frank asked.

"It's about Roger Evans, Frank. What can you tell me?"

"Roger Evans?" Frank was expecting that Danfield might want to discuss the man's untimely death; especially since the occurrence at his Hampton house. "I can't tell you anything about Evans. Only that he committed suicide."

"That's what bothers me," Danfield said. "Charlotte and I knew him well. We knew of the problems he had with his wife. But she is still alive. He loved her. He believed she would get better. Suicide? It's out of the question. He would never kill himself. There's more to his death than suicide."

"What could you expect me to know, Fred, that you don't? The only time I ever met him was at your house. I know about him only because of our visit there."

"Personally Frank, it's Laura," Danfield said. "Evans was troubled since he first encountered Laura. I've known him for years and I've never seen him that distraught."

"But what has that to do with Laura?" Frank asked. "She

knows nothing about him either."

"It's just that he died so soon after his confrontation at Southampton. I thought maybe he had spoken to her or seen her since then. Perhaps she has some insight into his death."

"I doubt it Fred," Frank said. "Besides, I'd hardly call it a confrontation. The man was playing dramatic parlor tricks."

Danfield put his cup down on the table in front of the couch. He reached into his jacket pocket and withdrew a long cigar. He fussed with it, smelling, licking and finally lighting up. There was a no smoking rule in the agency, but every time Danfield visited he lit up and defied anyone to tell him not to. Management was aware of his defiance and his assumed importance. The firm received one of its largest billing accounts from Danfield's firm and agency management was well aware of the importance of that income. He exHayled a cloud of gray smoke into the room. Frank was disturbed by his actions but Danfield knew he would say nothing.

"All right," Danfield admitted. "Confrontation might be the wrong word. Let's call it discord. Roger was distraught since he first met Laura. You were aware of that fact. There was something about your wife that really upset Roger. He left early and went back to New York. He told us that he had to resolve the scare he got at Southampton. Whatever the hell that meant."

Frank knew he dared not tell Danfield that Laura had visited Evans the day before he killed himself. Would he discover that fact on his own?

"Fred, I'm convinced the business between Evans and Laura is nothing," Frank offered. "He probably has some ability to connect with people but there is nothing in Laura's life that would set a man off to such an extent that he would take his own life. Is that what you're implying? For Christ sakes!"

Danfield realized he had incurred Frank's ire. Perhaps, he thought, he had gone too far.

"Don't get me wrong, Frank," he said, a contrite tone slipping into his voice. "I don't mean to imply that Laura might be involved on a personal level."

"God, Fred, I certainly hope not," Frank shot back. "Laura was as shocked as anyone that Evans died. She was horrified."

"Let me put it this way, Frank," Danfield persisted. "There apparently was some mystery about Laura's operation. I think that might be the crux of it."

"There was no mystery about the operation, Fred," Frank was adamant. "I want to make that perfectly clear. Roger Evans was playing a role. I guess successfully enough to convince you that he was into something mystic. For crying out loud, Fred. Be reasonable."

By now Danfield realized he had pushed the wrong buttons. "If you or Laura might remember anything that was said let me know," he concluded.

"Fred, why don't we let the police handle everything?" Frank said.

Danfield blew out some smoke and nodded. "I guess we'll have to, it seems."

* * *

Frank Whitney was home when Detective Tom Hodges and his partner showed up at their apartment.

"My wife hasn't been well lately, Detective," Frank greeted the men. "She's been out of the hospital only a short time."

"Nothing serious, I hope," Hodges said.

"An eye operation."

"This shouldn't take too long. I won't burden her. These are merely routine questions concerning Roger Evans. I promise I won't pressure your wife."

"You realize she hardly knew the man. I'm not sure she could be any help to you at all."

"Let me determine that, Mr. Whitney," Hodges said. Frank ushered the men to a sofa in the living room. Laura sat opposite them with Frank standing by her side.

"Mrs. Whitney," Hodges said. "When and where did you first meet Roger Evans?"

"It was last weekend at the Hamptons," Laura said. "We had gone to visit a client of Frank's. They had thrown a party and we were invited. Roger Evans was a guest but he was enticed into performing some mental tricks. I guess you'd call them tricks. I understand he was a magician of sorts. He was getting input from members of the party by feeling objects of theirs. He was very accurate in telling people about their lives. When he got to me he had my watch. He became flustered. He called my name. He was

Séance

blindfolded, yet he saw something behind the blindfold that caused him to stop his performance."

"Did he tell you what he saw?"

"He told me later, when I met him again at the party."

"And?"

"He claimed he saw his own death."

Hodges lifted a copy of Roger Evans' e-mail from his jacket pocket and handed it to Laura.

"Can you tell me anything about this letter, Mrs. Whitney?" he asked.

Laura read through it quickly and handed it to Frank, who, in turn, read through it.

"I'm afraid not," she said. "It's the first time I've seen it."

"You say he saw his own death, as he said in his letter. Did he tell you at the time how he was supposed to die?"

Laura hesitated a moment. Then she simply said "No. Not at the party. He told me at his apartment that he saw a vision of himself hanging."

"Apparently he knew he was going to hang himself even then," Hodges said. "Mrs. Whitney, did you know that Evans wanted to help you with your own personal problems?"

"No, I had no idea."

"When was the last time you'd seen Evans?" Hodges said.

"It was Wednesday afternoon."

"What did you see him about?"

"Like he said in the letter," Laura answered. "When my husband and I first met him he said things to me that disturbed me."

"Such as?" Hodges said.

"Well, it was strange. Although we'd just met him he described a frightening dream I'd been having. He knew my name and he described the dream exactly as I'd had it."

"What was the subject of this vision?"

"It was a séance. Three women were involved."

"What frightened you about a séance?" Hodges asked.

"It's difficult to put into words. There was something ominous about what the women were doing. Something unnatural. I had a sensation of apprehension. Evans reacted adversely to the same vision."

"From what I gathered," Hodges said, "Evans was a known

113

mystic, psychic, whatever the term is. But I must admit, this sounds like nothing more than coincidence to me. I don't put much faith in the occult."

"You're right, detective," Frank interjected, glad to hear a police detective affirm his beliefs. "That's what I told her. Just a coincidence."

"I believed he had the ability to see things," Laura continued. "For one thing he seemed to know about my friend, Jenny Douglas. She disappeared recently. Just vanished. He mentioned her name. What did Evans know of her?"

"You never mentioned her to him?"

"Of course not. I never met him before."

"Is it possible that Mrs. Danfield mentioned her name to Evans?"

"I doubt it," Laura said. "There was no way she knew of Jenny."

Hodges held the email in his hand. "I came by this letter quite accidentally," he said. "Father Gerald Stuart, the man to whom it was addressed, brought it to me. It seems Evans was greatly depressed lately, and through you, apparently envisioned his own death. By hanging, he says here. He apparently was subconsciously plotting his own suicide. So he confirms what you just told me. Perhaps you tapped into his brain waves."

Frank interrupted. "Where is this all leading, detective? We all know Evans was off center. What can my wife possibly tell you that you don't already know?"

"I was getting to that, Mr. Whitney," Hodges answered quickly. Turning to Laura, he said, "When you last spoke to Evans did he seem depressed to you? I mean out of the ordinary. Enough to take his own life."

"I'm not qualified to make such a comment," Laura answered. "I don't know."

"Your perception is all I'm after. Your reaction to his attitude."

"I can't say he seemed like a man who was going to kill himself," Laura answered. "He said he was preparing for a trip."

"We know Evans had been living in a despondent state of mind for years," Hodges said. "Ever since his wife had a breakdown. I'm trying to connect his depression to some trigger that caused him to kill himself."

"Maybe his mind finally just snapped," Frank offered.

"Most logical explanation, of course, Mr. Whitney. Obviously his mind did snap. But why was he able to live with the depression for a while and then suddenly end it?"

"I'm sure neither my wife nor I have any idea," Frank said. "If you're referring to that e-mail, I'm afraid we're going around in circles. The problem Evans cites is..." Frank reached out for the e-mail in Hodges hand. "May I?" he asked. The detective allowed him to take the missive. He read aloud. "Here's a quote... 'she might be the victim of some mystical force'. He's referring to Laura. Some mystical force! I ask you to be reasonable. This man was nuts."

Hodges turned to Laura. "Mrs. Whitney, you did go to see Evans for help, did you not?"

Laura noticed Frank's concern at every word she uttered and how often he took it upon himself to intercede. She chose her words carefully.

"Not help exactly. I merely wanted to know what Evans meant by the visions he had. When he held my watch he had a fearful vision. He did not react so strangely with anyone else in the room. He was upset. He upset me. I thought perhaps he might have sensed that my operation might yet fail. I don't know. I went to see him. I wanted an explanation. He was still vague. I wanted to know if everything would be all right for me."

"And is it?" Hodges asked.

"Well, yes; so far. My eyes are responding perfectly to the operation."

Hodges got up and put the letter and his notebook in his coat pocket. "Thank you very much for your time and cooperation, Mrs. Whitney," he said. "If I have further questions I will call you."

"Is that all?" Laura asked.

"Yes. You've been very helpful," Hodges said. "Again, I thank you."

When the detective left Laura sat down and breathed a long, heavy sigh. Frank came and sat beside her.

"Frank, do you realize what that letter means?"

"No. What?" Frank almost didn't want to know.

"Evans knew. Something is interfering with my life. And he

knew. He wanted to help me. Frank, he said it is going to get worse. Damn, I wish I could have gotten the truth out of him before he died."

"Laura," Frank said, "that is a terrible tragedy. A man committing suicide just after you had talked to him. God, I understand how you must feel right now, but you've got to think about yourself. Please, honey, don't make this worse than it is. And for God's sake, don't blame yourself."

"Evans knew I was having disturbances," Laura continued unabated, as if what Frank just said was irrelevant. "He knew but he was afraid. He confessed his own cowardice to the priest in this letter. Evans said he thought this priest and another man might want to talk to me." She didn't mention that Father Gerry Stuart had already contacted her.

"Please Laura," Frank sighed. "Enough."

Chapter 18

The phone rang. Laura lifted it and trembled when she heard the familiar voice.

"Laura, it's Jen."

"Oh my God!" Laura exclaimed. "Where are you, Jen?"

"I can't tell you. I'm his prisoner."

"What are you talking about? Whose prisoner?"

"I can't tell you. I just want you to tell Ralph and the kids I'm alive and all right. I can't get away."

"Where are you calling from, Jen? Is it that house, the big house in Manhattan, I followed you to?"

"You followed me? I wish I'd known."

"Is that where you are now?"

"Yes. I found a cell phone here. It must belong to the real owner. I think they're getting ready to leave here, to pull out. You can't find me. Please don't try. He's dangerous."

"Jenny, you were on the street. I followed you. Why didn't you just run away?"

"Oh, I couldn't. He lets me go out for things. Food. You know. But his man always goes with me."

"The blond man who was at the house?"

"Yes."

"Can't you run away?"

"You don't understand, Laura. He's a brutal monster. He'll kill Ralph and the children. I can't let that happen. I do what he wants. He is inhuman, a monster."

"Has he hurt you, Jen?"

"He...yes... they rape me."

Laura stifled a sob. "Mother of God, Jen, why is he doing this to you?"

"Laura, I don't know," Jenny said. Then her voice changed from high pitch to a lower, more somber tone. "Laura, I must know. What connection does this man have to you?"

"Connection to me?" Laura was puzzled. "None. The only time I met him was when I followed you to his house?"

"Why does he have so many of your paintings in his house."

"What? My paintings? I don't understand. Perhaps he bought them sometime in the past."

"But these are paintings of yours I hadn't seen before. You told me you were painting in a different style. These were a technique I had not seen yet."

"Jen, can you describe some of them?"

"Sure. There was one showing Broadway during a snowstorm at night."

Laura gulped. "Impossible," she said. "That painting was bought by Vernon Hayle. It hangs in his gallery. He assured me he wouldn't sell it."

"There are more," Jenny continued, "a fruit stand, a city scene at night made of nothing but lights..."

"Stop. Jen, this is impossible, fantastic. I don't know this man. And, as far as I know those paintings had just been delivered to Vernon Hayle. They are brand new. And there have been no prints made from them. Vernon would never make copies of my work. You're saying they are originals?"

"Yes. Originals. Signed by you. I thought you might know him. He sure as hell knows you. He has at least a dozen of your works."

"They must be copies, forgeries."

"Laura, I would check with your gallery. Find out if they sold your paintings. I've got to go, Laura. Don't forget to tell Ralph I'm alive and alright."

"Why don't you call them directly, Jen? Ralph needs to hear from you."

"No! Never. He would know I did and he would harm my family. I know he would. He kills people."

"You know that?" Laura asked.

"Yes. He kills people."

"Who is he?" Laura said.

"You mean what is he?"

Suddenly, the phone went dead. Call ID gave the number from which Jenny had called. Laura dialed and it rang and rang. She hung on until someone finally answered.

Suddenly the phone went dead. Call ID gave the number from which Jenny had called. She hung on. Finally the phone stopped ringing and went completely dead.

Laura's first urge was to call Ralph Douglas but she remembered what Jenny said...that the man in black would kill him and the children. Instead she called Detective Flynn at Missing Persons.

"Detective," she said after identifying herself, "this time you've got to believe me. I got a call from my friend, Jennifer Douglas, a few minutes ago."

"So your friend has returned."

"Not exactly. She called to tell me she is being held prisoner."

"Held prisoner? Then how does she make a phone call?"

"I don't know. But doesn't this prove that I saw her? She told me that her family was threatened. And she is afraid for their safety. Can't you go back to that house?"

"We've got no reason..."

"I'm begging you, Detective. You've got to do something."

A long pause before Detective Flynn answered. "All right, Mrs. Whitney. I'll get over there."

"That's all I ask. Thank you."

Laura didn't hear from Detective Flynn until the following afternoon. He entered the house once again and found nothing. The owner was very cooperative and took him and his search party through every room.

"Sorry," he told Laura. "But you're going to have to admit that your friend just took off. This investigation might center more on the husband."

"Why would she have told me what happened to her if you suspect her husband? That doesn't make sense."

"Many disappearances don't make sense, Mrs. Whitney. But we'll get to the bottom of this. It takes time."

Never, Laura thought. Not in a million years could Ralph have anything to do with Jenny's disappearance. There was something sinister involved here and she could not grasp what it was. Who in the hell was the man in black at the house? Why did he have copies of my paintings and what did he want with Jenny?

Chapter 19

This night was a special night. Tonight Vernon Hayle was invited to Saylem's house. Vernon had hoped for such an occasion but was unwilling to ask for an invitation. His new enthusiast was an enigma. He did not respond to questions. In fact he stopped Vernon on occasion when he was asked a personal question.

"What is your profession?" prompted an immediate reaction to quell the query by placing his hand over Vernon's lips.

"Where are you from?" The inquiry also produced a frown from Vernon's mate.

"Not to ask questions," Saylem cautioned.

That evening Saylem insisted Vernon take a taxi to his house on the Upper East Side.

Vernon was impressed when the cab let him out in front of the distinguished building. It was stunning; four stories high, excellent turn-of-the-twentieth-century architecture, massive double-door entry. Acceding to the superstition of the supposed evil connection to the number thirteen, only twelve steps led from the street to the entrance. A small garden stepped down from the street to the right of the entryway. Vernon knew immediately he was looking at many million dollars of real estate. This house seemed oddly familiar to him. He recognized it during his sometime walks through the area. His own holdings were not far from here.

Saylem met him at the door.

"Welcome to my abode," his host said.

"Quite a place you've got here," Vernon offered.

"It suits me for the time being," was the pretentious answer.

"How long have you owned this house?" Vernon asked. "I seem to remember a family living here. Can't remember the name offhand."

"Not long," said Saylem. "Questions again, Vernon. You're asking questions and I don't tolerate questions."

"Just curious," Vernon said, wondering why Saylem's aversion to exposing details of his life.

"Remember," said Saylem, lover of clichés, "curiosity killed the cat." He smiled slyly at Vernon as his luminescent eyes sparkled.

Vernon entered at his host's bidding and followed him through a second set of doors. There were times Vernon had noticed the most odd thing about Saylem. He seemed to glide when he walked, his feet barely moving and hardly touching the floor. How could anyone be that light on his feet, he wondered.

They came into the massive entry hall. Vernon suddenly stopped in his tracks. He was shocked by what he saw. The walls to either side were covered with paintings. There was a variety of subject matter, styles and artists. What stunned Vernon was that there were a number of paintings by Laura Whitney.

The paintings were striking. Vernon rushed to the wall and studied them. He was aghast. They were original oil paintings. And each was an exact duplicate of Laura's recent work. Exact. Even the signature on each was exactly as Laura signed it.

In the center of the grouping was Laura's masterpiece, Broadway Snow Storm. Vernon was astounded that it was not a print. Studying it for a moment, Vernon was almost convinced it was the original. He could not tell the difference between this painting and the one that hung in TheArtGallery. But it had to be a copy. He had just left the gallery and the original painting was still hanging there.

Turning abruptly to Saylem, he said. "What the hell is going on here? These are Laura Whitney paintings. And they are unerringly accurate."

"I dabble," Saylem said. "I like what Laura Whitney sees. It's as if she imparted what her eyes observed to mine."

"Dabble! Are you insane?" Vernon exclaimed. "These paintings are exact copies of the originals. I know Laura's work. I've studied it. I'm acquainted with every color, every stroke, every nuance. How were you able to make exact copies? You would have had to get the originals from my gallery to copy them. What's going on?"

"These are my attempts at duplicating Laura's work. I feel I am flattering her by imitation."

"If I didn't know better I'd say you stole these from me but I know that's impossible. I just left the gallery and every painting is still there. You couldn't have gotten the originals."

"I told you they are copies."

"But how could you copy them? You don't have the originals. They never left my gallery. You've never spent enough time in front of them at the gallery and I don't allow photographs to be taken."

"I painted from memory."

"Impossible! You're not divine."

"I should hope not."

Vernon continued his rant. "Look here," he contended. "This painting and this one." He pointed to the two most recent of Laura's works. "They are paintings even I don't have. No gallery has them. They are part of Laura's private collection. I've seen them at her apartment. She would never sell them. You would have had to be at her apartment to view them. Do you know her?"

"No. I know of her. Let's just say we have 'identical vision' in art "

"Liar!" Vernon cried, now inflamed by Saylem's mendacity. "You lie. You must know her. This is the strangest thing I've ever seen. I don't understand it. I don't understand you. You're...unnatural."

"I suppose so," Saylem said. "From your point of view that could be the case."

"This isn't going to work," Vernon said, on the verge of tears.

"What isn't going to work?"

"Our relationship. It's built on lies."

"Suit yourself," Saylem said calmly, sardonically. "There's the door. Walk out and end it or would you have me strike you dead right now, right here? The choice is yours."

Stunned by such a vicious comment, Vernon could not believe what he had heard. Strike me dead? Did such violence exist within this strange man's temperament? He had been introduced to a fondness for violence in Saylem's sexual performance but just how far did the partiality go?

As he left the building Saylem called to him. "Vernon," he quipped, "don't forget to look before you leap."

The bastard, thought Vernon, always with his fucking clichés.

It wasn't until he got to the street that he realized how emotionally upset he really was. He thought he had made the perfect connection with this man. He had hoped Saylem would explain his ties to Laura Whitney and would continue their affair.

But he had been rejected outright. How badly it hurt. How cruel this man was. The emotional pain was so deep Vernon felt he could not face life without continuing his relationship with Saylem.

That evening Vernon Hayle called Laura Whitney at her Manhattan number and got her on the second ring.

"Laura," he said excitedly, "it's Vernon."

"Oh, how are you, Vernon? I got your check. Price getting out of sight, isn't it?"

"Laura, I told you that you would be a star. And this is merely the beginning." He paused a moment, then said, "Laura, I don't intend to pry into your private affairs but I must tell you this. I must confess to you, Laura. I stumbled across something out of the ordinary recently. Here's the strangest thing. I was at an acquaintance's house in Manhattan recently and, in the grand entrance hall, his walls were covered with paintings. And, here's the weird thing, some were actually yours. Not prints. Original oils. And, Laura, it was impossible to tell them from your originals. They weren't just attempts at copying. They were astounding."

"What are you saying? Which paintings? Older ones?"

"No, Laura, not the old ones. Some of your newest paintings, Broadway Snow Storm, Night Lights, Monday Morning and more. Each exact. I'm talking exact, each an original."

Laura was stunned. A jolt of fear like an electric shock raged through her body. Jenny Douglas had told her of the same circumstance when she had called. Dear God, could Vernon be telling her of the same villainous fiend?

"Wait, Vernon," Laura interrupted him. "Where is this house. Describe it."

Vernon described the uptown house. Laura could hardly believe what Vernon had told her. Laura was silent for a moment. Could it be the man in the place into which Jenny Douglas had vanished? The description fit exactly. Was it possible.?

"Can you tell me more about him?" she asked. "What does he look like?"

"Tall. Six feet. On the slim side but well built. Very distinguished man. Long black hair. Loves to wear black clothing. His name is Saylem."

"Oh my God, Vernon!" she exclaimed, having heard a name she vowed never to forget. "I do know him!"

"You do? I thought you must have. Otherwise how would he be able to duplicate your paintings?"

"I don't mean that I really know him. I met him only once through an unfortunate circumstance. I believe you've described the same house and man. He apparently owns it. I was in that place and I noticed the strangest thing. There were paintings on the walls in the entrance hall as you said, but there were a number of vacant spaces where paintings had hung. Could those vacant spaces have been reserved for copies of my paintings?"

"I don't know, Laura. I don't know. When I questioned him about them he dismissed me. The bastard actually dismissed me. Practically threw me out of his house. Ended our relationship in an instant. I can't cope with what he's done and I can't explain it. I'm so depressed. That's why I called you. I thought you might have some influence with him. How did you come to know him?" Vernon asked.

"I called the police to search his house," Laura said.

"Why did you do that? When?" Vernon asked.

"A childhood friend of mine disappeared. She was a woman with two children, happily married. She just walked out of her house and vanished. I saw her accidentally in Manhattan one day and I followed her to that house. I saw her go in. This man, this Saylem, came to the door and denied that anyone had entered. That was my entire knowledge of him; that one instance."

"What happened?"

"The police searched the house and found nothing. They said I must have been mistaken and that apparently ended it."

"This is madness," Vernon said. "Why would your friend vanish into his house?"

"I don't know, but here's a strange turn, I did get a phone call from Jenny, my friend who disappeared. She was terrified that this man in black would harm her family. She asked me the same thing you did. Did I know this man? Of course I didn't. She told me of my paintings that were hanging in that house."

"Laura, are you saying that Saylem is a kidnapper of a woman."

"I'm convinced of it. Where did you meet him?" she asked.

"You're not going to believe this. He was in my gallery, standing in front of Broadway Snowstorm. He was fixated by it and he was mimicking the motions of painting it himself."

Laura became pensive a moment, then said, "Who is he? What does he want?"

"I wish I knew," Vernon said. "He's a mystery yet to be explained."

* * *

The next few days became absolutely unbearable for Vernon. He went to Saylem's house numerous times, left messages, begging for forgiveness. All of Laura Whitney's original paintings were still in his gallery. Saylem had somehow amassed a collection of brilliant copies.

This "calamity" in Vernon Hayle's life had left an emotional distress with which he could not cope. The blow to his body had the jolt of a near heart attack. How could this have happened so quickly, he wondered. Why was he so vulnerable to such a quixotic liaison? He had never before felt so out of control. It had always been the converse in such a situation. In all his amours he had been the one in charge. He called the shots and ended an affair when he wanted. This had never happened to him before.

He went to Saylem's house, climbed the steps and pounded on the front double doors. He beat at them until he could no longer stand the pain in his hands. The degree of depression he felt was overwhelming, like a massive migraine consuming his entire body. The pain was unbearable. The thought occurred to him that the only way to obliterate the pain was to end all pain and suffering. What in the name of God was happening to him?

"Saylem!" he cried out, his sore hands clutching at the doorknobs. "Please, Saylem. How can you do this to me? I'll do anything. Don't let this happen. I can do things for you. I have money, plenty."

It was no use. It was as if no one lived there. Vernon finally had to give up when a police car pulled up in front of the house and an officer suggested he leave immediately. Vernon strode away, his head bent forward, his shoulders slumped and his hands buried in his pants' pockets, the posture of a defeated man.

Mike Walsh

At midnight Vernon Hayle entered the Queensboro Bridge at Fifty-ninth Street and walked to the center. God, he thought, it is beautiful from here looking back on the city, the wonderful city he had loved so much all his life. No place like it on earth. Whenever he viewed the city from afar he always thrilled at the scope of man's ability to create. The magnificence of the thousands of lights shaping skyscrapers and high-rise buildings by their illumination alone brought to mind one of Laura Whitney's marvelous paintings of a city at night. He would take that memory with him to his grave, he thought.

And then his reminiscent turned to Charles Collins. I dismissed him like so much old clothes, having no more value in my life. Hadn't I been just as cruel to Charles as Saylem has been to me? Poor Charles. He's young though, and resilient. He'll get over it. Not like me. I am consumed. Get over it, ha! I must escape from this horrid misery. But there was no real escape...but one.

Below the bridge was Roosevelt Island, halfway to Queens. On either side of the island was the water of the East River. By land or by sea. Which way? He decided water. He walked back until he was over the river then stepped onto the railing. The cliché, "Look before you leap," Saylem's last words to him, came back as he threw himself from the bridge. How could Saylem have known? The instant he left the bridge he realized that he would never again see any of Laura's works.

Chapter 20

Laura was grateful that Frank was at work when the phone call from Father Gerry Stuart came. She preferred to see the priest and his associate alone. Frank was not being helpful. He lately seemed rancorous.

She ushered them into the apartment, noticing immediately the startling contrast between the two men. Spendler, taller of the two, was fair-skinned, blue-eyed and his gray hair made him seem even fairer in color. Father Stuart, on the other hand, had black, thinning hair, dark eyes and a swarthy complexion. Where Spendler's height was exaggerated by his thinness, Gerry Stuart seemed even shorter because he was slightly overweight.

Spendler felt immediately uneasy in Laura's presence. Evans was right, he thought. She was emitting psychic irregularities. The two men sat opposite her.

"Mrs. Whitney," Gerry Stuart began, "did you know Roger Evans wanted to help you?"

"No, I didn't know. He at first avoided me. I read the e-mail he sent you. The police showed it to me. What did he fear, Father?"

Gerry Stuart was quick to answer. "I don't know what he was afraid of, specifically, or even that he felt fear. Roger had a bad experience a few years back that I'm sure played a part in what transpired."

"I know about that," Laura interrupted. "His wife as his partner...double hypnosis."

"Why yes," Gerry Stuart said, surprised. "Where did you hear of it? Did he mention that to you?"

"I had a talk with Charlotte Danfield. She knew him fairly well."

Gerry Stuart nodded and continued. "At one time Roger was heavily involved in the exploration of psychic phenomena, just as Carl and I are. His wife assisted him on many occasions. In this particular instance he had put her into a trance from which she never recovered. After that, Roger would never again become involved in any psychic endeavor. Oh, he'd perform mild tricks and entertain people, but nothing heavy. It took something out of him to lose his wife that way. He lived with his depression. Perhaps it finally was too much for him."

"Are you saying he was afraid he might cause the same thing to happen to me that happened to his wife?" Laura said. "He wasn't afraid of me personally?"

"That's right, Mrs. Whitney," Gerry said. "That could very well have been his motive."

"But he felt I was being invaded by some unknown force. He said so in his letter."

"Are you?" Carl Spendler asked.

"I'm not sure," she said and followed with, "Yes, I believe I might be."

"Can you describe to us what you sense?" Gerry Stuart said, his curiosity aroused fully.

"Yes, tell us what is troubling you," Spendler added. "Please."

"I know what is happening to me but I can only surmise what it means," Laura said. She described the incidents in the past few months that she believed had supernatural origins. She told of the first frightening meeting with Evans, the recurring nightmares, the hand on the beach touching her shoulder, the figure on the deck of the house, the vision in the bathroom mirror, the dreams, the fact that Evans foresaw his own death.

"It was almost as if I caused his death because I came into his life," Laura said. "And it's too closely related to my last visit to him."

Gerry Stuart looked to Spendler, his eyebrow rising slightly. "Yes. He mentioned your visit in his letter," he said.

"I went to his apartment. I talked to him. He implied that there is some foreign factor in my life. It frightened him."

"Did he give you any indication why he believed it was a mystical influence he felt?" Spendler asked.

"He claimed I was meta..."

"Metagnomic," Carl Spendler said.

"Yes. Metagnomic. He told me that he could feel psychic disturbances when he was near me."

"You are psychic, you know," Spendler said. "I feel the energy right now."

"Good lord! Then it's true!" Laura cried.

"Not necessarily," Spendler empathized. "Mrs. Whitney, when did all these mysterious events in your life begin? Maybe we can trace the source of the disturbance by some major change which recently occurred in your life..."

At that point the front door opened and Frank Whitney entered. The surprise and displeasure he registered when he saw the two men talking to his wife was evident to all.

"What's going on?" he said.

Both men rose and Gerry Stuart moved forward to introduce himself. He put his hand out. Frank reluctantly shook it.

"I'm Gerry Stuart and this is Carl Spendler," Gerry said. "We're friends of Roger Evans."

"Frank Whitney," Frank said. "I hope this visit has nothing to do with your dead friend."

"In fact, yes, it has," Gerry Stuart said. "We came because of him."

"I don't mean to debase Evans now that he's dead," Frank said, "but your friend wasn't playing with a full deck."

"We were aware Roger was suffering from fits of depression," Spendler parried, "but he was perfectly sane."

"Sure he was," Frank replied sarcastically, obviously irritated. "He's got my wife half scared to death with his foolishness about spirits and visions. She's afraid to close her eyes to sleep anymore. Don't tell me the next thing is that you're here to exorcise her?"

"I wouldn't take what Evans said any too lightly, Mr. Whitney," Spendler asserted. "Your wife is psychic. She is sending off very strong psychic vibrations right now. How dangerous they are to her or what they are would have to be investigated..."

"Oh, for God's sake," Frank barked. "I've just about had my fill of this occult business. This is getting completely insane. I don't want to be rude...but I suggest you leave right now."

Laura rose to her feet. "Frank," she snapped. "Stop this. What are you doing? These men are here at my invitation."

"Well I'm uninviting them," Frank responded. "It's time we did something serious about your obsession. And these people aren't helping at all."

Laura turned to the two men who had risen from their seats. "I'm sorry," she said. "I didn't expect this..."

"It's all right, Mrs. Whitney," Carl Spendler said, pulling a calling card from his jacket pocket and holding it out to her. "If you have any problems, if you need help, please...call me."

Frank took the card from Spendler and escorted the men to the front door. When they were gone he walked to the desk in the living room and tossed it into the top drawer. He turned back to Laura, his intention to admonish her, but she broke into tears that stifled his anger.

Perhaps, he thought, they were right. Laura did need help. But not from spook hunters or witch burners. He decided Laura needed a psychiatrist.

* * *

As Gerry Stuart and Carl Spendler waited for the elevator outside the Whitney apartment Gerry turned to his friend.

"Well, Carl," he said. "What do you think?"

"It's a shame about the husband being so strongly against accepting our assistance. It's just going to make things worse."

"You're right. And she may need us."

"There's definitely something going on here," Spendler said. "I would have liked to spend more time with her. There's no doubt in my mind that she is psychic. Definite vibrations. The only way we can tell if the influence is coming from outside her own body is by spending time with her. Whether or not it's harmful would be a guess at this time. Did you sense vibrations from her?"

"Some. But apparently not as strongly as you or Roger felt. I don't think there is evidence of a malevolent force from what she's told us so far. Nothing has happened which would document invasion by spirits or demons. Her nightmares, visions, sensations of being touched could all be figments of her own mind wanting to create some invasions."

"True," Spendler said. "But I would have liked the opportunity to see what develops and be there to face it."

Chapter 21

Charles Collins began hanging around the street where he had followed Vernon Hayle one night. He knew the house and he could identify the man Vernon was spending his time with, having seen him coming out of The Clubhouse. Night after night went by without results. The man seemed never to leave his building. One night, as Charles was about to give up, a hand tapped him on the shoulder. He stood at the corner of a building across the street from Vernon Hayle's place.

Startled, he turned and confronted Saylem. It was the man he had seen with Vernon. He recognized him immediately. The mesmerizing stare bore into Charles' eyes. His instinct was to look away but he could not.

"Looking for me?" Saylem asked.

"Uh...no," Charles stammered. "Who are you?"

"I am who is not," Saylem said. "My card." He held out the card to Charles, who reluctantly took it. "Call on me anytime. You may be surprised at the reception."

Charles looked down at the card. There was nothing printed on the card. It was completely black. As he stared at it letters appeared in white. They spelled out his name, Saylem. Then his name vanished and in its place appeared a phone number.

When he looked up the man was gone. He was nowhere to be seen. Simply vanished.

* * *

They say you can easily buy a gun in New York City, or any big city for that matter, if you are willing to pay enough. By asking around in sullied bars in certain areas of the city, Charles Collins, through unsavory connections, was led to a man who peddled illegal weapons. Charles was to meet him in The Bronx near Hunt's Point in a dead-end side street near the railroad yards. Charles was deathly afraid of traveling to such a notorious area carrying hundreds of dollars in his wallet, but he bolstered his courage and set off on his journey.

He took the subway uptown and got off at Hunt's Point Avenue. It was six PM and there were plenty of people on the trains heading home from work. As he walked closer to the freight yards the commuting crowd thinned out perceptibly. By the time he arrived at his destination fear was gripping his throat like a stranglehold.

There was a car waiting for him in an alley near a small factory at the address he was given.

"Are you Charles?" a young man, in his twenties, asked him as he neared the car. He was dressed in jeans, sneakers and a pullover shirt that read, "God shit on the Bronx long enough".

"Yes. Are you Edward?"

"You got it, man. Let's see the money."

Charles had been told to bargain. Don't show the money until you see the merchandise. Know what you get for the money and offer less.

"Let me see the guns," Charles said.

"Hey, fuck, man. We don't use that word."

"Fine. Let me see the...goods."

Edward popped the trunk. Inside was a suitcase. He opened it and displayed a variety of small arms.

"I want a small piece," Charles said. "Sort of like that one." He pointed to a Beretta automatic.

Edward lifted it out. "Nice piece. Easy to handle. Easy to hide."

"How much?" Charles asked.

"Four hundred."

"I'll take it," Charles said. He did not bargain. He wanted to pay and get out of there.

"Sold," said Edward, smiling. "You drive a hard bargain. He reached down into the trunk and came up with a box of ammunition. "You'll want some bullets."

"Okay. How much?"

"Fifty."

Charles pulled the bills out and handed the amount to the gun dealer. Edward pocketed the money, closed his trunk and got into his car.

"You know how to handle one of these babies, don't you?" Edward asked.

"Sure," Charles answered. "I watch television."

* * *

Charles Collins called the number on the card Saylem had given him. Saylem answered curtly. "Yes."

"I believe you know me. My name is Charles Collins. You said I could call you anytime."

"Yes, I did."

"I would like to see you. Talk to you," Charles said.

"Is this about you or would it be about Vernon?"

"Both." Charles would say anything to get near enough to Saylem to kill him.

"Well, at least you are honest," said Saylem. "Come over then." He gave Charles the address.

When Charles arrived at the house he found the front door unlocked. He let himself into the great entry hall. No one greeted him there. Odd, he thought. Saylem had invited him to come to the house. It made sense that there would be someone to meet him.

"Hello," he called out, his voice echoing in the huge house. "Anybody home?"

There was no answer. He moved deeper in the great hall. The lights were dim, making the interior of the house barely visible. It gave the elegant house with its super high ceilings a mysterious, eerie quality.

He felt in his belt where he had hidden the Beretta under his pullover shirt. He was determined to kill Saylem. This vicious man had destroyed both his life and Vernon's. Vernon was dead and this bastard probably didn't care that he had introduced such havoc into their lives. Yes, tonight Saylem dies.

Charles searched the rooms off the entry hall one by one. He was surprised when he discovered some of Laura Whitney's paintings hanging on the walls. He didn't know Vernon had sold or given away the works he saw hanging here. This fiend had probably stolen them.

He wondered if Saylem even knew Vernon was dead. Probably he did. It was on the news and in all the papers. Did the bastard care?

Charles worked his way through the main floor of the house,

finding no one. He began a slow walk up the massive circular marble staircase. Even the banister was marble in intricate detail.

"I know you're here," he called out again as loudly as he could. "You knew I was coming and you left the door open. It's no use to hide. I'm determined to find you."

As he neared the first landing Charles looked up to the source of moonlight, its blue light streaming down from above, illuminating the way. Above was a glass circular skylight dome cut into the ceiling. It was at least ten feet in diameter. Suspended from the center of the dome's steel support beams was a massive crystal chandelier. It was held by a heavy steel link chain and dangled just above the second floor.

There, just above the chandelier, something moved in the moonlight. It caught Charles' attention as he started to look away. There. Again. Movement. Was there something or someone up there on the chandelier? Impossible. There was no way for a person to get up there without a leap beyond human capability.

A bird then. Maybe a bat? It moved again, the contour more visible now. It was larger than a bird. The shape was evolving. From a slight mist-like form it quickly grew larger into something more specific. It took on the dimensions of a person, although the shape shimmered, retaining a swirling, undulating, smoke-like mist that danced around it.

Charles' heart turned cold with fear. Two great bright red, unblinking eyes glowed in the head of the entity. Whatever it was, human or inhuman, it was watching him.

He felt chest pains as his pulse raced. Mother of God! he thought. What is it? A hellish demon?

He yanked the pistol from his belt and chambered a round. He held the piece at arm's length and shouted, "Come near me, you fucking freak, and I'll blow your head off."

The shape-changing demon above him leapt from the chandelier, looming large, and descended on Charles. The fear-stricken man fired four shots in rapid succession at the fearsome beast. Confusion and the body of the demon engulfed him as he lost consciousness.

* * *

Charles Collins awoke in the dark. He tried to move but there was pain in parts of his body he didn't even know he had. He wondered if he was badly hurt. He felt a hard surface behind him, flush against his back. A wall? He tried getting to his feet but stumbled and fell to his knees. He felt around his body wherever he could. There was not the slightest light to see. There were no windows. There was no light from outside. He thought then that it must be nighttime.

Apparently he had been anchored to the floor. He tried to move away but could only crawl forward a few feet. He was constricted; bound hands and feet. He could smell and feel liquid on his wrists and arms. As he moved his hands around his body, he realized that his clothes were wet in places. And that wetness was sticky. Blood? Was he wounded? He couldn't tell. He smelled rotten. He must have urinated while he was unconscious.

My God, save me, he thought. Where am I? What happened to me? I had been unconscious. How long? Who was this freak bastard, Saylem, who did this to me? And what was that thing on the chandelier? It certainly was not human.

His eyes began to slowly adjust to the dark. It must be early morning as a meager amount of light began to reveal the size and scope of the large area. Charles could barely make out the shape of the walls and the rafters of the ceiling above him. He thought he might be in the cellar and that he was against one of the walls.

Where was he? What did Saylem plan to do with him?

He remained quiet for a long time until the pain in his body increased. He had to break free. Somehow. He strained and pulled at the cords that bound him; to no avail.

"Help!" he screamed over and over, hearing his own voice echo in the room. "Please help me!" No one answered.

As dawn finally broke and dim light softly lit the room, details began to take form. There were joints and rafters everywhere in the unfinished area. The floor beneath him was concrete. It must be the basement, he thought, or a hidden room somewhere in the house.

"Help!" he screamed. "For God's sake, someone help!"

Cell phone, he thought. He always carried it in his right pants pocket. His arms hung by his sides. He felt for the pocket and slid his hand inside. Nothing! It was gone! He tried the other pocket.

His pants had been emptied. Goddamn!

He strained his eyes. The light grew stronger. It must be morning, he thought. He could now vaguely make out more of the room. The walls appeared in slightly clearer form. And then he saw...what he feared.

There were other bodies in the room. They, like a man directly opposite him, lay on the floor, apparently dead, their lifeless bodies bound to the floor like him.

Charles pulled his head back, opened his mouth and his screams echoed to dead ears.

* * *

It took two days for the police to find him. He was near death from the loss of blood. The man who owned the house and his two children were dead. The estranged wife of the owner of the house, Thornton Latimer, saved Charles. She had decided on the weekend to visit her children who still lived in the city with their father. She had gotten a phone call from their school asking why the children hadn't been to school in a few days. When she dialed her husband's number no one answered. She knew immediately something was seriously wrong as she entered the house. It was vacant at a time when it shouldn't have been and there was general disturbance to her eye about the nature of items not being where they should have been. In the basement, she heard faint human cries. She let herself in through the almost unnoticeable wall-paneled doorway and found her husband, her two children and Charles Collins. The only one barely alive was Charles.

Chapter 22

Laura read of Vernon Hayle's suicide in the newspaper.

People in her life were either dying prematurely or disappearing. First Jenny's apparent kidnapping, then Roger Evans' supposed suicide and now Vernon Hayle's suicide. She could not imagine Vernon taking his life for any reason. He had had many lovers who came and went before this tragedy. On the surface, he had everything to live for, yet the last time she talked to him he imparted total despair. The only link she could find between any of these calamities was the mysterious man in black. How could that be? And if there was a connection in these facts...why?

Laura called Detective Flynn at the Missing Persons Bureau.

"Yes, Mrs. Whitney?" the detective asked, the slightest tinge of irritation evident in his tone. "What can I do for you? If this is about Jennifer Douglas, we have no news yet."

"This concerns both the disappearance of Jennifer and the death of a man named Vernon Hayle," she informed Flynn.

"I'm not homicide," he said.

"Let me tell you what I know," she said. "You can take it from there."

"All right. Go ahead."

"There is a story in the newspaper. Vernon Hayle's body was found in the East River. The assumption is he was a suicide. He had no reason to kill himself. I believe it was murder."

"Based on what evidence?" Flynn said.

"Vernon Hayle was a very wealthy man. He had everything to live for. I talked to him recently. No question he was gay. He never hid his preference. I believe he was having an affair with the man who was living in that house in Manhattan, the house that you searched for Jenny Douglas. That same man. There was a definite connection between Vernon and that person."

"The house you claim your friend went into?"

"Yes, exactly. There is something extremely odd going on here. My friend, Jenny Douglas, disappeared from her family. I saw her on the streets in New York and saw her enter that house. Vernon Hayle, who handles my paintings, dies and had been linked to the same man. I find it too much of a coincidence that there was a connection with him and that person in that house. And suddenly he decides to commit suicide. I don't exclude foul play. Vernon was not the type to commit suicide. He had too much to live for."

"Please, Mrs. Whitney, don't play detective," Flynn said. "I'll check it out. That's all I can promise. If there's been a homicide we'll get to he bottom of it."

Within days a Detective Hodges of homicide called Laura and made an appointment to see her. She made sure Frank was present when Hodges called.

"Detective Flynn of Missing Persons asked me to call on you," Hodges said. "I must tell you, Mrs. Whitney, you're a puzzle to me."

"Why is that?" she asked.

"Flynn had originally searched the house at your request. At that time he found nothing. But we entered the house recently. There was no one there. It was completely vacant. No people. No one. We searched the house thoroughly. Then we got a call from the true owner's wife. They are divorced and living apart. We found a large concealed room in the basement. In it were three dead bodies."

Laura choked on her breath. "Oh God, no! Not Jenny!" she exclaimed.

"No," Hodges said. "Your friend was not one."

"Thank God," Laura sighed a breath of relief.

"There were three people who apparently were the family who owned the house. The Larimers. And another person, who was barely alive, identified as Charles Collins."

"Goddamn," Laura cried. "He was Vernon Hayle's lover."

"I hate to admit this, Mrs. Whitney, but we should have listened to you. The two people who claimed to own the house have vanished as has your friend, Jennifer Douglas."

* * *

The large white Victorian house sat on a hill like a gleaming white skull overlooking the jittery waters of a rocky shore.

Contrasted against the deep green backdrop of the tall pines it seemed a beacon in the dark night. The white posts of the front porch railing ran across the face of the house like a hundred sharp teeth clenched in a sparkling grin. The glass windows above, to the left and right, caught in the blood red glow of the setting sun appeared as unblinking eyes watching the gloom of dusk approach.

The mailbox at the front of the house bore the name Vera Lancaster. Through the front doors, through the foyer, past the living room, up the winding staircase and to the bedroom door Laura traveled swiftly. Only the dim light of the setting sun guided her. The door swung slowly inward. Had she opened it or was there someone in the room bidding her enter?

Laura knew this place, knew this room. There was furniture. A dresser against one wall, a sofa against another and an oil portrait of a middle aged woman on the third wall. Closer, close enough to see the face clearly. It was a gentle face, unsmiling, stern yet welcoming. She knew the woman. She could see the portrait was damaged. Closer still. Close enough to see the two black holes where once there had been eyes.

Laura tried to resist, to wake up. She knew it was a dream. She was aware of being in bed while she was drawn deeper into the crux.

She was powerless to avoid the vision that appeared. She fought with her mind to resist but delaying the inevitable was hopeless.

An apparition was there in the center of the fantasy, ghostlike in white gossamer. Laura knew it was Vera Lancaster. It had to be. The medium was beckoning her. She held out her hands in supplication, lips parted as if to speak, beseeching, entreating.

Laura fought, tried desperately to break away, end the dream, break the vision. She woke with a tremor.

Frank was holding her close.

"Laura, what's wrong?" he cried.

"Vision. Again." she said. "A house. Large white house. It was the woman at the séance. I could see her clearly. Vera Lancaster. It was she. I know it. She seemed to be reaching out her hands...to me."

"Laura, darling," Frank said in a soothing tone, "you must calm down." He brushed the hair from her sweating brow. "You are obsessing over this woman. I'm afraid for you."

"Afraid of what, Frank?" she asked.

To Frank Whitney's chagrin he feared she was heading for a breakdown.

"You continue to have these nightmares," he explained. "It's not normal. I believe you've planted these images in your subconscious and you slip into the same dream over and over."

"But I saw her. I know her face. I know who she is. She is trying to reach me. Don't you see that Frank? That's the reason I have these dreams. She is part of me now and she is trying to tell me something."

"But she can't, Laura," Frank said calmly. "She's dead."

* * *

"Tell me about the dreams, Mrs. Whitney," the psychiatrist spoke softly, his voice smooth in comforting tones.

"It's vague," Laura said, sitting in an armchair across from the man who was assigned to reach the basis of her dilemma. "I remember pieces. I'm both puzzled and frightened. I am afraid the visions will persist. I believe they have meaning."

"What parts do you remember specifically?" the psychiatrist asked.

"A room in an old house. Darkness. Women. Death. Screaming. I sense a terrible foreboding. I have never had such a feeling of helplessness. Never before."

"And this fear lasts...how long?"

"I don't know exactly. Until I calm down."

"Then you have a lingering fear of what exists in your dreams that you feel afterwards."

"Yes. But there are other visions of events that happened. The séance is not the only one."

"Tell me."

"I had a vision of my best friend leaving her family and, sure enough, she disappeared. And I foresaw the murder of the man I met at a party, Roger Evans the psychic. And finally a vision of dead people in an room."

"What do you suspect is the cause of these...visions?" the psychiatrist asked.

"I don't know. That's why I'm here, isn't it?" Laura tried to keep the barb from her voice. "I have a suspicion it's connected to my corneal transplant. But I can't prove it."

"Why do you think it might be the operation?"

"Because none of what is happening now had ever occurred until after the transplant."

* * *

When Laura returned to the psychiatrist's office she looked drawn and tired.

"Mrs. Whitney, have you been able to sleep?" the psychiatrist asked.

"Very little. It's difficult."

"You must sleep. Did the sedatives help at all?"

"At first, yes. But I'm reluctant to let myself sleep."

The doctor set up a tape recorder on his desk and turned it on.

"Have you ever been hypnotized, Mrs. Whitney?" he asked.

"Yes, once. A long time ago, at a party."

"Did you respond to hypnosis? Did you go under?"

"I was told I did. But I don't remember anything."

"I'm going to hypnotize you, Mrs. Whitney. The essence of your visions lies burned in your subconscious. I want to release your subconscious thoughts so that we can find the source of your problems. Will you agree to hypnosis?"

"Yes, of course, if it will end this madness. Anything."

The psychiatrist closed the blinds in his office, throwing the room into semi-darkness. He flipped on a pen flashlight that he held before him.

"Now Mrs. Whitney, I want you to relax. Completely. Just let your body go limp. Concentrate on the light. I want you to clear your mind of any thoughts. Think of nothing but my voice and the light." His voice softened even more. "You are very tired. Your eyes cannot stay open. The lids are very heavy. Sleep. You must sleep. You will find peace and comfort in sleep."

Laura fought. Fear of what was waiting over the brink made her shudder at the thought. The psychiatrist's voice droned on until it became merely a murmur. During the conflict of will her desire to be rid of the nightmare outweighed her fear to face it and she began to slip into slumber. The psychiatrist saw that he was winning and he continued to entice her. Then she was under, in a deep sleep, her eyes closed.

"Mrs. Whitney, can you hear my voice?"

"Yes."

"I want you to take me into your subconscious. I want you to tell me everything you see."

Laura's body shook. Her face pinched into a scowl, her mouth twisted and misshapen. She groaned, a low, wailing noise as her body shook. Her eyes burst open suddenly, staring blankly into space. She threw her hands in front of her face, covering her eyes, as if to block out the vision she saw. She screamed. The horrifying sound shattered the small office space.

"Mrs. Whitney, can you hear me? Mrs. Whitney!"

Laura was clawing at her eyes. The lids closed in self-defense as her fingernails raked across the surface, scratching the lids.

The psychiatrist grabbed her wrists and forced her hands away from her face. Laura was shaking in almost uncontrollable spasms. Tears were streaming from her eyes. Then, as she began to slowly calm down, the spasms lessened as her eyes opened.

"Mrs. Whitney," the psychiatrist said, "it's all right now. You're going to be fine."

Through her tears Laura sulked and said softly "But what is he?"

"He?" the psychiatrist asked. "Who?"

"The apparition! The dark person. The thing in the séance?"

* * *

There were a few more trips to the psychiatrist. The dreams had eventually ended. Laura spoke to him privately on what was to be the final visit while Frank waited for her in the outer office.

"Mrs. Whitney," the psychiatrist asked, "how do you feel today?"

"I feel fine."

"No recurrence of the visions?"

"Not for the last few weeks," Laura answered.

"Good news," he told her. "But let me say this. There is no way of knowing for sure that you will experience frightening dreams again. But I believe you have rid your subconscious of the fear harbored there. It appears the basis of your problem emanated from the accident and your ensuing blindness. I believe you built a mental barrier to darkness, afraid to subconsciously enter the realm of darkness because it reminds you of your period of blindness. You don't want to sleep because it requires that you assume a simulation of becoming blind. In sleep your mind creates a world of darkness more terrifying than reality. You invent evil and make it live in that world."

This can't be the answer to the riddle of my mind, she thought. She was envisioning death, again and again. "Must I live on the edge for the rest of my life?" Laura asked. "Or is this an end to it?"

"Of course you may relapse," the psychiatrist told her. "It's not exactly like removing one's appendix. You have faced the problem openly. That is half the battle. You know why you dream. You realize that you dread entering the darkness of sleep because of the fear of blindness."

"No guarantees, doctor?" Laura said.

"I'm afraid not, Mrs. Whitney," the psychiatrist answered. "We can only hope the future will fall into place."

Chapter 23

Laura would not accept the premise that her visions resulted from fear of sleep, a world of total blindness revisited. Doubts and suspicions had beset her since the first meeting with Roger Evans.

She acknowledged the last year of her life was unnatural. She absolutely felt some influence beyond her understanding was playing a dominant role. Could some unknown force actually shape a person's destiny, she wondered?

Laura mentally formed the circumstances in their order of occurrence: her first meeting with Evans, the hand touching her shoulder at the beach, the vision in the mirror, Jenny's disappearance. Then the visions of ensuing deaths followed; the death of Evans, Vernon Hayle.

There must be a connection between the visions and the incidents that followed each. The odds were overwhelming against such repeated coincidence. There appeared to be more to this than any simple explanation. Something or someone, spirit, ghost, whatever, was trying to invade her life. To what end?

Nothing like this existed in her life before the lightning strike. That was the beginning, no doubt in her mind. Aren't some people psychologically affected by sudden physical trauma? But this was more than just that. Why should psychic occurrences begin as the result of a trauma? Something after the accident, something just as drastic...the operation. The corneal transplant.

Of course. It was the operation. Yes. But what could a set of corneas have to do with the metaphysical?

Vera Lancaster, she thought. The name Roger Evans had given her. Just who was Vera Lancaster?

Laura would not forget that name. Evans had called out her name the night of the party at the Danfields' Hampton house. She was determined to find out. She booted up her computer, went on the Internet and entered the medium's name into one of the search vehicles. She got a number of Vera Lancasters.

Which to choose?

Each had an address. Let's be logical, she thought. The

operation was performed in New York City. From all she had read about the transplant of corneas the donor organs had to be fresh, usable within a few hours. That narrowed her search to the east coast, nearby states. She cut the area down to within a one-hour flight time and an hour travel on the ground. Her geographic circle shrank the area considerably.

In her dream the terrain surrounding the Victorian house limited it to an area indicative of many pine trees. She settled on a state north of the city. After hours of eliminating the few Vera Lancasters from the area selected her search brought her to a town in Maine.

* * *

Thank God for the Internet, Laura thought. By locating The Herald, a local newspaper in the town of Seen By Chance, she was able to trace Vera Lancaster to a written article that appeared a week before her corneal operation. Seen By Chance was a small town on the northern coast of Maine. Vera Lancaster lived there all of her life. She died at the age of forty-three apparently during a séance on the almost date of Laura's transplant. She had left vital organs to various organizations and her eyes to The Eye Bank.

A séance. Laura considered the notion. What an oddity, she thought. Her initial vision was of something similar...it could have been a séance. And Vera Lancaster died there. It tied together.

Laura was elated on the one hand but she found it disconcerting that Vera Lancaster had been a medium and clairvoyant all her adult life. She continued exploring the Internet and garnered information of the tragic circumstances relating to the séance. This, then, explained the nightmarish vision she had defining Vera Lancaster's death. She opened a file on her computer and downloaded some of the information she found. She then typed in a summary of what she had learned.

* * *

Laura and Frank had not returned to the Hampton house. Too much had happened recently in her life that had isolated her. She knew she would not be able to relax and feared it would be a waste of effort trying. She felt she was on the verge of discovery. Vera Lancaster loomed large on the horizon and dominated her conscious mind.

Frank was sitting at a desk in an area of the living room in their apartment that was set aside for a sundry of duties. Frank had the computer booted up and was in the process of reviewing advertising proposals, ad copy and comprehensive ideas for clients. Frank sometimes worked at home in the evening to be with Laura more often. Before her accident he rarely got home before eight or nine in the evening.

Laura held her file in front of Frank, not sure how he would react.

"Something for you to read," she said.

"What is it?" he asked.

"This is remarkable, Frank," she said, handing some of the pages to him. "About the woman, Vera Lancaster. Roger Evans called out her name at the Danfields' party. Remember? Turns out she died just before I had my transplant. She donated her eyes to the Eye Bank. Perfect timing."

"What about her?" he asked, skepticism in his voice and his eyes.

"I think I have her corneas."

"What makes you believe this is the right woman?"

"Well, her name to start. Evans identified her. Then there is the distance she lived from us. She lived in Maine. And the dreams I had of her house, the séance. It all fits."

"When did you compile this?"

"I started about a week ago."

"Maybe you're on to something," Frank admitted. "Where'd you get all this information?

"The internet. From a newspaper website."

"Why didn't you tell me you were doing this? I would have helped you."

"I know you frown on all this supernatural stuff," she said. "When I discovered that I may be carrying the corneas of a person who dealt in the occult my curiosity was really piqued. I want to know more about her."

"I hate to be the doubting Thomas," Frank said, "but you can't be absolutely sure you've got this woman's corneas."

Laura realized Frank might not accept Vera Lancaster as the donor because, she believed, this woman affirmed the mystical inclination he kept denying. "It has to be her." She was adamant. "The timing. She died just before I received the corneas. It all points to her."

"I noticed you've been boning up on occult literature," Frank said with quiet disdain.

"It ties in, Frank. Don't you see that? Vera Lancaster, a psychic, a medium, and an eye bank gets her eyes within a few days of my procedure. Right after that I began having psychic disturbances, going back to that first encounter with Roger Evans. Then there was that incident on the beach. And the vision I saw in the bathroom mirror plus all the dreams."

"You never told me about the bathroom incident. What happened?"

How would he react to this, she thought. Would he consider it just another of my imaginings, more foolishness? She proceeded to tell him, regardless of his reaction.

"I saw something behind me in the bathroom. A woman was moving. But it happened so fast it could have been my imagination. Scared the hell out of me. The point is, you know unusual things have been happening to me since the operation and there is no denying them."

"Why did you think it was her, the Lancaster woman?" Frank asked.

"Frank," she answered, her voice ringing with emotion "who else could it have been?"

Taking the papers from Frank and reading from them, she said, "Listen to this. She was born in the town of Seen By Chance, Maine. She died just before my operation. Cause of death listed as heart attack. Death reported by a woman named Martha Fuller, one of the two other women who had attended a séance. The newspaper revealed that Vera Lancaster had experimented in occult practices for years. Something disastrous happened at the séance that brought on a heart attack. Vera Lancaster died on the way to the hospital."

"She had a weak heart. What does that prove?" Frank said.

"Bear with me." Laura continued reading from her printouts. "Here's a quote from the paper, 'Vera Lancaster was a practicing medium. She conducted séances for a growing circle of followers. From all indications gathered from townsfolk and clients who attended her meetings, she claimed to be in contact with the spirit world. Some of her assemblage swore that she could reach the departed and was able to reveal detailed messages from loved ones who had passed on.'

"'Her death came when she had conducted a séance with two friends, Martha Fuller and Susan Gray. Whatever happened at that séance apparently caused Susan Gray to be confined to an institution.'"

Laura paused and said, "Sounds like what happened to Roger Evans. No one knows why he killed himself, if he did."

"Hmm, interesting. Maybe you are onto something," Frank muttered.

Laura resumed with the facts. "'The third woman, Martha Fuller, survived the incident unscathed. It was strange and disturbing that Vera Lancaster's death was from heart failure even though there had never been an indication of heart disease. It was as if her heart had been crushed.'"

"What does that mean?" Frank asked. "Her heart was crushed. By what?"

"That's part of what I am trying to find out. Doesn't it strike you as really strange that she should die at a séance? What really happened?"

"What else did you find out, Sherlock?" Frank asked, grinning at his wife's resourcefulness.

Laura cracked a slight smile and continued reading. "'She was well respected by the people who knew her. She was unmarried and, aside from the meetings held for clients, she led a quiet, singular life. Her main source of income was from a family inheritance which gave her a house, free and clear, and enough funds to live without having to work.'

"There are facts from The Herald's Web site about her early school years, suppositions of her character by neighbors who had been interviewed and tales of a romance that had ended tragically. But I'll skip those."

"All right, then, Laura, let's say it's her," Frank suggested reluctantly. "What do you think all this means?"

"I'm not sure. But I believe that Vera Lancaster was somehow reaching out to me, trying to tell me something that will affect my life." Was it danger? What did she know?

"From beyond the grave, obviously," Frank said, tapping his pen on the desk.

"Maybe. She was projecting a message to me. It's the only thing that makes sense."

"Laura, you want me to believe that this dead woman has the ability to send a visual message to you from beyond the grave through her corneas. According to your file she is hundreds of miles away and quite dead."

"Don't mock me, Frank," Laura snapped. "Don't be so dogmatic about things we know so little about. The power of the spirit is unknown. How do we know the living cannot be connected to the spirits of the dead? Don't be so quick to scoff at what some people are willing to accept as truth."

"Come on, honey. Be reasonable." Frank was solicitous once again. "For God's sake, don't get carried away by the coincidences that have happened. The woman was probably a charlatan and milked her clients with phony noises, white gauze floating in a dark room, faces projected on black walls. Stuff that Houdini debunked years ago."

"Where did you learn about things like that?"

"I don't live in a vacuum. I read up on some of these things because I'm concerned about you. I want to know what is troubling you."

"And," Laura said, "have you learned anything by reading?"

"Yeah. I'm convinced it's still a lot of bunk, just like Houdini knew."

"You won't admit that there is such a thing as a genuine medium?"

"You mean someone who can actually contact the spirit world, the dead"

"Yes."

"No. I don't. No matter what you or anyone says. Or whatever so-called proof you may have. I don't believe in the spirit world, life after death. So how can I believe someone can contact something I don't accept exists in the first place? One belief would contradict the other. Nothing can make me accept phonies who claim to talk to a great vacuum."

"But suppose you're wrong," Laura replied excitedly. "Suppose there is a spiritual world after death. Then isn't it possible that the mind, which is spiritual, can be linked to the total spirit?"

"If I'm wrong! God, Laura," Frank said excitedly, "who knows what's real? Religions? Prophets? They all differ."

"I don't mean in that sense. Only that our spirit is somehow connected to a total spiritual entity. Maybe that's what God really is. Maybe we are all part of God."

"And people actually talk to God when they pray? That's what you believe?" Frank was not about to be convinced.

"No. I don't mean formal prayer. Perhaps it is within the power of our minds to contact the spirit world and we all have that capacity. Only some people are aware of their power and have learned how to use it."

"Like this Vera Lancaster person?"

"Yes."

"All right. I'll grant you this. She probably believed she was able to do the things you say."

"Perhaps. And perhaps she was doing some good with her beliefs."

"Something good, like her death and one woman insane?"

Laura became somber for an instant. "Something got out of control at that séance, Frank. Something that she couldn't cope with. I would love to know what."

"Why, Laura? Why?'

"Because I think it is all related. My eyes, the dreams, the tragedies that followed. All of it."

Laura sipped her coffee and was silent for a few moments, contemplating what to say and wondering how Frank would respond to the request she had in mind.

"Frank," she said finally, "I want to go up to Maine. I want to go where she lived. I must find out more on a personal level."

Frank reflected the disdain he felt. "Laura, where is this leading? What do you expect to find by going to Maine? And what difference could it make if you found out the worst about this woman?"

"You can't treat what has happened so lightly?"

"All I can gather is what you imagine has happened."

Laura was stone-faced. She did not think Frank would resist her desire to visit Vera Lancaster's hometown. She viewed it as a necessity.

"Something extraordinary has come into my life," she said. "I've been allowed, somehow, through circumstances, I suppose, to glimpse life from a new point of view. Can you understand that, Frank? I want to know what has entered my life and brought fear with it. My life is not normal."

"My God, Laura. Of course you are normal. Hasn't the psychiatrist helped?"

"I'm not normal. My life is entirely different. Nothing has been the same since the operation. I believe I may have been responsible for the deaths of Roger Evans, Jenny's abduction, and maybe even Vernon Hayle's tragic death."

"For God sakes, Laura. How can you even think such a thing?"

"It's true. I must have had something to do with their deaths. There has to be a connection. Don't you see that?"

Frank was bristling. "Ridiculous! Absolutely ridiculous!" he said. "You are confusing coincidence with fantasy again. How could you have caused their deaths?"

"I don't know. But I intend to find out."

Frank got up and rapidly paced the room.

"All right," he said. "Suppose we go to Maine and find nothing to back up your beliefs. Will you drop this whole obsession once and for all? Will you call an end to it?"

Laura pondered a moment, reflecting so seriously that it seemed the choice was not an easy one to make. Finally she answered. "All right. You've got a deal. If we find nothing that satisfies me I'll give it up and stick strictly to painting. But, if we do find something..."

Frank smiled, hoping that he appeared sincere and did not reflect the true emotions he felt.

"I'm taking you at your word. I'm going to hold you to it," he said.

* * *

Laura thought there was no denying that the corneas came from Vera Lancaster, a medium, a psychic. And it was because of this certainty that her curiosity had to be satisfied. She must know if anyone's physicality might be influenced by a body part received from another human being. The circumstances seemed to point to this conclusion. And, by now, she was convinced she was not going to find the truth from a medical professional.

Laura found Carl Spendler's calling card in the foyer desk where Frank had tossed it. She dialed the number and placed the card in her wallet. In case I need it again, she thought, I would have it with me. After four rings a voice came on announcing she had reached a machine.

"Mr. Spendler, this is Laura Whitney," she said. "I don't know if you remember me but you came to see me..."

A voice cut her off. Spendler had picked up the phone. "Of course I remember you, Mrs. Whitney. You are the woman Roger Evans was concerned about. What can I do for you?"

For an instant Laura almost hung up with a change of heart, but quickly decided to finish what she had started. "Since you're aware of my problem I won't bore you with the details." Laura dispensed with preliminaries. "When you came to my apartment we were interrupted by my husband and I never got a chance to completely explain myself. Can we meet somewhere and talk."

"I'll be glad to see you. How can I help?"

"I think your expertise may give me answers to questions that are bothering me."

"I certainly hope so. I'll do anything I can to help."

"When can we meet?"

"Lunch, today? Are you free?"

"Fine. Tell me where and when."

Since Spendler loved Central Park he suggested The Boathouse at noon. Laura found him seated outdoors. It was a clear bright summer day and this was the perfect spot to clear her head, she thought.

"Nice to see you," Spendler said, rising to greet her. "How are you?"

"I'm fine," she said, taking a seat. Laura hadn't been here in a while. She enjoyed the ambiance of the dining room but enjoyed dining outdoors even more.

They asked for coffee and sandwiches. When the waiter left Laura spoke. "Mr. Spendler, have you ever heard of a medium named Vera Lancaster? She lived in Maine."

An expression of complete surprise overcame Spendler. "Vera Lancaster. Yes, of course. I heard she died recently. Roger Evans mentioned her in his letter to Father Stuart. Something about a séance. What about her?"

"I believe I am carrying her corneas in my eyes," Laura declared.

Spendler's eyes widened in astonishment. "Vera Lancaster's corneas?" he exclaimed. "You've lost me there. Fill me in?"

"The first time we met you asked me when the mysterious events in my life began. I never got the chance to tell you that I had a corneal transplant right around the time Vera Lancaster died." She related to him the cause of her accident last year, her blindness, the operation, and the events leading to her internet discovery of Vera Lancaster as perhaps the donor of her new corneas.

"Apparently Vera Lancaster was an organ donor and I was the recipient of her eyes," she added. "It was only since the operation that things have substantially changed in my life."

"You believe Vera Lancaster's corneas may be the cause of recent personal oddities?" Laura felt uplifted by Spendler's obvious attention.

"Yes. Only I'd go well beyond oddities. There have been deaths. Roger Evans for instance."

"What about Roger?"

"I saw him die in a dream before he died," she said, her frown telling of her concern. "The way the newspapers reported it. He was hanging from his terrace. But that's not exactly what I saw."

"What do you mean?"

"I saw Roger Evans murdered."

"But Roger committed suicide. That's what the police have concluded."

"But you must have doubts," Laura said.

"I must admit I considered foul play. I can't believe Roger would take his own life. He had to care for his wife, Audrey. He loved her dearly. He wouldn't leave her alone in her condition."

Laura continued. "He did not wrap the cord around his neck or tie it to the deck railing."

"Then who killed him?"

She paused a moment for emphasis, then said, "You mean what killed him."

"You'll have to explain, Mrs. Whitney."

"I could see no one in my vision but Roger Evans. But he tried to fight off something that attacked him. The cord wrapped itself around him and it tied itself to the railing as if by an unseen hand. There was no one on the deck with him and yet he was bound and thrown over the railing. That is what I saw."

"But your vision was a dream. It was not reality."

"I saw his death at almost the exact time it happened? I'm convinced he was murdered."

"By whom?"

"I don't know. That is what I'm trying to find out. There have been other people in my life who have met early deaths...suddenly. In the last few months... a friend's kidnapping, a gallery owner. I believe all are somehow connected. I've mulled over every case and I am the common denominator."

"Are you suggesting spiritual possession? A spirit you are involved with that allows you to foresee things?

"Isn't that what Roger Evans stated in his letter?"

"Sort of. But it would be difficult to prove."

Laura emphasized the profundity of the happenings. "I need advice. I'm convinced I've got Vera Lancaster's corneas. They must be the catalyst."

"I've never come across a case where a transplanted body part carried a possessive spirit with it," Spendler avowed.

"But could it happen? Is it possible?"

"I don't know. I suppose it's remotely possible. It seems highly unlikely but, considering what I've witnessed over the years, I wouldn't discount anything."

She sipped her coffee. "What if this is the case? What can I do?"

"I can help but I want you to realize I am not a psychiatrist or therapist."

"I'm aware of that. But you are a parapsychologist aren't you?"

"As a parapsychologist I investigate for proof of the reality of telekinesis, telepathy and the like. My avocation, you might say, is looking for proof that there is a spiritual life after death. A hopeless task at best."

"I've read a couple of your books. You propose it is impossible to breach the line between life and death in the conscious world.

Where does that leave me?"

"In good hands. We have to unleash the subconscious mind. That is where your demons exist. We'll find them. I'll help you fight whether your demons are real or imaginary. I'm sure I can count on Father Stuart to help. Right now I can only suggest actions you might take. But let me get this straight. As of yet you don't know for sure that Vera Lancaster's corneas are the ones you received, let alone the source of your disturbances."

"Well, no. I can't prove it. But everything points to the fact that they are."

"Let's assume that they are. You seem convinced that the medium is the true cause of your obsession..."

"I don't know if I'd call it an obsession," she interrupted. "That's what my husband calls it."

"All right then, possession. Once you're convinced of the cause you will have options. First, you might seek a psychiatrist who can help you suppress your beliefs."

"I've already been there. It doesn't help, believe me. What're my other options?"

"An exorcism," Spendler said bluntly.

"You've got to be kidding. You're suggesting that a devil has invaded my body."

"Mrs. Whitney, it doesn't have to be a devil. Could be an evil spirit, a demon, a djinn."

"All right. Let's say it's an evil spirit. Did this creature appear at Vera Lancaster's last séance? Is that what killed her?"

"It's possible. She might have contacted a spirit who was too strong for her to accept," Spendler responded as their lunch came. "You are implying that you brought a spiritual force into your body, through your eyes...Vera Lancaster's eyes. Now you are seeing visions of what this creature is seeing, or worse, perpetrating. Does that wrap it up?"

"Just about," Laura admitted. "Other than an exorcism or psychiatrist, where do I stand?"

Spendler paused a moment, stared into Laura's eyes, then said. "If you're up to it, we find your demon and face him, whether real or imaginary."

"My God," Laura said horrified at the thought, "what can I do?
"

155

"Whatever you do, when you're ready I'll join you."

* * *

Carl Spendler stopped by the rectory where Father Gerry Stuart lived on the east side of Central Park.

The meeting with Gerry Stuart was to be about their now favorite subject, Laura Whitney. As he walked through the park he thought about her. Odd that her issue was occult oriented. He often considered the people around him as he walked. Reach out to anyone you passed and ask his or her current life situation. Spendler maintained that anyone you asked would lay a glut of problems on you. Every person you meet has issues. Laura was no different except in one respect, her plight came from outside the realm of normality. It was not something to cope with unless some knowledgeable assistance came into play.

Gerry had just finished lunch when Carl found him in the rectory.

"Well, hello," Carl's friend said. "How was the lunch with Laura Whitney?"

"Gerry, sit down!" Carl said. "Brace yourself. You're not going to believe this."

"What's so important?" Gerry boomed.

Spendler sat in one of the two overstuffed armchairs in the priest's rooms.

"Come on," Gerry said. "Give out."

Spendler said, "Laura Whitney had an operation a few months ago. She was blinded in a crazy accident. Lightning hit a restaurant right where she was sitting. She got a corneal transplant. Both eyes, mind you."

"She had her sight when we met her. I'm assuming it was successful," Gerry said.

"Yes, it was. She was at the end of a recuperation period then. This is the part we knew nothing about when we first met the Whitneys. I don't think we would have dismissed her so easily if we had known then what we know now. But, here's the thing...she is convinced she inherited the corneas of Vera Lancaster."

"You don't mean Vera Lancaster, the..."

"Exactly. The medium."

"Well, I'll be," Gerry remarked. "What a small world. No wonder Roger knew something was wrong with her."

"Here's the amazing thing," Spendler said. "She believes her psychic malady is a result of the corneal transplant."

"Sounds plausible," Gerry Stuart asserted, more willing to accept spiritual interference than Spendler. "How did she find out that Vera Lancaster was the donor? I thought that information is unavailable."

"I don't know. She seems to be obsessed with the idea of proving Vera Lancaster is the donor. She wants to know her options."

"What did you tell her?"

"To face her demons."

"Her life must be in chaos," Gerry said.

Spendler continued, "When she discovered the corneas belonged to Vera Lancaster, she believed she knew the source of her problems. I think she is going to go to Maine where Vera Lancaster lived. She feels once she finds the reason for her problems she can put an end to them."

"What can we do to help, Carl?"

"Right now, not much. Wait and see what develops. Then perhaps we can join her."

* * *

The arrival of a certified letter bolstered Laura's determination to travel to Maine. The letter was from a law firm in Portland that named Laura as heir to a portion of Vera Lancaster's estate. The will, the letter stated, had named her exclusively as the recipient of the house on Lancaster Island and property related to the house.

Laura nearly fainted. The will was registered over a year before her death. How was this possible? How did Vera Lancaster know her name? Was the woman a true psychic who could tap into the unknown? She apparently knew, long before her death, that her eyes would become Laura's eyes.

This scenario was far beyond what Laura had anticipated. She dialed the phone number on the letterhead. An operator put her through to the name on the letter.

"Charles Franklin speaking, Mrs. Whitney," the lawyer said. "I assume you got our letter."

Mike Walsh

"Yes, Mr. Franklin," Laura said. "I can't believe this."

"Well, it's more than believable, Mrs. Whitney. It's a fact."

"But why? How? I don't know the woman. I never even met her."

"Well she apparently knows you," came the answer.

"Why me?"

"Vera Lancaster had no living relatives. No children, no sisters, cousins, aunts, uncles. No one. She was unique, the last of her line. She owned a large house on Lancaster Island and most of the land remaining there. Besides the house she left a sizeable amount of money to a couple of lifelong friends."

"I just don't get it," Laura insisted.

"But that's not so, Mrs. Whitney. You do get it. The house and land are yours."

* * *

"This is beyond crazy," Frank Whitney said. "Laura, it makes no sense. How does this crazy woman even know you, let alone enough to leave you her property? It makes no sense."

"That's what I told the lawyer. But he insists she did just that."

"How in the name of heaven could she know you and trust you enough to leave you her property? It's unreal."

"That's just it, Frank. What I've been trying to tell you. Yes, it is unreal."

"What does it mean?" Frank pushed the issue. "That this person's legacy will be with us for the rest of our lives?"

"I think not," Laura did not welcome the sharpness in Frank's voice. "But we should find out what to do about it."

"That are you suggesting, Laura?"

"Logically, that we go to Maine and find out what we own."

"I guess it doesn't matter that I'm reluctant to follow up on this, Laura."

"Of course it matters, Frank," Laura was sympathetic to his reluctance. "But I've got to get this out of my system once and for all."

"Once and for all is the best phrase I've heard in a while," he said, a note of relief in his tone.

158

PART THREE

Chapter 24

The seaside town of Seen-By-Chance, Maine got its name in 1847 when Jack Farrell, an itinerant sea captain, mistakenly chose the wrong shore of the cove in which the town was situated to erect a lighthouse. At the time, Farrell, one of the original town founders, had designated a site, agreed upon by townsfolk cursed with the same stigma of erratic judgment, on the southern tip of the harbor that they considered most suitable for a lighthouse. Since this was a high point, they reasoned, the lighthouse would easily be seen from the sea. When the edifice was erected it was clearly seen from the southeast. But the view of ships returning from the northeast was partially obscured by hills and an outcropping of growing pines. From the northeast the lighthouse was virtually seen by chance. No one seemed concerned with correcting the error and the town received its name from the masters of ships who were to depend upon that lighthouse beacon.

The town was a perfect example of the concept one might have of a quaint New England harbor. It was postcard perfect. The rugged pine-encrusted surface rolled gently down to the edge of the water, practically plunging into its surface. The land joined the water without seeming to have an edge. Out of the lush evergreen sprung the outcroppings of the small, bustling town. From the main highway, which spiraled along the rolling coast, the bright colorful buildings of the town contrasted with the dense green landscape surrounding them. Boats, in the harbor, dotted the expanse of the deep blue water and accentuated the verdure with their varied colors. The textures and shapes of the closely arranged houses and wharves along the shoreline presented a vision to Laura that could be captured a hundred different ways in remarkable and exciting paintings.

The highway wound close to the outskirts of town where a

tributary road took Frank and Laura the remainder of the journey towards the main street. In the center of town they followed an expansive circle that looped around a statue of Jack Farrell that, ironically, had its back to the harbor. They could see the rugged hills, which seemed to loom over the town, framing it and diminishing it even more. To the right, off the main street, roads shot out to join the water's edge, where docks, fisheries and boats abounded. The serene water and the pine-covered landscape of the harbor combined to form an idyllic scene.

They drove along; absorbing the quaint beauty of Seen By Chance, and within minutes had passed through the town to the motel where they had made reservations. As they pulled into the parking lot Laura was enthralled that even this lodging place was constructed to delight in the breathtaking beauty of the harbor. Laura decided she was going to like it here.

They had lunch in an adjoining restaurant whose view was no less alluring than anywhere else. Aware that the purpose of their trip was not that of vacationer did not demean their appreciation of the town's beauty.

As they awaited their meal that first evening Laura reminisced of the evening in Southampton, in a setting much like this that the one in a million lightening strike had changed her life so drastically. A shudder of trepidation washed over her at the prospect of what awaited her future.

Frank noticed the instant and asked, "Are you all right?"

"I'm fine," she said. "Just nervous is all."

* * *

"I'm sorry, Mrs. Whitney. I have no idea why Vera Lancaster left you in her will." The lawyer representing Vera Lancaster's estate answered her query. Laura and Frank sat in his office across from his desk after having just finished signing what papers were necessary to verify her inheritance of property.

"Can you tell me anything about her that you might recall?" Laura asked.

"Not much. She was a very private woman. Although she was a lifelong resident of Seen-By-Chance I really only spoke to her a few times. You know she was a medium?"

"Yes."

"It was common knowledge. I suppose that's why she kept private about her affairs. I understand she did have many clients though."

"Perhaps I might speak to someone in town who knew her," Laura said. "I'm sure that having lived here all her life she must have made some friends."

The lawyer thought a moment, and then he said, "Try The Herald, our only newspaper. Dan McCormack is the editor in charge. He knows more about people in town than anybody else."

* * *

The Herald, the only newspaper in Seen By Chance, was, surprisingly, an efficient, fairly upgraded modern operation even though it was founded at the turn of the twentieth century. It was originally owned and operated by a father and son team named McCormack who had both since died and left it to the next generation. The present descendant/editor was very cooperative when he discovered Laura's identity.

"Well, what do you know, the mysterious heiress people are talking about," he said. "Here at last. You're not a spiritualist too, are you?"

"Not by a long shot," Laura replied. "I'm as puzzled as anyone. Vera Lancaster was a perfect stranger to me. I never met her. As far as I know I am not a distant relative. I have no idea why I was named in her will. But that is why I'm here; to find out why, and what happened at that last séance."

"What is it specifically that you require from me?" McCormack asked, his curiosity surprisingly excited.

"Anything I can piece together that makes sense," Laura told the editor. "I'd like to go through some of your past issues to learn more about her that I'm not aware of."

"Occult stuff, huh," McCormack said. "You must know that she was a medium. Claimed to contact the dead. She could foresee a person's future. Things like that."

"Yes," Laura said. "I wonder what part a medium might play in her connection to me. Can you provide articles about her that I can browse through?"

"I guess you'll find some material here all right. She was in the news a lot, especially since her death. Many unanswered questions."

Frank was escorted on a tour of the small newspaper's facilities while Laura made copies of articles about Vera Lancaster that interested her.

She learned that the medium had conducted séances for clients of many diverse backgrounds from all around the country, some coming as far away as California. She had gained an acknowledged reputation in some circles. Her last séance had been conducted under somewhat secretive circumstances.

Laura wrote down the names Susan Gray and Martha Fuller, the two survivors of that séance. She had seen their names on the Internet when she searched for Vera's name, but here she filled in unknown facts. Susan Gray was committed to a mental institution in Portland. She had been a middle school teacher. Martha Fuller ran a flower shop in town. These women, Laura felt, might talk to her about the mystery surrounding Vera Lancaster's death. They were her only link to what had happened at the séance. Martha Fuller lived right here in town.

When Frank returned with McCormack he found Laura mulling over the copies she had made.

"Find what you wanted?" the newsman asked.

"I think so," Laura replied. "Tell me, Mr. McCormack, have you any idea what happened at that last séance?"

"Mrs. Whitney, your guess is as good as mine. But I'll tell you this; it was the biggest thing to hit this old town in many years. Hell, some of the folks around here are still talking about it. You don't get that kind of event every day of the week. Even in the big cities. So when something that momentous occurs around here it takes precedent over everything else. Imagine, one person dead of heart failure and another one raving mad. The whole town knew about Vera Lancaster and her weird life. No poison, no shooting, no violence at all. She died of natural causes. Heart just gave out."

"What do you mean by Vera Lancaster's weird life?" Laura asked.

"The séances, her claiming to contact the dead. Did you know the Lancaster family goes back well over a hundred years in this town?"

"We heard that from the lawyer today," Laura said.

"Anyhow, long as I can remember, Vera Lancaster claimed she was seeing spirits and contacting dead folks. Some folks swore by her. Some people believed she really could contact their dead relatives. They came from all over the country to see her. Paid her well I hear. But hell, she didn't need the money. Her family left her well off. House free and clear all these years."

"Did she have any enemies you know of?" Laura asked.

"Enemies, no. Some folks didn't like her because of her strange ways. But no one I believe was an enemy. She kept to herself pretty much. She didn't care for publicity. I remember one time I went up to the house to interview her for an article I wanted to do, more about her family than her, and she wouldn't cooperate at all. Can't say I blame her. Few times I met her she always seemed like a nice enough sort. Never really bothered anyone. Had her own kind of cult following, fanatic followers who believed in her. One is interned in Portland. And there are others who live in Maine."

"Susan Gray is the woman you're speaking of, isn't she?" Laura said. "I'd like to talk to her."

"I don't know what you can get out of her," McCormack said. "Far as I know, she's really beyond it all now. I'm not sure if anyone has penetrated the barrier she's built since that night. But I guess you can't do any harm trying."

Laura thought instantly of Roger Evans' wife, who also was incarcerated. But there could be no connection here, one case having occurred long before the other. Yet, both had to do with probing the unknown through the human mind.

"Can you give me the names of the other followers; people who were close to her, who participated in these séances?" Laura asked.

McCormack dug through his file and came up with Susan Gray's home address. He jotted it on a pad and tore the page off, handing it to Laura. "Well," he said, "you probably know that Martha Fuller runs the flower shop in town. She might help you better than I could. Strangest thing about Martha Fuller. After that séance, her husband just ran off on her. Left her cold."

"Disappeared?" Laura asked.

"Well, no," McCormack replied. "He didn't just vanish. I talked to him before he left. Got a job in Bangor. He told me he couldn't live with her anymore. Then, within a month or so he comes back to her. Just reappears. I guess his job didn't work out."

Laura jotted this bit of information on her note pad. You never knew when a tidbit like this meant something, she thought.

Laura thanked him for all the courtesies he had extended.

"Think nothing of it," McCormack said. "If you uncover anything that clears up the Lancaster mystery, let me know. Makes a good story. It would mean a lot to the town to know the answers. There are people who still would like to know what really went on out there at her house. And it sells newspapers."

* * *

The first woman Laura wanted to visit, Susan Gray, was allowed to have visitors. Although she was sequestered she was not violent. Nonetheless, Laura found that permission for visitors would have to be given by the next of kin. Fortunately, her husband lived not too far away, on the outskirts of town. Laura and Frank obtained his phone number and directions, made an appointment and drove over to see him before nightfall.

Harvey Gray lived in a modern, brick and shingle split level house built in a suburban area that had undergone major development in recent years. They pulled into the driveway and Gray met them at the door carrying a newspaper. He was a small, unassuming man, dressed in casual jeans and a sweatshirt that had an imprint that read "Jesus Rules."

He confronted them at the front door.

"Mr. Gray," Laura said, "I'm Laura Whitney and this is my husband, Frank. I called you about permission to visit your wife."

"Why would you want to see Susan?" he asked.

Laura explained to him her interest in unraveling the mystery surrounding Vera Lancaster and the fact that she was the heir to Vera's property.

"So you got that Lancaster woman's house," Gray said. "And poor Susan, her friend, did not."

"I am sorry for that," Laura said. "I don't know why I inherited the house. I had nothing to do with the inheritance. I didn't even know the woman. I'm here to uncover the circumstances that led to this and resolve them."

"Well, anyhow, thank God someone is interested," Gray said. "I

164

hope you're writing a book. I'd love to expose that Lancaster woman as the lunatic she was. Look what she did to my wife. Put her in an asylum. I don't know what good Susan might be to you. She's useless, poor thing."

"But there must be a chance that she remembers something about the night of the séance," Laura said. "Anything would help."

"I doubt very much if you'd get anything from her," Gray said. "Susan hasn't spoken a word to anyone since that night. She does mumble a bit at times, but nothing really coherent has come out of her since then."

"I can at least try," Laura insisted.

"It's all right by me," Gray said. "I wish you luck. Anything that might help her. That Lancaster woman may be dead but she'll cause trouble, one way or another; even if it's from the grave where she belongs."

* * *

The drive to Portland took only a few hours. They stopped once along the way and had dinner. At the institution Laura was escorted to a reception room where Susan Gray waited for her. The woman who had survived the deadly séance was visible through the glass window on the door. She sat quietly at a table across from where Laura would be expected to sit. She gazed absently into space. The attendant pushed the door open, entered the room and ushered Laura in.

Then the unexpected occurred.

The moment Laura appeared Susan Gray jumped to her feet knocking the chair to the floor with an echoing clatter. She stifled a shriek, her eyes filling with tears. She approached Laura slowly forcing the attendant to step between them.

Susan Grey did not seem violent to Laura. She appeared disturbed by her presence but her eyes were wide with wonderment.

"It's all right," Laura said, feeling a bond with the woman who was a total stranger. "Let her be."

"Okay. But I have to be careful," the female attendant said as she stepped aside.

Susan Grey held out her right hand to touch Laura. Her face

was filled with wonder. As Laura touched the extended hand the woman's expression suddenly glowed with adulation. She burst into uncontrolled tears and dropped to her knees wrapping her arms around Laura's legs.

The attendant stepped forward to dislodge her grip on Laura. "Here now, none of that. On you feet," she barked.

"No," Laura said. "Leave her be. She's no harm."

Through her sobs Susan Gray muttered softly, "Vera...my Vera...you're here."

Chapter 25

Laura struggled to bring herself to a moderately relaxed state after the anxiety induced by the confrontation with Susan Gray. She unwound in the car by venting her puzzlement to Frank.

"Damn!" she swore. "This is getting more exasperating each time we uncover something new? That woman thought I was Vera Lancaster."

"Well, what can you expect," he said. "She is in an asylum."

"She never said anything else," Laura said. "She called me Vera and that was it. She had to be returned to her room. I spoke to her but she wouldn't say anything except Vera Lancaster's name."

Frank looked over at his wife as he drove. The strain was showing on his face in grim, hard lines that had not been there only a short time ago.

"Laura," he said, "why don't we drop this whole damned mess right now? Let's just let it die."

"I can't stop now. I'm so close."

"Close!" Frank said. "Close to what?"

"I must know the truth."

"The truth about what? You already know that you've inherited her house. You don't know for sure that you received her corneas but you're convinced that you did. That woman was involved in some bizarre activities. What can you learn that would have any relevance to your life? And to what end?"

"Don't you see?" Laura said. "I am involved, Frank. I think every weird incident in the past few months is in some way connected to her. You didn't see how that Gray woman reacted to me. You weren't in that room with me. She was overcome with ardor. Why? She didn't know me. She never laid eyes on me. And why was Roger Evans disturbed when he first encountered me? Why in the name of God has my presence the power to perplex people? What must I do to prove that it's all tied to Vera Lancaster? Don't you see that I must know?"

"At this point I'm afraid I don't. That Gray woman is obviously insane. They lock up insane people. Who knows what

167

might send her off? How do you know what's in her crazy mind? Maybe she reacts like that to every new face she sees."

"No. That's not true. We were told that she is normally very quiet. My presence set her off"

"Laura, darling," Frank said, calming himself, trying to control the astringent tone in his voice, "I've gone along with you so far. God, I love you and I want to help. But you're obsessed with the idea that some set of mysterious circumstances is more important than even your work. Isn't it time to let it rest and get back to our normal life?"

"No. Not yet," she insisted. "I am involved. I know that now. A physical part of me is Vera Lancaster. No matter what you say. She lives within me. I'm certain of that."

"Good God, Laura!" Frank exclaimed. "Listen to yourself. You're saying that transplanted corneas have supernatural effects on you."

Laura paused and stared at Frank as if his words had hit on some key that, for the instant, unlocked her confusion and temporarily made her see and face reality.

"I'm not sure what I believe. But I do know that I am connected. I'm sure of that."

* * *

The next morning they drove to Vera Lancaster's house. It was situated on Lancaster Island. The island itself was no more than five hundred yards off the coast of Seen By Chance, connected by a long low wooden bridge, painted white in high contrast to the deep color of land and sea around it. The island consisted of about two hundred acres of hills, pine trees and rocky beaches.

It was a short trip, lasting no more than fifteen minutes, but for Laura it was one of the most memorable in her life.

Along the way, as Frank drove on the shore road from the town to Lancaster Island, Laura gazed absently at the beauty of the harbor and the boats that abounded. A marvelous scene, she thought. So many people engaged in both the frivolity of wealth and the working boats that serviced the markets that bought their product. The haves and the have-nots co-existed side by side.

The town marina and boat slips ended before the bridge began.

Amidst the myriad boats cruising the harbor many triangular shapes of rigged sails were visible. Some were visible on the seascape far from shore, others cruised nearby. A close-in vessel interrupted Laura's vision; a sleek, sixty-five foot single-mast craft that sliced the waves not three hundred yards from shore. The boat leaned majestically under the driving wind. At the helm a tall man toiled at his task. Here, the road along the shore ran straight and paralleled the course of the sailboat. The man at the helm looked to the shore, stared directly at Laura and raised his hand and waved to her.

Laura focused on that figure, her vision like a zoom lens on a camera. She saw everything in an instant. He was a tall, lean man, draped in black casual clothes, his black hair slicked back and his green, serpentine eyes piercing even from the distance.

"Good lord!" Laura cried out, suddenly startled.

"What's wrong?" Frank said.

"It's him!" Laura cried, fear wracking her voice. "That man on the boat out there. It's him!"

"Who is him?"

"He's the man from the house in Manhattan."

"Are you sure?" Frank asked.

"Yes. The house Jenny Douglas went into."

"You've got to be kidding," Frank said. "How can you be so sure from this distance?"

"Look!" she said. "He's in black. Black hair. It's him."

Frank glanced quickly at the man at the helm. The sailboat had suddenly tacked away from the shore and the man at the helm was visible only from the rear. Frank saw a sandy-haired man dressed in gray slacks and a white sweatshirt.

"Laura," Frank said. "Your eyes are playing tricks. Look again."

She glimpsed again. There he was, in black, staring back at her as the boat pulled away. She took note of the boat's name written in bold sans serif letters on the stern.

The name printed there was "Jenny."

And the man in black was smiling at her in a perverse grin.

"Frank," Laura said. "Slow down. Look at that sailboat. At the back. What name do you see there?"

Frank braked the car to a crawl and glanced over at the boat pulling away from them. He saw no name on the stern.

"Nothing," he said. "There is no name."

"What?" exclaimed Laura. "You don't see the word 'Jenny'?"

"No. Nothing." he repeated.

Her eyes, she thought. Were they playing tricks? She did not want to upset Frank. She was grateful that he had given into her whims and had accompanied her on her journey. She decided to remain silent on the remainder of the trip to the Lancaster house.

* * *

The house stood isolated at the farthest end of Lancaster Island, facing out to sea. It had become notorious as a result of Vera's lifelong activities and her strange death. There were a number of houses on the island just over the bridge closer to the town where some land had been sold to local developers over the years. But along the coastal road, there were no more houses; until they came to the Lancaster house.

There, above them, alone, at the peak of a hill, like some primordial beast, proud of its lofty resolute presence, sat Vera Lancaster's residence.

Laura was astounded by the grand size of the building. It was almost exactly as she had seen it in her visions. Then, only the details were missing. The rays of the rising sun burst from behind the rugged outline of the house, sending the silhouette into shadow. Gazing at the foreboding shape Laura felt a sense of lingering anxiety.

Frank parked the car at a cut-in road that led to a trail upwards through the surrounding pines. The silence in the woods was so intense that the sound of their footsteps on the thicket crackled like breaking glass. It was peaceful, undisturbed by the presence of human activity. Laura felt as if she were walking in the sanctum of some grand cathedral. It was a sensation she wanted to cherish, if even for the instant.

The architecture of the house was definitely Victorian. It loomed large before them, seeming an aberration in the deep green of the surrounding woods. A large porch wrapped around the entire front. The structure was fully three floors high, adorned by two widow's walks, one at either corner. The pine trees that surrounded it seemed like sentinels, protecting their treasure.

Laura felt the sensation of immediate déjà vu as they came closer. It was almost exactly as she had seen it in her dreams, foreboding, threatening. It seemed to summon her, drawing her closer, she having no will to resist.

As they climbed the path to the house neither spoke, both fascinated by its presence. It demanded all eyes be focused on it. It was intense, commanding.

Frank turned to Laura halfway up the hill. "Look below, Laura," he said, pointing toward the sea. "There's a boathouse and a dock just beyond the road."

"I wonder," she said, "if there's a boat in it."

As they drew closer Laura saw the house was in fairly good condition. There seemed to be no deterioration or rot. The paint looked fresh. The elaborate trim was kept up. The railings showed no sign of negligence. But of course, Laura thought, Vera Lancaster died only a little while ago.

They unlocked the front door with the key provided them. In the large foyer a winding staircase spiraled upward. To the left was a large living room with a stone fireplace framed by a massive white mantle. To their right was a parlor. The furniture was covered with white sheets. Elaborate carved moldings and cornices accentuated the room.

This is Vera Lancaster's house, Laura thought. I've come this far. The answers I seek are here. I must find something.

They wandered through the living room, into the dining room and kitchen in the rear. When they returned to the foyer they approached two ornate wooden doors. Laura stepped up to them and threw them open.

"Oh, my God!" she exclaimed, as the doors parted.

"What is it?" Frank said excitedly.

"Frank, this is it! The room in my dreams."

"Are you sure?"

"Absolutely. This is the room I saw."

Chapter 26

They entered the room, Laura reluctantly at first, repressing an ongoing feeling of anxiety, until both stood in its center. She looked around, trying to overcome the feeling of imminent danger that threatened her senses. The familiar, frightening vision of the séance flashed in her mind and, for an instant, the terror of that vision clutched at her throat. Frank saw how close she was to the edge of hysteria and he put his arm around her shoulder as comfort.

"What does it mean, Frank?" Laura asked.

"What does what mean?"

"The dream. This room. What secrets does it hold about the woman who died here?"

"How can we know?" he answered. "Perhaps nothing at all."

"I don't believe that," Laura said, eager to talk about the medium. "I'm convinced she was communicating with me. But the terrifying apparition I saw in this room was beyond a mere psychic image. Maybe it was connected to previous séances. This is the room where the last one was held. It has to be."

"It should be easy enough to find out."

"Frank," Laura exclaimed suddenly. "I want to stay here for a while."

Frank expressed his displeasure by his grimace. "You're feeding your fears. Besides, I've got to get back to New York. I can't afford the time off. We couldn't stay for more than a few days at best."

"All right, then. How long?"

Frank pondered a moment. He had to give Laura the leeway she needed. "I'll try for a week," he said. "Whatever I can get. I'll stay as long as I can. But you know what the advertising business is like." He walked behind Laura, put his arm around her and kissed her on the forehead. "Let's go into town and work this out," he said.

* * *

Martha Fuller lifted the receiver to her ear and heard a soft, calm, female voice.

"Mrs. Fuller?"

"Yes."

"My name is Laura Whitney. I inherited Vera Lancaster's house."

"Yes," Martha said. "I know who you are." Martha recognized the name. It had come up in the settlement of the will. Yet Martha had never heard Laura's name spoken by Vera or anyone associated with her prior to the will. It was indicative of the enigma of Vera Lancaster.

"My husband and I just came to town," Laura continued. "I'm sorry to bother you, but if you could give me only a few minutes of your time. I understand you were a close friend of Vera Lancaster. I wonder if I could talk to you."

"Certainly. Do you have the address?"

"Yes."

"Please come by then," Martha Fuller said.

It didn't take long. The drive to Martha Fuller's shop in the center of town was only a few minutes from the motel. Martha waited in the flower shop behind the counter. She had just sold a dozen red roses to a local businessman on his way to his anniversary dinner. The doorbell over the front door rang once as he exited and Laura Whitney and her husband entered.

Martha Fuller gasped for breath as Laura Whitney entered the shop. There was an immediate metaphysical connection of familiarity that she strongly felt at the sight of the woman who claimed a union to Vera Lancaster. What was that connection, Laura wondered?

As Laura and Frank approached, Martha knew there was a kinship stronger than a first impression. And then, as suddenly as Laura appeared in her life, she knew what she sensed. It was the same ardor she had felt for Vera Lancaster since they were children together.

* * *

When they entered the flower shop Laura immediately

recognized the trim, attractive middle-aged woman who greeted them. I know this woman, she thought. Martha Fuller was dressed in a yellow summer dress that had slight soil stains here and there on the fabric. It figured that the owner of a flower shop would carry a reminder of her craft somewhere on her person.

"I'm Martha Fuller," she said extending her right hand. She seemed uncomfortable, nervous. Her hand had a slight tremor as she took hold of Laura's,

"Laura Whitney, and this is my husband, Frank," Laura said.

"Come in, please," the florist offered. She took them into a living room in the rear of the store. Beyond that were a small kitchen, a bathroom and a greenhouse that adjoined the building. They were seated in the living room when Martha asked, "Can I get you anything to drink? Coffee? Tea?"

"No, thanks," Laura said while Frank sat silently.

Martha sat down opposite them. Laura realized that the woman was staring with deliberation into her eyes.

"What can I do for you?" Martha inquired.

"I've inherited Vera Lancaster's house and Lancaster Island," Laura said.

"I know who you are," Martha said. "You see, I'm the executrix for Vera Lancaster's estate. I heard that you were here and had gone out to the island. Rumors travel fast in a small town. What is it you want from me?"

"Have you any idea why I inherited Vera Lancaster's property?" Laura asked.

"Not even an iota," Martha Fuller answered. "The first time I ever heard your name mentioned was at the reading of the will."

Laura decided to be frank with the woman. "Let me explain why I called you," she said. "I am an artist. I live in New York City. A little over a year ago I lost my sight in a freak accident."

"Oh, how terrible," Martha Fuller said. "I'm so sorry for you. But you don't seem..."

"It's all right now," Laura interrupted her. "I've regained my sight. I underwent an operation. I had a double corneal transplant." Laura paused, for an instant considering the effect of her next statement. Then she said bluntly, "The corneas I received belonged to Vera Lancaster."

Martha Fuller's eyes widened. She felt this day would come.

She knew Vera was an organ donor and now one of the recipient's had arrived. Would there be others?

"This is awkward for me," Martha said. "I feel odd knowing that a portion of Vera is present in your body." Was Vera seeing me in those eyes? she thought.

"Mrs. Fuller," Laura said. "It's just as awkward for me. I can't tell you what the last few months have been like. The transplant has changed my life. In many ways."

"I can imagine," Martha said, genuine concern seeping into her voice. "I knew Vera was an organ donor. This is remarkable. But why do you come here to me?"

"It's not easy to explain." Laura knew it would to come to this. She must explain to this woman why she was here as outrageous as it may sound. She related the series of events that led to her arrival at Lancaster Island. Nightmares. Apparitions. She then told her of Roger Evans' death. She mentioned the tragic deaths of Vernon Hayle and the kidnapping of Jenny Douglas... and, of course, the mysterious man in black.

"You see," she said, "I must know more about her. What has been happening in my life must have some connection to Vera Lancaster. Too many unusual deaths."

"With part of Vera's body implanted in yours I wouldn't doubt anything you tell me that's happened to you since then," Martha said.

Laura turned to Frank and showed a minor grin. It said, see I told you so.

"I don't doubt anything about her," Martha Fuller continued. "I've sat in quite a few séances with Vera. God, she was something else. I believe she might have actually reached the other side."

"I do believe she did, Mrs. Fuller."

"Call me Martha, please."

"All right then...Martha. I know very little about Vera Lancaster. Things that have happened to me fell into place once I discovered that she was a medium. It makes sense to me that they could have emanated from her as the source. What can you tell me about that séance, since you were there? What did it accomplish?"

"It was horrifying," Martha Fuller said. "Vera was trying to prove that there was life after death. She was consumed with the idea that she could prove spirits do exist. She tried to break the barrier and make contact."

"Didn't she attempt the same thing in many of her séances for clients?"

"Yes, of course. And she never used tricks. She was true reality. I believe she did make contact with many loved ones for clients. But most people did not believe she had. There was never any tangible proof. The only proof she could offer was the word of her clients. The majority of the town hereabouts mocked her. But she had a following that loved her. The last séance was different, though. She called on powers beyond the norm to reveal itself. She opened a door to the other world. And, dear God, I think she contacted someone or something."

"Like what?" Laura asked, a tinge of trepidation in her voice.

"I don't think what we saw in that room ever came from anything holy. It consumed her body and lifted her in the air. I never experienced anything so frightful. I can't explain it. It vanished as quickly as it came and Vera was dead before our eyes."

Laura's face went white. "Are you saying that there actually was a supernatural connection at that séance?" she asked.

"I don't know what it was," Martha Fuller said. "I can't explain what happened. But something extraordinary did occur. Whatever happened was over in an instant and Vera was dead."

"I read the newspaper articles," Laura said. "The report was death by heart failure."

"That's what they say."

During this discussion Frank merely fidgeted. He offered nothing to contribute to Laura's queries. Laura noticed it, convinced Frank was turning sour on her quest for clarification.

Her next statement presented a problem because of Frank's presence. She considered forgetting it but realized she'd come this far and it had to be said.

"Martha, I believe the spirit who appeared at that séance is now present in our world. I think that entity was given an opening and broke through the barrier of death and is somehow making its presence known. Why? I have no idea. Why me? I have no answers."

Now Frank let out a heavy sigh, showing his obvious disdain. "Laura," he declared, standing up, "I think we'd better leave. Mrs.

Fuller is going to think she's let in a couple of nutcases."

Martha Fuller interrupted Frank. "Oh no, Mr. Whitney. You're wrong. I don't think anything of the sort. If you knew Vera as I did, nothing would seem strange to you anymore."

Frank sat down.

"You knew her that well?" Laura asked.

"Yes, I've known Vera most of my life." Martha Fuller said. "I guess I knew her better than anyone. We were childhood friends. Went to school together. She was interested in the supernatural as long as I can remember. She got a few of her friends involved in what started as curiosities to full-fledged séances. She held them in the parlor in the house on the Lancaster Island."

"How long had she owned the house?"

"All of her adult life," their hostess said. "She inherited it on her twenty-first birthday. She took up residency there. The island belonged to the Lancaster family for over a hundred years."

"Did she have any living relatives?"

"Not that I know of. Her parents died in a fire when she was just a child. She had a grandmother whom she loved. She died about twenty years ago. There were other people in her family from past generations but I never heard of any."

"Did she have many friends?" Laura asked.

"Actually, no. Only a few. At the end there was only Susan Gray and myself. And I suppose you know what happened to poor Susan."

"Yes. As a matter of fact we went to visit her before we came to you." The thought of Susan Gray's overwhelming fervor still reverberated in her memory.

"She hasn't spoken to anyone, including her husband. How did you do with her?"

Laura relayed the unusual scene with Susan Gray. "I swear," she said, "I think that woman thought I was someone else. She responded as if I were her closest friend. And I'd never met her before."

Martha pondered the thought for a moment. Then she said, "I can understand Susan's feelings. I feel as comfortable with you as I did with Vera."

After a pause Laura broached the purpose of her visit and asked, "If I feel I find anything that helps unravel the facts would you be so good as to help me?"

"Certainly," Martha Fuller answered quickly.

A sandy haired man suddenly entered the room. He looked older than Martha Fuller. Laura judged him to be about fifty years old. She noted he was average height with a few extra pounds packed on around the middle. He was dressed casually, blue jeans and a slipover sweat shirt.

"This is Bert, my husband," Martha Fuller introduced him.

Frank stood and reached out his hand to shake Fuller's. "Frank Whitney," he said. "This is my wife, Laura."

"Pleased to meet you," Bert Fuller said. His voice was soft, measured, as if he chose his words carefully with distinct clarity. "You're the person who inherited the Lancaster woman's property, aren't you?"

"Yes, she is," Frank said.

"What specifically are you here for?" Bert Fuller asked.

Laura did not answer right away. She turned her gaze to Martha Fuller who recognized Laura's hesitancy.

"Laura wants me to help her with Vera's house," she said.

"Great," Bert Fuller said. "Burn it to the ground as far I'm concerned." As instantly as he had entered the room, he abruptly turned and left.

Martha Fuller then explained to them that, since Vera Lancaster left her in charge, she had done nothing to the house other than having a cleaning crew in once and awhile. Aside from covering most of the furniture with sheets she left everything as it was. Laura explained her plans to stay at the house for a few weeks. After that she was not sure what her plans would be as to use of the house.

"I understand," Martha Fuller said. "It's your place to do with as you please."

* * *

Laura and Frank stayed at the motel in town for the night. The motel was on the waterfront, not far from the marina and many boat slips. Before the sun had set Laura informed Frank she wanted to walk along the waterfront.

"Sightseeing?" Frank asked. "Or do you think you might find

178

that boat you saw this morning?"

"Both," she answered. "You coming or do I go alone?"

"No, Laura. I'm coming, of course."

They stopped at a local restaurant for a light dinner. During the meal Laura spoke of her friend, Jenny Douglas.

"I cannot get over Jenny," she pondered. "She was kidnapped and held prisoner. There was no ransom. The Douglases are not wealthy people. Why would anyone kidnap her?"

"And you think you saw that same guy here on that boat," Frank said.

"I know I did!" she answered.

"All right. What motive did this madman have to pick on someone as innocent as Jenny? Could she be having an affair?"

"Never. Not in a million years," Laura said. "How could you even think such a thing? She absolutely adored her husband and children."

"Hell, Laura, anything is possible."

"When Jenny called me she said that strange man rapes her. And threatened to kill her entire family if she tries to escape. I wouldn't want to guess why he picked on Jenny. But, Frank, this same man is connected to the death of Vernon Hayle. Why is he involved with people I am acquainted with? Who is he and what connection does he have with people who are close to me?"

"Laura, what the hell are you saying?"

"I don't know, Frank. But if he is here, perhaps Jenny is nearby also. He is dangerous. The police told us about the murders in the house in Manhattan. I've got to know if Jenny is alive."

"Okay, Laura. I'll grant you that. I just hope you're not creating another mystery on top of your Vera Lancaster enigma?" Frank said.

They left the restaurant and toured the town docks. They walked in and out of boat slips, throughout a few marinas until the sun set. There was no boat named "Jenny" to be found.

At each marina Laura asked the appropriate owner if there was a "Jenny". No one had heard of one. Hallucinations? Had her eyes betrayed her?

There were no supplies at the house other than furniture and utensils; dishware, pots, pans. In the morning they loaded up on groceries, towels, soap; the basics, and set off for the infamous house.

Chapter 27

Once at Vera Lancaster's house, they spent most of the day going from room to room stripping sheets off the furniture, opening windows, and giving the old house a renewed chance to breathe. To their chagrin they discovered there was no electricity.

"Damn," Laura swore. "What do we do now?"

"I'll get the flashlight from the car and we'll see if we can find some candles for the time being."

Frank went down to the car while Laura rummaged in the kitchen, searching through cabinets for candles. She found a box full on a shelf in a broom closet. They were large candles, each at least a foot long and completely black. When Frank returned she held up a few to show him their good luck.

"Black candles?" Frank laughed. "Are you sure your Vera Lancaster wasn't into witchcraft?"

"Probably for her rituals," Laura said. "Remember, she was a spiritualist."

"Well, the candles will do for the time being. At least that's one problem temporarily eliminated," Frank said. "We'll have some light. We know the water is running, so we'll be able to wash and make some coffee. That is if there is any fuel for hot water."

He tried the stove, which was gas heat. It worked. He ran the water and it became hot after a few minutes. He followed the gas line from the stove to where it disappeared into an exterior wall. He opened the window and looked out. There were two propane gas tanks just outside the window, tucked in under the back porch overhang.

Frank, armed with a flashlight, descended to the basement searching for more candles. He got lucky. He found boxes filled with a variety of candles and candleholders. He gathered as many thick votive candles as would fit in one box and brought them upstairs. He propped a few of the thick candles upright on the stairs leading to the upper floors so that their passage would be lit at night. He spread as many as were needed throughout the various rooms in the house.

After they ate they decided to explore the house and grounds. Frank asked Laura to walk with him through the woods in the back before it got dark. She said they would have plenty of time for wandering outside. She believed it was the interior that should be explored first. Laura was more concerned with discovering intimacies about Vera Lancaster before anything else.

So they compromised. Laura investigated the upstairs rooms while Frank went for a walk.

"Don't go far," she said. "It'll be dark soon. I wouldn't want you to get lost. We don't know our way around."

"I'll find my way back," he said. "Don't worry. Put a few candles in the windows. I won't stray out of the sight of the lights."

Laura went upstairs and examined a few adjoining rooms when she heard Frank calling to her from outside. His voice was coming from the rear of the house and she heard him clearly through an open window. She pulled it further open and looked out. Frank was standing in a small clearing a few hundred feet from the house in what looked to Laura like a small graveyard.

"Laura," he called out, "I think you ought to come down here and have a look at this."

Laura descended the winding staircase and met Frank in back. He led her to what he had found. There were eleven gravestones. The stones were worn with age, some obviously much older than others. They bordered a small mausoleum. The name over the entrance, chiseled into the stone was Ezra Lancaster, 1821-1899. As Laura examined some of the other headstones, she found that six displayed the name Lancaster and the others showed different names. Frank stopped beside a new stone.

"Here she is," Frank said.

Laura bent beside the stone and read the inscription.

VERA LANCASTER
LAST OF HER LINE

At last, Laura thought, I found you, Vera Lancaster. But the bond she expected did not materialize. She had expected a great surge of insight, an affinity with the dead woman lying beneath her feet. But it wasn't happening. She felt detached, suddenly strange and foreign. Perhaps, she thought, she needed to be away from the cold indifference of the grave and inside the house. That, surely, was where the answers were. Not here with the dead.

"Let's go in the house," she told Frank, the sense of alienation pulling her away from this spot.

The sun was disappearing over the bay to the west as the house fell into darkness. They lit candles and each carried one as they worked their way upstairs.

When they entered one of the larger bedrooms she knew immediately that this was Vera's room. Their candles cast weird, sinister shapes like sprites dancing across the walls chasing the last rays of sunlight. Other than a luxurious canopy bed, the room was simply furnished, the furniture obviously dating back many generations.

Frank moved to an overstuffed armchair beside the bed and deposited his candle on an end table while Laura wandered deeper into the large room. She entered an open archway, which led to a smaller adjoining room, perhaps a nursery at one time. As she entered the room she realized at once, that here was the heart and essence of Vera Lancaster's life. The room was crammed with shelves of books. In the center of the room stood a large, elaborately ornate mahogany desk. She set her candle down and sat at the desk in the leather chair behind it.

This then, she thought, was where Vera Lancaster lived. This room was her heartbeat. The room flourished with her presence.

"Frank," she called out, "come in here. See this room."

As he came into the room his eyes automatically traveled to the filled bookcase.

"Wow," he exclaimed, "she did a lot of reading."

He set his candle next to hers and moved to the floor-to-ceiling bookcase. He lifted out one volume at random and thumbed through it.

"Strange subject matter," he said. "Even the binding is odd." He handed the volume to Laura. She studied it but seemed more interested in the content rather than the binding. The book was titled "The Rituals of Magic".

"Do we own the books now?" Frank muttered.

"The inscription on her tombstone," Laura said. "'The last of her line'. She had no heirs. I suppose we own them."

"Yeah. But I would have expected someone to lay claim to these books. The town. The library."

"Perhaps no one is aware of their existence."

"I suppose everything in the house is ours. That might explain why everything is still intact, furniture, paintings, silverware, books. Imagine a house like this in New York and this stuff sitting there. It would be stripped clean."

"I guess so. Which just goes to prove what a peaceful life Vera Lancaster had in a town like this. And living way out here must have made it even more so."

"I wonder if she read all those books. There must be hundreds. What do you think they're all about?" Frank said.

"I don't know, Frank," Laura answered. She got up from where she had been sitting and placed the book back in its slot in the bookcase. "But I'm damn sure going to find out."

Chapter 28

While Frank slept upstairs in Vera Lancaster's bedroom, Laura sat behind Vera's desk in the dead woman's library. Two long black candles burned on either side of her. She busied herself opening drawers and rummaging through their contents. She found nothing more than she had expected; writing paper, envelopes, paper clips, rubber bands, a varied selection of the typical paraphernalia that fill a desk.

Frustrated, she rose and walked to the wall of books and began to skim along the titles. She was astounded that almost the entire contents of the shelves were related to matters of the occult ranging from witchcraft, demonology, Satanism, spiritualism, and divination to books on ESP, hypnosis, psychokenisis, parapsychology, clairvoyance, telepathy.

She knew practically nothing about the subjects yet they all seemed familiar.

Laura's eyes ran along the titles when suddenly they rested upon a well-worn, leather-bound volume that had no visible title or markings. It bothered her that there, amidst all the various titled books, so solitary and yet so noticeable, stood this unmarked volume. She lifted it out and set it on the desk. She opened the cover. A controlled handwriting appeared, speaking to her in fine uniform strokes. Laura began reading and immediately realized, with great excitement, what she had unearthed.

It was Vera Lancaster's personal journal.

The first page of the manuscript had a date at the top. Laura plunged further into the pages. The dates did not follow a daily or even weekly basis. Vera had made entries at random, apparently as the mood possessed her.

What a find, Laura thought. This must have the answers I seek. Now I will know the truth. I will see the pieces finally fit together and I will know where I belong in her life.

* * *

Impetuously, Laura read Vera Lancaster's diary in the flickering glitter of the candles. The corneas in her eyes, that had once watched the journal fashioned, now viewed it again.

Vera Lancaster had started recording her thoughts when she was only eleven years old. Laura read through those early years, gathering an insight into the medium's personality and early experiences with the psychic world.

Vera was that young when she realized she was different from other children. While her playmates pretended to have make-believe friends with whom they would invent games when alone, Vera's phantasmal companions were as real to her as life itself. She knew she was not imagining the voices that spoke to her.

Her parents did not concern themselves that she had become an outcast from the recognized ranks of society's progeny. They had been used to it throughout the years. The Lancaster family had been reclusive for generations, living away from the townspeople, almost isolated from their neighbors in their large property on Lancaster Island. Their regret was that Vera was an only child and, having no brothers or sisters, she was forced to look to her own devices for entertainment.

Vera lived in the family house along with her father, mother and the only remaining Lancaster from the previous generation, her favorite of all, Grandma Lancaster. Vera loved the old lady because she knew that Grandma Lancaster truly believed her and accepted as truth what others dismissed as Vera's fantasies. Vera believed the old lady actually saw and spoke to her own spiritual friends with the same conviction that she did. Many times she had involved the old lady in the games she played with her spiritual chums and was amazed that the old lady spoke to the voices correctly. Whenever her father or mother joined in such activities Vera knew they were lying, merely patronizing her. The voices spoke but her parents did not hear. They only pretended to hear.

As Laura read, a strange occurrence took place within her mind. It was as if her eyes were the link to a visual experience. She beheld Vera's life episodes as they existed in Vera's own subconscious. It was as if Laura were witness to a film unfolding as she read the screenplay. As first it was disorienting for her. But soon she adjusted to the remarkable life of the medium as it unfolded and her brain absorbed it.

Mike Walsh

"*The beautiful blonde lady came to me today. I was working on my math in front of the house. I knew who she was because I talked to her so many times. She told me her name was Helena and she lived in another world.*

"*I told Mommy and Daddy about her. They didn't believe me. It was like always with them. I heard them talking later. They said I was having delusions. I know what that word means and they are wrong.*

"*Helena visited me again today. This time I didn't tell Mommy and Daddy. But I did tell Grandma Lancaster. She said I shouldn't worry about what they think. She said I was a unique child with a gift few people have. She told me I was one of God's chosen and that I should never think unkindly of myself; that I was far above the children who made fun of me. I don't really believe this but Grandma never lies.*

"*I like to read books which explain about what Grandma calls 'the gift'.*

"*I was sitting with Uncle Walt on the front porch this morning. He was talking to me about his car accident. Then he told me he had to get back to the hospital where he was staying. He said it wasn't time for him to die yet. But he didn't look hurt at all.*

"*When I told Mommy about Uncle Walt she got angry and yelled at me. She said Uncle Walt hadn't been up to see us in over a year. Didn't I know that he lived over two hundred miles away? Why would he not say hello to anyone else then go silently away? She said I was lying. She said I was making up stories like that. Grandma knew I wasn't lying.*

"*Mommy cried and hugged me an awful lot today. She got a telephone call from Uncle Walt's family. He was in a hospital in Connecticut. He was in an auto accident. I knew Mommy believed me now that Uncle Walt had talked to me.*

"*I am beginning to understand more about what Grandma says*

I have. I can see things. Sometimes things just pop into my head. I suddenly get a vision. And many times the thing I see actually happens. At first it frightened me that I could read the thoughts of kids in school. But I got to use it in my favor.

"At school I've been reading kid's thoughts. I learned how to control my mind so that I am reaching into the other person's brain. It's fun but it's scary.

"The kids at school are having me tell them what they are thinking. I had a group around me for well over an hour. Normally I never get to hang around with these kids. They're always in the thick of things; parties, dances, sports. I was never invited to join them, but today they joined me.

"I got a terrible scare last night. I had this nightmare that Mommy and Daddy were both trapped in a fire. I woke up screaming. When I told Grandma she tried to calm me. But I knew she was frightened too. My parents were in Boston visiting one of Daddy's friends. I knew they were injured and Grandma knew it too.

"We found out how my parents died. They were trapped in a fire on the second floor of the house in which they were staying. I was left to care for my Grandma. Now we both know that my gift was not a fleeting thing.

"Grandma told me that I have the sixth sense. She talked me into trying experiments with the ouija board. We asked questions of the board and before long I had made contact with Helena, the woman who had spoken to me when I was younger. She told us about her life in Maine and how her husband had murdered her. It thrilled me to be able to talk with the spirit of Helena.

"I see Grandma getting older every day. I do not want her to die. I love her so much. She is the only person I have left in my life.

"Grandma convinced me to attempt my first séance. I read a lot about séances but the thought frightened me. I was afraid to be a

medium. After all, I am just a teenager. But Grandma reassured me she would watch over me. I agreed and we tried to make contact tonight. Grandma told me what happened afterward. I went into a trance. Both my hands clutched hers. The spirit of Helena spoke to her through me. She told of many facts I could never have known about her personal life, her love, her death.

"I went into town and looked up the records of the lady named Helena. The old newspapers confirmed what I had channeled.

"I was frightened of my gift. When I thought that the spirit of a dead person had actually come into my body and used it to speak I was really scared.

"I want to go to college but I can't leave Grandma Lancaster alone. My parents' inheritance was passed on to me with a trust that would pay my all my bills. I decided college could wait.

"I am eighteen years old now and I have never been on a date with a boy. I would be in college right now had I decided to go. Instead I take Grandma her meals and spend hours talking to her. She knows how much I love her.

"I have been buying a lot of books on the occult. I have not neglected my education in that respect. I believe I am learning more from reading about the paranormal than I might learn in college.

Chapter 29

The hours sped by. Time became thought. Laura read late into the night. Vera Lancaster had become very devoted to her grandmother during this period of her life. As the diary unfolded Laura saw the old lady in her mind's eye as if she stood before her in reality.

Vera became the old lady's live-in nurse. For the next few years her time was spent mainly taking care of Grandma Lancaster, attending to the house and learning about the paranormal. She and her beloved grandmother conducted many séances together. Vera became expert as a channeler. She learned how to slip into a trance and summon the spirit of the departed Helena at will.

Vera was well into her twenties when her grandmother finally succumbed to the ravages of old age. She was over ninety when the end finally came. Vera did not realize how much she would grieve her passing until she faced the emptiness of her life without the old lady's presence. She was devastated by her sudden loneliness.

Laura learned that Vera's preoccupation in the supernatural became her salvation. She built her every waking hour around activities that she hoped would take her mind off her loss. But the old lady's death took its toll. Her activities served only to remind her of Grandma Lancaster's death.

Finally, Vera decided to close up the house, and for one complete summer, she toured Europe. The complete change, she believed, would open new avenues of thought that would not remind her of the old lady, her parents or the life she led. It worked for a while. She freewheeled across the face of the continent through many of the cities she dreamed of visiting.

But it was in Paris that she rediscovered her interest in the supernatural. Laura had never been to Paris but she saw in her mind's eye exact memories that Vera Lancaster had seen street by street.

Laura read on.

Today I went to a performance of a noted mentalist named Levin. As soon as he came on stage we both connected mentally. He performed simple acts of mind reading. Secretly, Levin was a black magician of the highest order. He had taken his name from his idol, Eliphas Levi, who lived in Paris during the late 1800's and had helped the black arts flourish.

We talked for hours in a nearby bistro. I spoke of my attempts at spirit communication and he was impressed with my efforts

---

I saw Levin again tonight. I could feel his mind probing mine. Tonight I went home with him.

He is the first man with whom I have ever shared a bed. He was overly excited that I was a virgin. To him it seemed spiritual that I was untouched. He reveled in his joy. He told me about black magic.

I had read some of the rituals and practices of Eliphas Levi and the infamous Aliester Crowley, They believed the black magician, to be total, must relate to God on a personal level. Crowley believed that God and man are one, man possessing the divine light within himself; that everything in the universe is part of a divine order and man is as much a part of the whole as is God Himself. The whole is the total concept of God. The parts are united to form oneness...God. The black magician feels that by the expansion of the spirit to realize and experience all things within the universe he attains the level of God.

I must say, I'm not sure I agree with the precepts of black magic but I knew I had to learn more and I had to see Levin again.

He taught me things about myself and my sexuality I never knew existed. He believed that sex played an important role in the marriage of opposites. The male and female, linked together, approached godliness. Sexual activities were very much a part of his philosophy.

Tonight he took me to a ritual of black magic. Levin attempted to infuse the spirit of a departed soul back into her body. The ceremony was conducted in front of followers of Levin's cult in the cellar of an abandoned warehouse. An alabaster altar was set in the center of the space. On the altar was painted the sign of the pentagram.

Levin was dressed in a flowing white robe. As he recited the incantations his body swayed to the rhythm of his voice. The body was laid out on the altar in the position of the crucified Christ. Levin repeated the incantation three times, commanding the spirit to enter the body.

I felt fear overcome me. The dead body sat up. Levin asked questions of the spirit, which now inhabited the corpse. The dead body answered in a strange low voice that was almost an incoherent whisper...but it did speak. Finally, Levin set fire to the corpse, supposedly setting the body and soul simultaneously free.

I did not believe what I had seen. Was this possible? Did the body really move? Did it speak? Or was it no more than the master magician at his best, creating an illusion?

Levin assured me that it was not trickery. The ritual had been performed in the name of the Dark One, the Master of All Darkness. The same rituals had been performed throughout the ages of man. Even the Church recognized that the practice of necromancy exists but is held only in the realm of evil spirits. It is considered the most dangerous of practices because it calls upon and evokes the aid of demons and spirits which may attach themselves to the magician and dominate him."

Laura was stunned by the passage she had just read. She took pen and paper from Vera's desk and wrote down the passage. She could not believe what had been written—"demons and spirits may attach themselves to the magician and dominate him." Was it possible that Vera Lancaster had inadvertently contacted an evil spirit in the last séance and brought it into her own life?

She read on.

Levin frightened me. I was beginning to realize a force of evil motivated him. His object was to perform evil. I could see no good in it.

His bizarre rituals were entrenched too deeply into every facet of his life. His presence was now revolting. I decided to return to Maine.

———————

In the spring I held my first public séance as a medium. The parlor became a meeting place.

"I didn't contact any spirits tonight. But I made it seem so. I did not deceive my client into a false notion that I had. I picked her brain and revealed things to her that only she could have known.

———————

Summer is busy. It is easy for my clients to cross the bay in summer. Winter always presents a problem.

———————

Today I made contact with the departed son of a woman who came from California. It was one of the most thrilling experiences I had ever had.

* * *

Laura sped through the next few years of Vera's life. By word of mouth alone she became a respected and sought-after medium, known to have satisfied many clients' wishes beyond their expectations. Money was not Vera's motivation, so her fees were never exorbitant. Charlatans could have easily fleeced these clients. With Vera they found what they sought without deception.

Throughout her life Vera had yet to experience love. Other than the love she felt for Grandma Lancaster and her parents she had known only the sexual attraction of Levin, the black magician. Vera's life had been devoid of affection and devotion.

Her first serious involvement happened at the age of thirty-four, a time in life when most women were already raising a family. She met him at the library.

Laura continued to read.

———————

I was looking for an Edgar Cayce book at the library. As I reached for it on a shelf I brushed a man's hand reaching for the same book. He apologized and insisted I take it. We struck up a conversation about Cayce and the paranormal. We walked together for a while. We stopped for coffee. We talked for hours. His name is William Carter. He lived in Seen By Chance for only six months. He moved here with his mother and a younger sister. He is a schoolteacher.

We are going to see one another again.

William called me today. We are going on a picnic.

He calls me almost every day and he comes by the house whenever he can. But it's usually not until weekends. I don't know if he has told his family about us yet. I have a feeling they know he is seeing me. But what did they expect? He couldn't remain with them forever.

William and I made love today for the first time. Actually, I seduced him. He came to the house to pick me up for a drive. I feigned a reason for not taking a long drive. It was a beautiful summer day and we wandered along the shore and settled on one of the small isolated beaches. It was there that I knew I must have William forever. He told me today that he loves me. My heart leapt at the sound of those words. I wanted to jump for joy.

William and I see each other all the time. I have neglected my clients. They call and badger me to continue the sessions. William doesn't mind that I am a spiritualist. Some people believe it is the practice of witchcraft, but he is intelligent enough to be indifferent.

Today he asked me to marry him. I accepted without hesitation. To be his wife. To have his children. I can't believe it's true. I love him so much. We plan to be married in the spring. His mother is not enraptured with the idea. But what she thought didn't matter after all...for William died before we were married.

_____

William's death came with such sudden, devastating finality that it almost destroyed my sanity. I could not accept the fact that he was gone so quickly. My world was drastically ripped apart once again.

_____

William died in a swimming accident. I resolved this would not be the end for us.

_____

I must act fast. I called Martha Fuller and Susan Gray to assist me. When I told them of my intentions they were terrified, yet fascinated enough to help. We drove to the cemetery where William was buried. Together, we dug up his grave. At first I felt ashamed for what I was doing. I had desecrated the burial place of my lover.

I quickly brushed these thoughts aside. If I was to succeed I must work quickly. We summoned an iron determination and we struggled and heaved until we got the body out of the coffin. It was amazing that no one discovered us. We wrapped the body in blankets and loaded it into the back of my SUV. In the dark of night we loaded it on my boat.

I began the ceremony as I remembered it from the rituals I had attended with Levin in Paris. Martha, Susan and I cleaned William's body and placed it on the white tabernacle in my parlor. We covered him with white linen. White lambskin rugs adorned the floor and I had carefully painted the sign of the pentagram on the face of the altar. I placed two chafing dishes, mounted on tripods, filled with alder wood and laurel at either end of the altar.

I recited the incantations which called upon the spirit of William Carter to appear in the outstretched body. Tense, uneventful hours passed. Illusions led us to believe there was movement when there truly was none.

I continued my chanting. Just as I was ready to quit, William's body began to shake. I implored William's spirit to recognize me.

The body vibrated furiously, as the sounds continued to rise into a fiendish wailing sound. Poor Susan was frightened out of her wits but her courage kept her there with me. I knew I couldn't communicate.

The body began to shake convulsively out of control. Then it stopped and crashed violently to the altar and became very still. It was over. I could not bring myself to destroy the corpse as Levin had by burning it with kerosene. My friends assisted me as we got the body back into its resting place. From now on William would be only a memory to me.

Today the realization of what I had accomplished struck home. I was suddenly very afraid. I had performed a ritual of black magic and had successfully conjured the spirit of a departed human back into its body.

I had crossed the life-death threshold. Was it a power within me? Grandma had always said I had the gift. Or was I merely a catalyst, using the incantations of old, which contained some power to raise the dead.

Martha Fuller and Susan Gray now treated me with a renewed respect which was evident in their every word. I had at least earned that much."

* * *

Laura raced through the pages. The medium continued to conduct séances and was able to make contact on almost every occasion. Her force was felt in the spiritual community where she was now welcomed.

The experiments she conducted privately exceeded her regular séances. She kept her personal life strictly personal and shared intimacy with only a few close friends; Martha and Susan. She had advanced beyond the normal boundaries into the dark world of a sensitive. She did not restrict her secret activities to mere psychic phenomena. Vera was reaching into the black arts for answers to her burning curiosity.

Laura believed she was getting to the essence of Vera's power.

Over the years, the achievements Vera attained appeared commonplace in view of the possibilities that existed in the secret life she entered. It was no longer an effort for Vera to foresee some event as a clairvoyant, to read someone's thoughts as a telepathist, or to contact the spirits of the departed as a medium. She now sought to apply her past abilities as a stepping-stone to greater accomplishments. Since she was able to function as a catalyst and breach the world of the dead then why not attempt to communicate with not only the spirits of the departed but with the total force that is all spirit. What a thought!

Surely the force that held the spiritual level of the universe in tune was present at all times when she probed into its environment. Could she dare contact the ultimate spiritual force? Had she the courage? Could anyone dare to call upon God and actually make contact?

Laura read rapidly through the remaining pages. Vera had fallen into a routine of performing séances, her faithful followers, Martha Fuller and Susan Gray constantly with her.

_____

I must try again to assail the void; to reach and challenge the essence of the spiritual world. I am driven like an addict. Over the months I came close many times to experimenting once again but managed to avoid involvement at the last minute.

Today I faced my destiny. I had discovered that the spiritual force of the universe exists within mankind itself as part of the human subconscious.

The power of the spirit I sought was to be found within myself. That power was to be found within all mankind. Everything was God. Mankind, in essence, is God. Then man must possess the ability to communicate with God. The universe was the signature of the divine. Every thought, every motion in the universe was the body of God.

Were such things possible? Were the accepted concepts of God, heaven and hell only devices that were accepted over the centuries without proof? Was it possible that the beliefs of black magicians held as much truth as the precepts of organized religions? Therefore, the mind of man was a fragmented part of that infinite mind?

I believe it would take only the discovery of a key to release the finite mind of man to bridge the gap that exists between the two.

Those who possessed the 'gift' held that key. It was they, not the purveyors of religion, who were truly in contact with the spiritual forces of the universe.

Martha and Susan encouraged me to make spirit contact with them present at a ceremony. It was their intention to announce to a circle of authorities in parapsychology about what was to occur. They felt I would become a major figure in the realm of the supernatural.

I finally agreed to conduct the ritual with Martha and Susan present.

We were to conduct the ultimate séance. I would act as medium to bring forth the spirit. Hopefully I would go into a trance and it would speak through me. It was our intention that Martha Fuller would speak to the entity and try to communicate. We intend to understand its nature and to learn its identity. The time had come. My health was as good as I could expect..."

Here the manuscript ended. Of course, Laura thought, it had to end here. Vera could not have written another word for she never lived beyond the last séance.

But Laura saw vividly, as she did in her first vision, exactly what was to come. Vera spoke through her. The words came to her in a flood. She lifted her ballpoint pen and began writing...

I prepared myself in a flowing white robe and arranged the altar with the magic circle. I followed the outlines of the ritual and recited the long list of the hidden names of power, that summoned the spirit of the hidden place.

We sat in a circle at a round table, hands joined, and we prepared to make contact. While chanting the names of power at the peak of excitement, I saw a vaporous form rising in a cloud above the altar.

Within minutes the vaporous form of the spirit enveloped me and flowed in undulating motions over my body. My heart jumped as fear clutched at my throat. I continued the incantations. The substance moved around me, gliding gently over my entire body. I could feel its gentle touch along the skin of my face, along my arms, on my legs. Suddenly I felt a thrill of ecstasy that left me breathless and exhilarated as the cloud-like substance entered me, boldly, like a lover who knows no rejection. It poured over my face and neck. It glided into my mouth, my throat, into my lungs. It completely possessed me.

It was the crowning height of fulfillment in my life. And suddenly, I was lifted into the air, lost in a sea of ecstasy and pain, suspended above my two companions. I could do nothing. I was sapped of strength, its power controlling me. It crawled into my brain, probing. It reached into the farthest corners of my consciousness, stimulating and exciting. It ravaged my mentality. I was completely drained of energy but left with an emotional high that I would long remember. Nothing in life could surpass what had happened to me. To have summoned an entity from the spiritual realm was, in itself, a feat marked for wonder. But to have been twice blessed by welcoming it physically was more than I could have hoped for.

Then, for an instant, I saw its substance. A form appeared in my mind. I closed my eyes. It was red, fiery, a formless energy that whirled in my brain. It was the distorted form of some malevolent evil.

I tried to rise, to tear myself away from the vision I was permitted to see. But I could not move. I was totally exhausted. The vaporous ectoplasm rose and drifted away, slowly disappearing as it withdrew.

The force that so easily dominated me left me weak and limp. Within a minute it was gone as was I."

Laura let the journal drop to her lap. Vera Lancaster, she thought, you are me as I am myself. I feel your presence within me. I know you. I understand you. I sympathize with your need to unveil the unknown. Where are you, Vera? Is your spirit living within me?

As she slowly closed the journal her eyes caught a line written on what she thought was a blank page, a single line, all alone, that she hadn't noticed before. It read simply:

"I will be with you, Laura. Be careful."

Laura's breath choked and she felt a cold shiver of fear run through her. Vera Lancaster knew of her at the time of her last written entry in her journal. How could that be?

She brought the page closer to the light and ran her fingers across the written words. Was it fresh ink? The line appeared singularly in the center of the page and seemed out of place, as if it had been added there so she had to notice it.

Vera was a true psychic. Laura believed now that the medium could truly tap into the realm of the unknown, the spiritual side of nature. She could foretell events to come. Where did her ability end?

Chapter 30

The candles had burned low. Laura had read steadily into the night. Now, at least, there was no doubt. She was convinced Vera Lancaster had reached out to her, touched her, and communicated.

She rose from the chair, stretched and walked to the window that looked out to the back of the house. She stared blankly out into the night. Did this end it, she thought, now that she knew the cause of disturbance in her life? Was this the final remedy the psychiatrist had sought? Once known, never to recur. God, she hoped so. Yet a strange fascination with the essence of her benefactor lingered. Could she simply purge the spirit of the medium as simple and final as closing a door?

As she stared out the window a sudden blur of white flashed below amidst the trees. She thought at first that her eyes deceived her, having been strained for so long in the inadequate light of the candles. But there it was again, a definite movement, through the trees. It seemed a person was walking in the woods by the graveyard. Who, she wondered, could be out there this time of night? And why?

Laura left the room and hurried downstairs. She scurried through the house to the back door in the kitchen and rushed towards the wooded area near the graveyard.

The figure had emerged from behind a stand of birch thirty yards from her. It glided across the lawn toward the house, ethereal, ghostly, the form of a woman in muddy, tattered, gossamer-like garments that might have once been a flowing white gown. Her arms were extended outwards, the hands reaching toward Laura. The form moved closer, more clearly defined as it came into the light of the full moon.

Holy mother of God! Laura choked.

It was the half decomposed, rotting corpse of a woman. Two black holes defined the areas in her face where once her eyes had been. The foul body beckoned to Laura, the shapeless arms motioning for her. But Laura heard only the sound of her own screams as she collapsed.

Séance

Frank was jolted out of his sleep by Laura's screams. At first, he thought she was having a nightmare. He jumped out of bed, slightly disoriented in the new surroundings. Once he got his bearings he ran into Vera Lancaster's library, where Laura had been when he dozed off. She was lying on the floor next to the open window. He rushed to her, carried her into the bedroom and laid her gently on the medium's bed.

She slowly responded as he called to her through the clouded veil of her mind. "Laura, are you all right?"

Slowly, her eyes opened. She recognized Frank.

"Where am I?" she asked.

"In the bedroom. You must have fainted. You screamed. You woke me up. What happened?"

Laura's eyes widened. "Oh, Frank! I remember. I was reading her diary. Vera's diary. I found it in the library. I must have been reading for hours. When I finished I was pondering her life, looking out the window. I saw someone in the garden below."

"Someone out back? Who?"

"I don't know. It was a woman, coming towards the house to me. Oh Frank, it was horrible. It looked like a walking corpse! And she had no eyes!"

Frank was dismayed. "Laura! What are you saying? Walking corpses? You can't be serious."

Laura heard a note of serious doubt in his voice that she realized had been appearing stronger lately. "It was her, Vera. It had to be her," she said.

Frank did not respond. Laura looked directly into Frank's eyes that had rolled almost imperceptibly.

"You're not going to believe anything I say anymore, are you?" she said, irritated by his skepticism. "I can see that now. You won't accept what I believe or see, no matter what. So what difference does it make if I tell you anything anymore?"

"All right, Laura, please calm down. You've had a bad experience, I can see. Where is this diary of hers?" Frank asked.

"I left it on her desk."

Frank walked towards Vera's library.

"What are you going to do, Frank?" Laura cried out. "You're not going to damage her journal, are you?"

He returned to her bedside with the book in his hands. He sat down in the armchair beside the bed.

"No, of course not. I'm merely going to read it," he said calmly. "I want you to get some sleep. I'll be right here beside you. I'll talk to you about this in the morning."

* * *

She awoke suddenly. Frank had fallen asleep in the chair, the book closed in his lap. The candle he set up next to him on an end table had burned low. It was still dark outside but nearly morning.

She got up and silently crept down the stairs. She stumbled out the back door, realizing suddenly how weak she felt from the frightening experience of seeing Vera Lancaster's dead body moving towards her. Had it really been there? Had she really seen a walking corpse? Surely the physical body of Vera Lancaster could not activate itself from the grave. A ghost, then, her spirit manifested into physical form? Who else would beckon to her? She had to know for sure. She had to see for herself where the madness began and ended.

The gravesite was open when she got to it, the earth piled up around the gaping hole. The shattered, empty coffin stared up at her like the glaring eye of a giant cyclopean monster. She knew that truth and madness were the same.

Chapter 31

Laura returned to the house, wandering vacantly in a semi-daze. Her confused and frightened mind would not accept what she had witnessed this night. The light of the morning sun was breaking over the treetops.

She moved through the house, guided by the dim rays of sunlight. When she got to Vera's temple the heavy doors were wide open. Laura was drawn inexorably to the gaping entrance, thinking of the consequences that lay beyond that threshold.

She paused there, feeling suddenly weak, her hand holding onto the doorframe for support. She stepped inside the dark room, answering the call to destiny she knew was inevitable, now totally resigned to her fate, whatever it might be.

The room was darker than the rest of the house. It had been left exactly as Vera Lancaster embellished it. The walls were completely black and only the white alabaster tabernacle at the far end was visible. Laura made her way slowly toward it. As her eyes became accustomed to the feeble light she made out a dim shape resting prone on the altar. It was the missing body of Vera Lancaster.

Laura gasped and fought back fear. She edged slowly towards the altar. She must know the truth. She stood by the grotesque corpse and stared down at it. Her fear subsided.

Vera Lancaster, she thought, here you are, finally. She stared at the half-rotted face. Two vacant holes stared back where once the eyes had been. What do you want of me, Laura silently muttered. Is our destiny intertwined because I have your corneas? How did you get here? What unearthly power raised you out of your grave? Was it I? Can I call you back from death?

She began to softly weep, feeling sorrow for Vera. She knelt down beside the altar, her head bowed. Her right hand reached up and touched the body. She was tired and confused; her gentle sobbing filled the room. She drifted into sleep. As she lost consciousness she thought she felt Vera's hand move slowly until it made gentle contact with hers.

* * *

When Frank awoke the journal dropped from his lap as he stood up and stretched. Remembering where he was, he looked to where Laura should have been sleeping in the bed. It was empty. He felt sudden alarm.

He searched downstairs for her, trying to control the apprehension as each room revealed nothing. Finally he entered Vera Lancaster's temple. Laura sat at the foot of the altar, propped up against it, her right hand stretched up over the top of the empty surface.

Frank gently lifted her into his arms and carried her out of the room. She awakened in his arms.

"Frank," she said groggily. "What are you doing?"

"I found you sleeping at the foot of the altar in there," he said, gesturing to the temple room. "I carried you out."

"Put me down," she said.

Frank deposited her on the foyer floor and she immediately rushed back into the temple. He followed behind her.

"Where is she?" Laura demanded. "What have you done with her?"

"What are you talking about?"

"Vera. Where is her body? It was right here on the tabernacle last night."

"There was nothing here when I found you, Laura. You were alone."

"Liar!" she snapped spitefully. "Why are you lying to me?"

"I'm telling you the truth. You were alone. Besides, how would a dead body get in here?"

"I don't know. And I don't care. It was here, and her grave is empty." Laura started out the door, heading for the graveyard.

"Come on, I'll show you." She motioned to him.

As Frank followed her through the woods he prayed that they would find nothing. If the gravesite were disturbed Laura must have dug it up. But she would need tools to dig the grave out. And how could she accomplish such a feat and bring the body to the house by herself? Even if she managed to drag the body out, where was it now? Had her delusions gone this far?

When they got to the graveyard Frank was relieved to see the ground over Vera Lancaster's grave had not been disrupted. The grass growing over it was unmarred. It was exactly as they had seen it the first time. Even the weeds that had been growing in the soil were exactly in place.

Laura stood above the grave, dumbfounded.

"Now, for God's sake, Laura, isn't this enough to show you that you were imagining all of this?"

She turned to him in a sudden burst of fury.

"You did this!" she accused. "You covered the grave over. You're trying to make me believe I didn't see the empty grave. You've been against me from the beginning."

"Laura, I'm not against you," Frank admonished her. "I brought you here to discover everything you want to know about this woman. I want you to resolve what's troubling you and be done with this madness. Don't you think we've both had enough of this?"

Laura turned away from him and ran back to the house. Frank walked slowly after her, his shoulders hunched, his head slightly bowed, his body tensed in opposition to the turmoil he was enduring.

* * *

In the morning Frank drove over the bridge into Seen By Chance for the specific purpose of picking up supplies. He stopped by a supermarket and picked up some food, a couple of flashlights and a few small oil lamps. He wished Laura had come with him, but she was not interested in leaving the house. She spent the last few days in Vera Lancaster's library reading and rereading the diary.

He stopped at a diner in town. He ate a fast breakfast and, on his way out he almost bumped into Jack McCormack, the owner of The Herald.

"Why, Mr. Whitney," the newspaperman said. "How are you?"

"McCormack, isn't it?" Frank wondered if this meeting wasn't too coincidental.

"Yes. Say, did you and your wife get to Susan Gray?"

"Yes, we did."

205

"What did you find out? I'd be very interested in anything new. In fact I'd be willing to pay for information on Vera Lancaster and that last séance. Anything that would shed new light on that case."

"I'm afraid I can't help you," Frank said. "My wife saw her but never spoke to her."

"What happened?"

"Nothing, really. She is completely mad. My wife never had a chance to ask her even one question. She simply threw herself to the floor and grasped my wife's legs."

"Damn," McCormack said. "Did she speak?"

"I don't think so."

"No one has been able to make her speak since that night Vera Lancaster died," McCormack said. "I'd give an eyetooth to know what went on at the night of that séance."

Frank thought of the journal and the words Vera Lancaster had written. For a moment he almost told McCormack about the journal but thought better of it. It would upset Laura to reveal its contents to the press.

"So would I," he said calmly.

Frank left McCormack standing there. When he got back to the house he found Laura in the library, still absorbed in the diary.

"Come and eat," he said. "I got us some food."

Reluctantly she put down the book and joined Frank in the kitchen. He worked over the stove preparing an omelet.

"Laura," he said, turning to her, his voice filled with concern, "let's get out of here. I've had enough of this place. And I'm afraid for you. Let's call it quits."

Laura was startled. "I thought we agreed to stay two weeks. We've only been here a few days."

"What's the difference? A week, a month. You found her diary. All you're ever going to find out about her is what she wrote down. Isn't that enough?"

"Are you afraid I may be going insane, Frank? Is that it? Because you think I'm seeing things?"

"It's not that, Laura. It's just...we don't belong here. We don't belong in this woman's life, digging through her belongings. It's not right."

"Do you think it's right that I should have her corneas?"

"What has that got to do with us staying here?" Frank snapped.

"Can't I convince you that there is no relation between a pair of transplanted cornea and anything supernatural?"

"You can't convince me. I am so close to the truth I can't possibly go home."

Frank suddenly fumed. He turned and smashed the plate of food he was holding into the kitchen sink. He bolted from the kitchen, his sudden anger filling the room like an explosion.

"That damn woman," he swore. "How did this ever happen to us?"

Laura went to the stove and finished cooking. A few minutes later she called to him. After calming down, he returned to the kitchen where she had laid out a plate for each of them.

Frank kissed her on the lips. "I'm sorry," he said, smiling gently. "But sometimes you worry the hell out of me."

"That's all right, Frank," she said. "Sometimes you worry me."

Chapter 32

Frank awoke in the middle of the night as if an alarm had gone off in his mind. He reached over to touch Laura and found she wasn't beside him. The door to the bedroom was open. He quickly got out of bed and went into Vera Lancaster's study. Laura wasn't there. He assumed she was downstairs.

He saw the dim light coming from beneath the temple door.

Was she in there again? He quietly opened the door. She had lit the black candles and had spread them out on the altar. She was kneeling before the altar, dressed in a flowing white robe that trailed behind her.

Frank's voice rang through the room like a clanging bell.

"Laura, what the hell are you doing?" he pleaded.

She rose and turned to face him. For the briefest moment he didn't recognize her. Her face seemed different; an iridescent light seemed to glow from her eyes.

"I'm learning," she said softly, yet determined. "And certainly not in hell's name. Please, Frank, leave me be."

* * *

Laura sat before a large mirror on the dresser in Vera Lancaster's library. It was lit only by two black candles, which she had placed on either side. Frank was upstairs sleeping and she hoped he would not bother her again. She had come so far. She felt she was on the threshold of a true breakthrough to the spirit of Vera Lancaster.

Her reflection in the mirror was framed in the eerie, flickering light of the candles. She stared deeply into her reflected eyes. Her concentration became total. She tried to remove from her mind every thought except those of her purpose. She concentrated on her reflected image and thought only of her goal. She stared hard, unblinking.

Time passed slowly. Her mind became practically devoid of thought. She looked deeper into her own eyes. The image staring back at her seemed to be smiling, though she knew she wasn't. The eyes appeared to grow brighter, larger.

Laura was drawn into those eyes. She no longer possessed the power to deny their lure. They drained her mentality. She felt the force they emitted, piercing her brain. They held her spellbound, hypnotized.

Then she saw an apparition forming around her image in the mirror. It was a misty, vaporous substance, that gently flowed around her body. She felt fear. She wanted to break away, but could not. Her strength left her. She tried desperately to get out of the chair, but she began to shake. The trembling became uncontrollable. She finally struggled weakly to her feet and stumbled backward. She stepped away from the dresser. As she looked back at the mirror she saw that her image was still there, facing her, exactly as she had been even though she had walked away. The figure was now definitely smiling at her, the eyes wide, piercing and unblinking.

* * *

Laura had frightened Frank and worried him. She was on the verge of going mystical for some time now. Giving in to Laura's insistence and coming here, he conceded, was a terrible mistake. He knew that now. He should have held to his original argument and by now she might have forsaken her obsession with Vera Lancaster. He cursed the medium and wished her as much distress as he was experiencing right now.

But...she was dead and it didn't matter. Laura was his concern. She was all that mattered.

Frank made his choice. Laura was constantly in the temple downstairs or in the study upstairs. She was either reading the old volumes of magic or she was attempting to perform some absurd ritual in the temple.

He decided to try talking her into returning to New York as a first plan of action. He found her in Vera's temple, candles burning all around the altar, reciting chants and long lists of strange sounding names when he interrupted her.

"What are you doing?"

"I'm very close right now," she scorned.

"Close?" Frank queried. "Laura, just what is it you're close to?"

"Don't question me, Frank. You know why we came here. This woman is part of me. I must know what is happening to me. You must understand that by now."

Laura was no longer the woman he knew. Lately she snapped at him, her voice edged with bitterness.

"Laura, I must talk to you," he said calmly, hoping to reason with her. "This situation is going too far."

"Situation? There is no situation. What could you possibly have to talk to me about?" She turned away from him, her voice trailing off. "Just leave me alone, please."

"Laura, I have to leave. I have to go back to New York."

"I'm not stopping you, Frank. Go back if you must, but I am staying here for as long as I can."

This was not Laura at all, he thought. He felt the change in her was dangerous. Although calm, she no longer seemed rational. "I want you to come with me," he said.

"Not now. I can't," she said. "You know that I can't go."

Frank's patience had run thin. He accepted the last year as truly difficult for Laura. She was under a terrible strain. But now she was approaching a point of no return.

"Laura, you must come with me," he said, his voice pleading. "Please. This obsession of yours has gotten completely out of hand. This dead woman has messed us up. We have to go back to New York if we're going to maintain our lives. You cannot believe that staying here is of any benefit to you."

"Frank, please leave," she said bluntly. "I don't want you here. You're interfering with my work."

"My God, Laura. You speak of your work. What about your real work? Your painting. What's to become of it?"

"This is my work. Here. Vera is now my work."

"What's come over you?" he cried, frustrated. "You've got to stop this."

"I'll stop nothing," she retorted. "It's you who'll stop. Now please get out and leave me alone!"

There was no reasoning with her, Frank thought. He turned away, the realization ringing in his mind that she had crashed. He knew he could not forcibly take her back to New York. His dilemma was that he could either go to New York alone or stay here with her for as long as it takes. His choice was obvious.

He made several calls on his cell phone to his partners in New York informing them that he needed more time to work out his personal problems.

The latest call sealed the verdict.

His senior partner, Pete Sheffield, was on the other end.

"What the hell are you talking about, Frank? You can't pull something like this out of the blue. You know the advertising business. We have commitments, deadlines that must be met."

"What would you do if I dropped dead, Pete?" Frank said. "Get another man, right. Don't delude yourself into believing that I am that important. Hell, none of us are."

The voice in his ear said "Frank, be serious. You've got to get back on your accounts. You can't abandon your responsibility."

"I can't abandon my wife, Pete," Frank affirmed.

"What's this all about, Frank? What's going on?"

"Pete, please. Put someone on my accounts for the time being. Let my people handle them. I'll call the appropriate executives and explain that this is critical. Just give me some time."

"No, Frank, don't call anyone. I'll take care of this end. How much time do you need?"

"I don't know yet. Bear with me and I'll explain everything when I get back."

There was silence for a moment, and then his partner said, "Frank, you know I trust you. I have faith in you. But you've got to let me in on it. What happened?"

"Give me the time, Pete. I can't explain now because I don't know the outcome. Believe me, it will all work out soon."

"All right, buddy," Pete acquiesced. "But don't push it."

To himself Frank thought, but will it all work out?

He knew he must seek professional help for Laura. He must get her to a psychiatrist or someone who understands the supernatural. The supernatural, the occult, mystical, metaphysical...psychic. Did he know of anyone who dealt with such things? Yes, he thought, as a matter of fact, he did. The priest and his friend who had come to see Laura. What were their names? Damn! He could not remember.

Spalding.

Spanner.

No.

Two S's. Both names began with an S. He remembered that from when they introduced themselves. He got a notepad from his briefcase and started jotting down names.

Smith.

Sheppard.

Sterling.

Spalding.

Simson...

On and on. Come on, dammit, Whitney, think, think...

Nothing.

He should have put the calling card that the taller man handed him in his wallet. But he remembered tossing it in his desk at the Manhattan apartment. There it was sitting in the drawer, of no use to anyone. Visualize it, Whitney, he told himself. See it in your mind. You can do it.

He wrote down...Sa, Se, Si, So, Su. Vowels. Good lord, there must be thousands of names.

Nothing clicked. He would be at this all day and come no closer than when he started. Son of a bitch, he swore. He had only one choice and he knew it.

He had to go through Laura's belongings.

He found her purse upstairs in Vera's bedroom. He poured the contents on the bed and rifled through them. There it was, the black and white card.

Carl Spendler! Damn. That's it. Carl Spendler, the tall guy with the gray hair.

Frank loaded Laura's contents back into the purse and placed it back in the chair where he had found it.

* * *

Frank waited until Laura was completely absorbed at Vera Lancaster's tabernacle before he slipped into the bedroom. The diary lay on an end table near Vera's bed. Frank removed it and silently left, the book under his arm, praying that she would not miss it until he had gotten it to Spendler.

Chapter 33

When Carl Spendler received Frank Whitney's phone call he was both surprised and thrilled. He had about given up on Laura Whitney although he still had many questions he would like answered concerning her dilemma. Frank Whitney seemed such a skeptic to Spendler he didn't expect a call from him.

"Where are you?" Spendler asked.

"I'm in Maine," Frank said. "I'm with my wife. We're staying at Vera Lancaster's house."

"Fantastic. You're actually at her house?"

"Yes."

"Why are you there?" Spendler asked.

"It's a long story. First off, Laura inherited the house."

"I'll be damned."

Frank asked that they meet immediately. "I'm pressed for time," he asserted. "I need help desperately. It's my Laura. You came to help her when Roger Evans died. Does that offer still stand?"

"Absolutely. I'd like to bring Gerry Stuart with me," Spendler said. "If it's all right with you."

"Certainly," Frank said. "I will pay your expenses and time." To make the potential meeting even more enticing Frank offered the prospect of Vera Lancaster's journal. "By the way," he said, "my wife found Vera Lancaster's diary."

Spendler was astounded. "You have the medium's diary?"

"Yes," Frank answered. "You've got to read it."

"Damn right I do." Spendler believed that Vera Lancaster was as close to a true medium as he had ever known. He wanted to know for sure if there was any truth in what had transpired at her séances over the years.

Frank gave Spendler the town name and directions to get there. "Please," he said imploringly, "as fast as you can. I'll meet you at the airport"

* * *

Spendler called Gerry Stuart. It was ten PM. He hoped Gerry has not gone somewhere. He breathed a sigh of relief when the call was answered.

"Gerry, do you have the time to take a trip?" Spendler asked.

"What's going on, Carl. What's so important?" Gerry said, obviously excited.

"You're not going to believe what's happened."

"Come on," Gerry said. "Give out."

"Frank Whitney called me," Spendler said. "He wants us to help his wife."

"Well, what do you know?" Gerry said, glad to hear Whitney's decision.

"Whitney wants to see us right away. The problem is he's in Maine."

"Maine?"

"Believe it or not, he and his wife are staying at Vera Lancaster's house in Maine."

Excitement rang in Gerry's voice. "I've got a few things on the docket. I guess you have too. But I'll do some juggling."

"It's set then," Spendler said. "I'll book us a flight. We should be there this evening."

* * *

Frank met them at Bangor International Airport.

Frank shook Spendler's hand. "You remember Gerry Stuart?" Spendler said introducing the priest.

"Yes, of course," Frank said and then added, "Mr. Spendler, first of all, I want to apologize for the way I acted the first time we met. I'm sorry I was rude. I was upset then and could have served my wife better if I had recognized what was happening."

"Forget it, Mr. Whitney," Spendler said. "Under the circumstances at the time, I might have reacted likewise."

Gerry Stuart glanced quickly around the airport arrival area. "Is you wife here?" he asked.

"No. She's still at the Lancaster woman's house," Frank responded. "I've gotten you a room at the only motel in town. I hope it will do."

"I'm sure it will," Spendler said.

They drove to the motel at Seen By Chance and the men settled in. Frank handed Vera Lancaster's diary to Spendler.

"This is Vera Lancaster's journal," he said.

Spendler took the book, his nervous fingers reflecting the excitement in his voice. Yet he flipped through it casually. "May we read this?" he asked.

"Certainly," Frank said. "That's why I brought it to you. You'll get an idea of what we're up against."

"I'm glad you brought it," Spendler said. "It's probably the only way we're going to understand Vera Lancaster's motivation. We may be able to learn why your wife is so obsessed with the woman."

"I knew I would need some tangible evidence to convince you that I wasn't a raving lunatic myself," Frank said. "That's why I grabbed the journal. I don't think anyone would believe me if I merely told them what I'd read here."

"Believe me, Mr. Whitney," Spendler said, his voice charged with emotion. "People who are involved in the paranormal know of Vera Lancaster. No one would have thought you dreamed it all up."

"Tell me, Mr. Whitney, do you believe there have actually been any true psychic occurrences involving your wife?" Gerry Stuart asked.

"Well no, not exactly."

"What then?"

"Only what Laura believes. And what she claims. Her nightmares. She said someone touched her on the shoulder once on the beach when there was no one there. The other night she said she saw Vera Lancaster's ghost walking in the garden. She really believes that the spirit of this dead woman reached out to her."

"Do you believe that?"

"I can't accept as fact that a spirit physically touched her," Frank said. "If you mean that Laura is obsessed with this woman, then I'd say yes, she is. But I don't believe any spiritual force has taken over her body." Frank's voice cracked. "But God, I don't know. I'm desperate. Is it possible? That crazy woman's writing has triggered some nerve in Laura? It doesn't seem possible."

"That's what we must find out, Mr. Whitney," Spendler said.

"But Laura was always such a level-headed woman. How could this happen to someone as intelligent as Laura? She is a good artist. She was producing great work. Now, she doesn't paint at all. A psychiatrist blamed her problems on the traumatic experience brought on by the loss of her sight and the mental anguish involved. That didn't satisfy Laura. When she found out that the corneas belonged to a medium, she believed she knew the source of her problems. She talked me into coming to Maine."

"Do you think she found them? The answers." Spendler asked.

"No. Not at all," Frank quickly responded. "She found a library of books in Lancaster's house about the occult, black arts, mysticism and the like. She's obsessed with the idea of this woman. She merely added a ton more problems. It got worse. And when she found the journal I think she went over the edge."

Frank Whitney moved to the window of the motel room and glanced out at the serene view of the harbor. He pondered it for a moment thinking this was reality. This was the real world. The world Laura had stepped into was pure fantasy, a lingering nightmare. He turned back to the two men.

"Mr. Spendler, Father Stuart, can you help me?" he asked. "Is there anything I can do to get Laura away from the spell this dead woman has over her?"

"I don't know for sure just what we can do," Spendler said. "But we'll try to get her out of that house. I would like to borrow the journal and read through it."

"Is that necessary right now?"

"Yes," Spendler said.

"All right. If you think it will help. I'll do anything to bring Laura back to me. Just help us, please," Frank implored. "We can proceed to the Lancaster house in the morning. Say around nine o'clock."

Chapter 34

Frank Whitney felt he could not return to Laura if she had discovered the journal missing. What could he say to her? That she had misplaced it?

Yet he could not leave her alone in that house under such weird conditions.

He left Carl Spendler and Gerry Stuart at the motel and walked across the main street to where he had parked his rental car on the waterfront. As he slipped the key into the lock a lone figure caught his eye at the water's edge. It was a woman standing on the dock. Something about her reminded him of someone. She turned and faced him.

Then it struck him. My God, Laura was right. He was looking at Jenny Douglas.

He left the car and started towards her. She apparently saw him, turned and began walking quickly away and out onto one of the boat slips.

"Jenny!" he cried out. "Jenny Douglas! Wait!"

Frank raced towards Laura's friend as she dropped out of sight. By the time he got to where he had seen her she was with a man in a small, motorized rubber craft cutting the water toward the sailboats moored in the harbor. Frank watched as they tied the small craft to a large white sailboat and climbed on board.

Frank proceeded to a landing at the dock where small craft congregated. There he found a dock that specialized in getting people to their selected moored boats.

"Can you take me to a boat in the harbor?" he asked the man at the dock.

"Sure. You point out the one you want."

Frank guided the man to the boat Jenny had boarded. The inflatable rubber craft deposited him at the stern of the sailboat. Frank handed the driver some cash and climbed on board. Now the thing was to find out who was this guy with Jenny and what hold he had on her.

There was no one on the deck. Both the mainsail and the jib

were trimmed. The boat was anchored amidst an assortment of moored vessels.

Frank moved quietly towards the cabin. The man whom he saw with Jenny suddenly came on deck from the forward hatch. He stood erect and was halfway to the cabin along the rail when he saw Frank.

"Who the fuck are you?" Johnnie Limbo shouted. "What are you doing on this boat?"

"Where's the girl?" Frank said curtly.

"What girl?"

"Don't shit me, pal," Frank snapped. "I saw her come on this boat with you and I'm not leaving without her."

"Get the hell off my boat!" Limbo swore and lifted the wrench he was carrying over his head.

"Suit yourself," Frank said, waving Limbo to come to him. "We'll do it the hard way."

Johnnie Limbo was no slouch. Having been involved in a number of brawls in his lifetime, he knew his own ability to take down most adversaries who faced him. And having a wrench in his right hand was a definite advantage. Yet he realized this man who stood his ground as he charged was no patsy. Johnnie raised the wrench over his head threateningly and never had a chance to bring it down on Frank. A lightning, devastating one-two, left-right combination dropped Limbo to the deck and left him groggy. Frank lifted the wrench from Limbo's hand and tossed it behind him. He backed off and let his adversary get to his feet.

Limbo cleared his head, brushed blood from his nose and muttered, "Lucky shot!" Enraged, he charged Frank with arms cocked. Frank sidestepped a roundhouse right and delivered two jabs and a right hook that put Limbo on the deck again. By now his face was a bloody mess.

Frank stood over him.

"Are we finished?" he asked as Johnnie Limbo held out his left hand in a gesture of submission.

Frank never saw the blow to his head from behind that knocked him unconscious. Jenny Douglas stood there with the discarded wrench dangling from her hand as Frank Whitney collapsed in front of her.

Séance

* * *

Jenny Douglas saw Frank Whitney on the dock in town. She had accidentally turned towards the parking area and made eye contact. Maybe it wasn't him, she thought; only someone who looked like Frank. She risked another sighting and looked back.

Damn! It was Frank. What were they doing here? Laura must be here too! Could they have followed me?

Frank's eyes locked on hers and he stepped away from his car and started moving rapidly towards her. She must avoid contact. She raced down the boat slip to where Johnnie Limbo waited for her in a tiny powerboat. She jumped in beside Limbo.

"Quick!" she said. "Get out to the boat."

"What's up?" he asked.

"Someone I know from New York. He saw me."

"What's he doing here?" Johnnie asked.

"How should I know? On vacation? I don't know. He certainly couldn't have traced me here. He knows nothing about me. Besides, he's a busy executive. He hasn't got time to follow me. Let's just get the hell out of here."

Limbo kicked the motor over and the motor-craft sped out into the harbor.

What in the name of heaven was Frank doing here in this remote place, Jenny thought. What are the odds of him being on the same dock in the same small harbor town on this particular day? She couldn't let Frank or Laura get to her. They must not interfere with what has happened to her. The lives of her children and Ralph were at stake. Her monster jailer, Elymas, proved that he was capable of brutal murder at the house in Manhattan. As long as she obeyed him, her family was safe.

She cringed at the thought of how Elymas had used her as his sex toy when he first seized the Manhattan brownstone. He took her into a bedroom and ripped the clothes from her back. He threw her forcefully face down on the bed and entered her from the rear. It hurt her badly. It was feral, inhuman. He was more demon than human.

He assaulted her only a few times after that. Then Johnnie Limbo became her constant watchdog and sexual tormentor. Elymas made it known to her that her family's safety depended on pleasing him. The trouble with Johnnie Limbo was that he was never satisfied. He was young and capable of fornicating often. She did what he demanded.

She and Johnnie got quickly to the sailboat. She went below to the cabin while Johnnie Limbo went below through the front hatch to work on something. Jenny stayed below. She was never allowed off the boat or in town, anywhere, without Johnnie as her escort. She made a pot of coffee and was sipping it when she heard a commotion on deck. She stuck her head out of the gangway and saw Frank Whitney knock Johnnie Limbo to the ground. Johnnie's face was smeared with blood.

My god! she thought. This can't be happening. Frank can't be doing this. Ralph and the kids! She ran to the deck. She needed something. A weapon. Anything to stop Frank. Her eyes rested on the fallen wrench on the deck. She grabbed it up. It took two hands to swing it.

Frank fell unconscious before her.

"Sorry, Frank," she said. "I had to do it."

* * *

Curiosity grew immediately to overwhelming enthusiasm as Spendler and Gerry raced through the pages of Vera Lancaster's journal. The document was more detailed than they had expected. They read for hours, consuming every word, digesting every nuance. Spendler had read it first and waited for Gerry to wrap it up.

"Well, Gerry, what do you think?" Spendler asked.

"It's absolute dynamite. No one will believe what she claims to have accomplished."

"Do you think it's possible that she actually brought about such phenomena?"

"I don't know," Gerry said. "But she apparently believes it."

"She was a remarkable woman," Spendler said. "I remember attending one of her séances years ago. I tell you, it was the closest thing to being in the presence of spirits as I've ever felt. I remember there was no visible appearance in any form, but I could feel something in that room; an energy, I suppose. Indescribable. I knew I was in a truly supernatural situation. The woman certainly did have some ability to conjure. I don't doubt that. But I didn't know she had gotten involved in black magic."

"That's mostly what astonished me," Gerry said.

"When Laura Whitney brought up Vera Lancaster's name in connection with her eye operation I was immediately interested," Spendler said. "But now, after reading this journal and finding she was into black magic and performed a ritual experiment with necromancy, I am astounded."

Spendler glanced at his watch. It was already after ten am. "I would have come here alone if you couldn't make it," he said. "I've got to help Whitney. I have no choice."

"How sure were you that I would go?"

"Fairly certain," Spendler responded. "I figured nothing could stop you once you knew it was Vera Lancaster we were talking about."

Gerry held the diary in both hands. "Carl," he said, "what do you seriously think? Do you believe that Vera Lancaster caused her own death? Through fear, perhaps."

"It's possible, Gerry. None of the women at that séance knew what they would encounter. They really went into the séance blindfolded. There was no way to know that the entity Vera Lancaster claimed to have roused was capable of killing any of them."

"What could have jolted her heart so badly?"

Spendler pondered a moment. "I don't know, Gerry," he said. "But I have a feeling we're going to find out damn soon."

Chapter 35

When Laura found Frank had gone, her first reaction was disbelief. Then, noticing there was no car, she thought he might have driven to New York. He said he was going. She, on the other hand, had no intention of returning to New York right now. What had he intended? Was he leaving me without a car? No. Frank loves me. He would never leave me. It was something else.

Could he force her to return with him? Was he planning some legal alternative to get her out of here? She doubted it. Could he block her attempt to stay at the Lancaster house? He might tie up their assets. Laura had never separated her earnings from Frank's. Here, though, facing the reality of her situation, she was rapidly running low on funds; her cash on hand was below four hundred dollars. And she was almost out of traveler's checks. She still had her checkbook that had over three thousand dollars showing as a balance.

She decided to transfer funds electronically to the bank in town. Chances are, she thought, Frank hadn't had the time to thwart her plans.

She noticed that Vera Lancaster's journal was not on the table next to her bed where she had left it the night before. Frank must have taken it. Perhaps he left it downstairs, she thought. Her anger forced her to act quickly. She searched the entire house. The journal was nowhere to be found. Damn! Why had he taken it? Was he going to show it to someone? Why?

She wondered to whom. The psychiatrist? Who else might he call? Was he teaming up with him to convince her to leave? It seemed the only purpose Frank might have.

Laura and Frank each had their own cell phone. She dialed his number. It did not connect to voice message so she could not leave a message.

She found a local phone book in the bottom drawer of Vera Lancaster's desk. She dialed the only bank in town on her cell phone. She had to transfer funds immediately.

Frank had taken the car. He might have driven all the way to

New York, but she doubted it. He probably flew down. The car might be parked at the airport.

She walked down to the dock and started the power boat. There was fuel in the tank and it kicked over immediately. She guided the boat through the slightly choppy waters of the bay as expertly as if she had done it all her life, like she knew the waterways by sight. She landed at a public wharf in town. From there she walked to the bank, less than a quarter mile in on Main Street.

She and Frank had a savings account that totaled enough to get what she needed for the present. There was much more in stocks and bonds but she didn't have the time to sell them. She could garner funds as she needed from the sale of paintings in New York. She wondered who would handle her work at TheArtGallery now that Vernon Hayle had died. She knew he had partners and suspected that business would probably continue as usual. She wondered, though, if her work would sell without Vernon to feature it.

It took less than an hour to set up an account in the local bank with sufficient funds for the time being. She walked along the waterfront, in and out of the docks and slips, hoping that Jenny Douglas might appear as she had in Manhattan. That occurrence, she was convinced, was a once in a lifetime miraculous accident. But after seeing the sailboat bearing her friend's name, she was convinced that the madman who had kidnapped her was here in Seen By Chance. And if he was here, Jenny might be with him.

When she had exhausted her efforts she returned to Lancaster Island. The evening sun was beginning its descent. As she left the boat and walked up to the house she saw a shape moving behind an upper window. It was someone carrying a candle. It was there for a moment and then was gone.

Someone was in the house. Had Frank returned? But there was no car parked anywhere nearby.

She approached the house with caution, a sense of misgiving overcoming her. The electricity had not been connected in the house and she still relied on candles. Since she believed Frank had not returned she wondered who could be walking around inside. There should be no lit candles in the house.

She carefully opened the front door and entered quietly. There was still enough light to see, and yet...there was candlelight flickering in the space between the slightly open sliding doors of Vera Lancaster's parlor. Laura slid the doors farther apart and stepped inside. There were candles aflame on the altar and in every holder in the room.

She gasped as fear gripped her throat.

There, standing at the altar, was the man from the brownstone house in Manhattan.

Tall, slim, dressed in a black suit and a black shirt, the ashen skin of his aristocratic face highlighted by a pair of serpentine eyes that did not blink. A mane of glossy black hair was swept back from a widow's peak that sliced through a furrowed brow.

In his hand he held a tall glass of white wine.

"Well, Laura Whitney, we meet again," the man in black said. "Do come in."

"Who are you?" Laura said, trying to allay the fear in her voice.

"I am whom you seek," he announced. "I am who is not."

Laura Whitney felt an overwhelming attack on her senses the minute the man in black spoke.

"I seek Vera Lancaster," she said vacantly. "Certainly not you."

He chortled, a sharp snicker cracking his lips. "Vera Lancaster is no more. She is in the realm of the life-challenged."

"You're the man from the house in Manhattan," Laura said, her head buzzing. "Who are you? What are you doing in her house?"

"Surely, you know me by now," was the answer. "I 'passed over' from the wrong side at Vera's last séance."

"You killed Vera," Laura said.

"Now, now, let's not play the blame game. She killed herself by tampering in areas she knew little about. She apparently had a weak heart that gave out. Maybe all the years of sittings scared her to death."

"Why are you here? What do you want of me?" Laura said, trying to keep the quiver of fear out of her voice.

Elymas smiled, his voice rife with haughtiness. "Questions, questions. Which shall I answer first? I am here because it is my destiny. Vera Lancaster played the game. She didn't know what she would get. And, because of her interference, you got me. As for you...you sought me out. Curiosity killed the cat, they say. Don't you love clichés?"

"Who are you?" Laura insisted, her initial fear subsiding.

224

"Who am I? I am Elymas, emissary of my Lord and Master. Why, Laura, I am the guy who dispensed all those people you know about..."

"You murdered people in my life?" Laura exclaimed. "You madman! Why?"

"Why not," came the abrupt response? "Except for Jennifer Douglas. She still lives. Does that answer your question?"

"Where is Jenny Douglas?" Laura demanded.

"Ah, Jennifer. Useful lady."

"What have you done to her?"

"Why nothing serious. She services my worldly needs. You know, cooking, sex, basic subservient stuff. She provides for my needs and I...provide for hers."

"Her only needs are her family!" Laura swore, reaching for the will to fight. "Why do you enslave her?"

"She is hardly enslaved. She can leave any time she wants."

"What are you holding over her? Why does she stay with you? Because of her family?"

"My goodness, you really are full of questions. They die, of course, if she leaves," Elymas said flatly.

"What kind of madness is this?" Laura cried.

"Not madness, Laura. Deliberate... how shall I say it? Evil. Yes. I am the embodiment of evil. Evil exists, my dear Laura. It is a real, living thing. I am, therefore I kill. Sound too complicated? Let me simplify it. I bring my own personal brand of evil to the world."

"To what end?"

"To unite mankind in destroying itself."

"This is madness! What do you want of me?" Laura asked.

"You are part of her who summoned me. You are here because of Vera. I am here because of Vera. It is me you seek. You must rid yourself of Lancaster's dominance. I can't have people close to you interfering. You are mine. You belong to me."

"Like Jenny!" Laura ranted. "A slave to you! No! I won't!"

"Ah, but you will, my dear. I'll make a deal with you. You stay with me and I let Frank live."

"Damn you!" Laura swore, rejecting caution.

"All right. I'll sweeten the pie. Another cliché. God, I love clichés. Here's the deal. I'll trade you for Jenny. She can go home

225

to her family. And your husband can live. Now, I ask you, what could be more fair?"

"Damn you!" Laura swore in anguish.

"That deed has already been concluded," the demon said nonchalantly.

Laura struggled with the words. "You will murder Jenny and Frank if I don't agree to your terms?"

"Ah," the demon said, "now you get it."

Laura bowed her head in a sign of resignation.

"But there's more," Elymas said.

"What...what more?"

"You see with angelic eyes," Elymas said. "I can't have that. You possess a touch of the saintly. Vera's eyes cannot exist. You must give up the eyes you inherited."

"Never!" Laura swore.

"Then people continue to die."

Laura fell to her knees. She put her hands over her eyes and tried to hold back the tears.

"Ah," said Elymas. "The eyes have it. The end does justify the means."

As he spoke she knew she was truly in Vera Lancaster's world and the enigma was answered but unresolved. Her life was no longer hers. Was that why Vera had appeared to her in various forms? Was she warning her or protecting her, as a guardian angel? Or was she luring her to this destination to settle issues once and for all?

She lifted her head, fought back the tears and stared directly into Elymas's gleaming black eyes. Laura's instinctive reaction was to turn away. But instead, she found the determination to hold his stare with her own. She felt the surge of Vera's spirit within her. It was grand, almost overwhelming. Her concentration probed those demonic orbs that did not blink and penetrated beyond their surface into the subconscious memories that Elymas could not hide. Deep, deep into the recesses emerged visions that burned into her consciousness. Evil events beyond imagination raced through the eons, flashing not as she had thought them to be but as the demon recorded them. Layer upon layer from the time of the crucifixion of Christ through hundreds of crimes perpetrated by the greatest madmen in human history crashed into Laura's vision,

226

overwhelming her with blood, death and brutality.

She finally broke her hypnotic lock on his glare, turned away and collapsed to the floor.

"Well, well," said Elymas sarcastically, "I guess the old cliché that 'the eyes are the windows to the soul' holds up." And he grinned spitefully.

Chapter 36

Frank Whitney awoke to an overwhelming sensation of coldness. He opened his eyes. He was looking out at the Atlantic Ocean, which was level with his chest. The ocean was calm, as gently rolling waves caressed his body.

He tried to move but couldn't. He was tied upright to the piling of a dock. To his right, at the other side of the dock he recognized Vera Lancaster's speedboat. The mark of the waterline on the pilings indicated that he was harnessed to a post with his head below the marked spot where high tide would reach. How long, he wondered, did he have before the incoming tide drowned him? An hour? Two hours?

Don't panic, he warned himself. Keep calm. Figure this thing out.

He tried moving his feet. He was lashed to the post by rope around both his ankles and chest. His arms were bent back around the piling and his wrists were bound together. He had been strapped there to die. How did he get here, he wondered. He had been in a fistfight on the deck of the sailboat. Then, suddenly, he lost consciousness and woke up here. His head hurt. Somebody must have hit him from behind. But who? Could it have been Jenny Douglas? But why would she stop him from setting her free?

Don't think about that now. How can I get out of here and save my life? Could Laura hear me if I cried out to her? Probably not. She was most likely in the house and would never hear my calls.

Nonetheless, he cried out.

"LAURA! LAURA! FOR GOD'S SAKE, ANSWER ME! SOMEONE!"

From behind him he heard a voice. "Well, Mr. Whitney, welcome to the land of the living."

Frank turned his head to the left from where the voice had come. He was able to turn just far enough to see a man, dressed entirely in black, standing on the rocky beach to the right of the dock.

"Who the hell are you?" Frank yelled.

"Well, Mr. Whitney," said Elymas, "you've returned to us. By the way, may I call you Frank? In answer to your question, I'm the man who put you on that piling. Of course I had help. After all, you are a big man."

"Fuck you! Who the hell are you?" Frank shouted.

"Oh, I see. Right to the point. It's my name you want, is it?. I am Elymas. I kill people."

"You goddamn madman. What have you done to my Laura?"

"She's my Laura now," came the answer. "Listen, I don't have much time to chat. Lots of things to do. You know the routine. You being in advertising. Good luck with the tide. You know what they say, 'Time and tide wait for no man.'"

* * *

Gerry Stuart and Carl Spendler spent a restless morning anticipating what the day might bring.

For Spendler it was a time of expectation, a moment to cherish, a culmination of the years of exploration and search. Did he really believe in Vera Lancaster's demon? If the medium's experiences were real, then his belief that the mind was the catalyst capable of conjuring such phenomena was fact. Spendler accepted that Laura Whitney might truly be a link between reality and the spirit world. Could they convince her to leave this place, he wondered?

For Gerry Stuart the waiting was long and restless. If he was to be free of doubt, he must face whatever quandary awaited him in the confrontation to come. His calling to the priesthood had been based on faith, a belief in Christ as the Son of God and a communion with the precepts of the Catholic Church. But faith alone had never been enough. His obsession with the occult was a result of these concerns. His anticipation of tomorrow's meeting was coupled with both overwhelming fear and the gnawing sense that his doubts would be allayed.

They waited for Frank Whitney to appear. By nine AM they decided he was not coming and ventured the trip without him. They got directions from the clerk at the motel, rented a car and drove out of town, across the bridge to Lancaster Island. As they neared the house, the scene was dimly outlined against the bland horizon. A bleak destination, its foreboding appearance heightened Gerry Stuart's sense of impending dread. A sudden spasm of chills overtook him. He wasn't sure if it was fear or a cool breeze from the ocean.

They left the car and trekked on foot along the rising path to the house. The wind diminished once they entered the shelter of the pine-covered woodland. They pushed on, each carrying gear in backpacks that would assist them in determining whether or not there were spirits present.

In an instant they were in a clearing and the old house loomed before them, menacing and grim, like some huge hulking beast, ready to devour.

Gerry Stuart felt repulsion tear through him like a knife. This was reality, he thought. No illusion. Fear was a tangible presence and it ripped at his core. But he knew there could be no running away now. Those very doubts had brought him this far. If he was ever going to face his fears, now was the time.

Spendler, on the other hand, gazed upon the house with an overwhelming fascination. He could almost see Vera Lancaster in his mind's eye conducting her rituals, conjuring forms from another dimension. It is upon him, he thought. He will see what she had seen. He will speak to Vera Lancaster through Whitney's wife.

They marched forward, neither speaking, the cadence of their footfalls much slower than the racing rhythm of their pounding hearts.

* * *

Laura sat alone in the dark in Vera Lancaster's temple. Vera's demon was reality. And he was here, dominating her, possessing her.

She worried about Frank and hoped he was safe. Now she hoped that he had contacted Carl Spendler and the priest. Perhaps they were the catalyst needed to thwart the demon's intentions. But what could even they do? What would it take to defeat this beast? Here, she determined, was a classic battle of good and evil. The priest had God on his side, did he not?

Across the windowless room she was watched. Only a pair of

fiery red eyes, like jewels in the head of some solitary idol, remained visible in the dim light.

Then Elymas moved so swiftly he seemed to glide across the room, his feet rarely touching the floor.

Elymas was a force that rendered her weak and limp. He overwhelmed her, whirling around her like a piece of driftwood in a raging storm. She could feel his anger, almost a forceful weight, which sapped her of energy. She was lifted into the air and deposited rudely on Vera Lancaster's altar.

She could do nothing. Hopelessness overcame her. Her eyes were clenched shut; her mouth grimaced tight in fear.

The demon closed upon her like a smothering cloud. Through her stupor she heard a distinctive male voice calling her name..."Mrs. Whitney...Mrs. Whitney!"

Was it only in her mind? She tried to respond but was incapable of action. The black void of unconsciousness leapt at her from the ground and she descended into the void.

* * *

The front door was unlocked. Carl Spendler and Gerry Stuart entered meekly, sensing that their presence was known. The light in the interior was dim, only diffused daylight offering them guidance.

Spendler stepped forward into the immense foyer and called Laura's name. "Mrs. Whitney."

No answer.

Again he spoke, louder this time.

"Mrs. Whitney! Are you there? Mrs. Whitney!"

Silence, so intense it had a presence.

Again Spendler's voice echoed through the vast emptiness of the old house.

"Mrs. Whitney! Laura Whitney, where are you?"

Nothing but unbearable silence. Spendler nudged Gerry's arm and the two men moved farther into the house. Spendler found a light switch at the foot of the staircase and tried it. It didn't work. As they moved through the main floor there was just enough daylight in the old dark house to see well enough to get around.

Spendler reached into his backpack and lifted out a small device. He held in his hand a Gauss Master, an instrument used by ghost hunters to detect the presence of spirits. A meter on its face registered the degree to which electro-magnetic fields became obstructed by the presence of spirits.

The needle was hitting the extremity of its calibrations.

"My God, Gerry!" Spendler exclaimed. "This house is loaded. Look at the needle!"

Gerry Stuart glanced over. "I've never seen such a potent reaction," he said. "What have we got here?" His fear was palpable. His voice quivered as his mind screamed. He thanked God that Carl Spendler was here beside him for solace.

Spendler said, "Let's get on with it. We've got to find Laura Whitney."

They went immediately to the large sliding doors just off the entry foyer. The doors were slightly ajar revealing a dim, golden glow from inside the room.

The two men slid the doors apart and slowly entered, not knowing what to expect. This room was dimly lit from candles set in ornamental alabaster candelabra. They were in Vera Lancaster's temple. The walls and floor were black and draped in bands of white linen hanging from the twelve-foot high ceiling to the floor. In the center of the room was a long table also covered in white linen, which draped on all sides. There were no windows.

Standing at the head of the table was Elymas, the disciple of evil. He raised a glass of wine and saluted the two men. As his white teeth gleamed, his blood red eyes flashed with a fire from somewhere deep within him.

"Come in, gentlemen," he said calmly. "I've been expecting you. Carl Spendler and Father Gerald Stuart, I assume."

"You know us?" Spendler asked calmly.

"Why, of course," Elymas said. "Who does not know of Carl Spendler? Your encounters are praiseworthy. Have a seat, gentlemen. May I pour you a drink?" The voice was resonant, sonorous in tone.

"Who the hell are you?" Spendler demanded.

"Ah, you invoke the favored word, Spendler. Hell. I would not have liked the converse. It's not in my lexicon."

"Answer my question," Spendler demanded.

"I am Elymas," came the answer. "I am who is not. Did you bring that woman's journal?"

"No," Spendler said.

"I didn't expect you would," their host said. "But we'll deal with that at a later time. I wouldn't want it to end up in the wrong hands."

"We've come because Frank Whitney asked us to," Gerry Stuart said, a slight quiver still in his voice. "We are here to find Laura Whitney."

"And I thought you came for knowledge, priest," the voice mocked.

"Where is Laura Whitney?" Spendler demanded.

"She is here. She is my guest. But what's the hurry. You will meet her soon enough."

"Your guest? I believe this is her house," Spendler challenged.

"Her house...my house. Who's to say what 'is' means?" came the slow, scornful answer.

The men stood opposite the stranger. Spendler stirred restlessly. He wasn't sure what this bizarre man meant by his curious comment. And he said his name was Elymas. Spendler recalled the name vaguely...from the New Testament. He placed the name with the prophet Paul.

Gerry Stuart knew the name with certainty. He recalled Elymas as a sorcerer whom Saint Paul had confronted on the island of Cyprus two thousand years ago. Elymas was believed to be a consort of Satan who preached Satan's doctrine against Christ. Gerry remembered that Paul, along with Barnabas, had met and challenged Elymas. The power from God, which Paul wielded, left Elymas blind. But he could not truly be Elymas. Elymas lived two thousand years ago. And this man was not blind. Or was he?

Spendler silently lifted a palm-sized recorder from his knapsack and clicked it on. It was preset to record. He thought he must get this confrontation on tape.

"You deem to record our meeting?" their adversary said, then added pretentiously, "I will allow it."

"This is very awkward for us," Spendler said. "We'd like to speak to Mrs. Whitney."

"I don't see that as a possibility," Elymas said rudely.

Spendler was becoming tense. He tried to control his trepidation and not allow tremors of fear show in his voice. The air was charged with fear.

Suddenly a female voice, in a piercing plea, came from somewhere nearby. "Spendler! My God, is it you? Help me!" Laura Whitney screamed, crying out in distress.

"Mrs. Whitney!" Spendler cried out. "Where are you?"

And just as suddenly the voice was gone and the mocking laughter of their host crashed against their eardrums.

"Taunting, isn't it, Spendler? But there is no help. You and your priest friend are out of your league. You seek to know things that are beyond your grasp."

"What have you done with Mrs. Whitney?" Gerry Stuart said.

"She is my companion," Elymas said. "The Lancaster woman, the medium who sought answers, opened the door for me. It was she who gave me the way this one time. But surely you know that."

"We are aware of Vera Lancaster and who she was," Spendler said. "Is Mrs. Whitney a prisoner? Are you her captor? Wasn't that her voice crying out to me?"

"Questions," Elymas answered, seemingly annoyed. "Always with questions. I am surprised, Spendler. You and the priest are the supposed purveyors of truth and you do not know truth when it is before you. Do you not know upon whom you gaze? You seek truth, men of wisdom. Seek and ye shall find."

By now Gerry Stuart was truly frightened. Fear blinded his judgment and he reacted without thought. He screamed at the creature, his words flooded with rage.

"I know you, if you are Elymas," Gerry cried out, his voice crackling with apprehension. "I know who you are, consort of Satan. Satan's henchman, Elymas. You belong in hell along with your lord and master. You are the paradigm of evil." He turned to Spendler. "My God, Carl, he's not just a spirit! We are dealing with a demon from hell!"

The demon laughed. "You flatter me, priest. Take a good look. See if you do not recognize the truth when you see it with your own eyes."

"This is madness, Carl!" Gerry said. "This cannot be!"

The features of the demon became blurred and were changing. Gerry Stuart seemed dumbfounded, struck in awe. His eyes were bulging and his jaw dropped open. His face contorted into utter disbelief. He reached into his breast pocket and withdrew a crucifix that he held aloft.

"In the name of Christ, Son of God, I command you to depart," Gerry Stuart chanted. "In the name of The Father, The Son and The Holy Spirit I command you to leave and return to the hell from where you came. By all that is holy I demand that you..."

A ringing laughter echoed through the room, cutting Gerry off. Spendler reached out and clutched the priest by the arm.

"Take it easy, Gerry," he said. "Get a grip on yourself. It's an illusion. He's tricking you."

Gerry turned violently to his friend. "Are you mad?" he cried. "Can't you see? Don't you see what he's done? Look at his face."

Spendler looked to where Gerry pointed with the crucifix. He saw only the strange visage of the demon.

"Gerry, don't believe what you see!" Spendler implored.

"My God, Carl! It's my face! It's me! Look at it Carl!" Gerry Stuart demanded. "He wants to kill me. Can't you see that?"

He thrust the crucifix before him as far as his arm would extend as if the act could keep the evil away.

"Burn in hell, where you belong!" he cried out. "I cast out this devil...in the name of..."

Suddenly Gerry dropped to his knees. He began to choke. The crucifix fell from his hand and clattered to the floor. He reached out to Spendler with one outstretched hand while the other ripped at his chest.

"Carl!" he implored. "Help me!" He held out both hands before him in disbelief. Blood dripped from his palms. He glanced down at his shirt that had developed a massive dark red stain.

"Stigmata!" Gerry cried in disbelief. "I have Christ's wounds!"

He sobbed, his body bowed forward as he wept, both hands clutching his head. Spendler moved to him and placed his hand on his friend's shoulder.

"Easy, Gerry," he said, empathy in his voice, even though he clearly saw the blood. "Calm down. The wounds are not real. He's playing with our minds."

Gerry Stuart continued to sob. The blood ran from his hands over his face. Spendler bent and lifted the crucifix lying on the floor. He rose and turned to face his nemesis.

"I knew it would come to this," he said calmly to the demon. "You and me."

Elymas laughed and spoke again. "Of course! It's our destiny.

You were born to confront me. It's as old as history itself. Cain and Abel, David and Goliath, Paul and Elymas, Faust and Mephisto, Valjean and Javier, Ahab and his white wHayle, Churchill and Hitler. And now, you and me! Don't you love it, Spendler? Haven't you been waiting all your life for this moment?"

Spendler knew his adversary was evil incarnate. There was unbound power within this creature. Hadn't Roger Evans died as a result of its nature? Gerry Stuart might soon be another victim. And worst yet, what was the fate of Laura Whitney? Where exactly was she right now?

"What is it you seek?" Spendler asked.

"What do I seek, Spendler, you ask? I seek not, ghost hunter. I am who I am. I am eternity. I am the truth you desire," the demon replied. "I am of the ages. I am Laura Whitney. I am your companion priest. I am you, Spendler. You are the forest. I am the falling tree. You hear me fall because you are here. Was it not you who said without the mind's perception there can be no supernatural in the natural order of the universe? I am only the content of men's hearts and minds. I exist within all mankind. I am original sin."

"Bullshit!" Spendler fired back. "Gerry is right. You come from the depths of hell where you belong. You are an accident."

"Not an accident, Spendler. I am the balance within mankind. I keep things even. I deplete the surface population of the planet by arousing the malevolent side of man. The task is simple. Man is intrinsically evil. I exist to enhance that side of humanity. Without emissaries like me there might not be as much hatred, war, murder. Without me there might be only the sickening, mortifying stench of love."

"You are an abomination!" Spendler shouted. "You're an aberration of the greatest proportion."

"Do not anger me!" the demon bellowed. "My wrath is fearful. The Master endows me with power to dominate mortals. I should destroy all of you. Your friend there will die anyhow. He is a weak man who wants to die. It is inevitable."

"And me," Spendler said. "Am I to die?"

"Whatever is in your heart. You cannot deny what is so."

Spendler switched off his recorder and jammed it into his

backpack. He reached down, hooked a hand under Gerry's arm and lifted him to his feet. He had to act quickly. First, get Gerry away from this place and come back for Laura Whitney.

"Come on, Gerry," he said softly. "We've got to fight this bastard. We've got to help Laura Whitney."

Gerry stumbled and followed Spendler's lead. The imaginary blood on his body had vanished as Elymas directed his attention to Spendler.

"Carl," Gerry whispered weakly to Spendler, "he says he's Elymas. Then he should be blind!"

"What?"

"He must be blind if he claims to be Elymas. Saint Paul rendered Elymas blind through the power of God, whom he had on his side."

Spendler lifted the flashlight out of his knapsack with his free hand and aimed the light in the direction of Elymas. He directed the beam directly at the demon's eyes. The demon did not react to the light, but merely stared straight ahead. He was not looking at the two men and he did not blink.

"You're right, Gerry," Spendler whispered. "He is blind. He didn't even flinch when I threw the light directly in his eyes."

Spendler turned away from his foe and struggled with Gerry to get out of the room. Gerry had his arm over Spendler's shoulder and together they stumbled toward the door.

Suddenly the booming tones of the demon resonated through the temple. "Turn back to me, Spendler," Elymas said. "You think me blind. But that is not the case. I can see you well. Many incarnations ago I did not have eyes. That was then. Now I have eyes to see. I have brain to think. But do you see me as I am? Gaze upon me, Spendler. You nullify fear. Then see me not as adversarial. See me as I can be. Shine your light on the truth!"

The face transformed as Spendler watched. The features were changing from their original shape into something new and different.

"Good God!" Spendler swore as he recognized what was happening.

"Hardly!" the demonic voice mocked Spendler's outburst.

Now Spendler was looking at his own face. The demon had assumed Spendler's features.

The voice that spoke was mocking. "You see how easy it is, Spendler. I implore you, do not forsake me. Join His minions and me. There are things you can only dream of that can be yours. The world will open to you. A world you never imagined. Come with me. Give in."

Chapter 37

The tide was rising. Frank Whitney knew he faced death either by drowning or by hypothermia, depending on how quickly the tide came in or how cold the water got. Not a fair choice either way. No matter what, tied to the piling as he was, death was imminent.

What a rotten way to die, he thought; bound hand and foot to a piling watching the ocean rise. Nothing I can do. Try moving my hands. Maybe I can squeeze them free of my bonds. No good, dammit. I'm just hurting myself. Maybe my feet. Try, Whitney. Come on. You're a strong guy. You can do this. Push up. That's it. Get your shoes against the pole and push. Maybe if I got a foot free I can loosen the ropes. Maybe they're connected and this will give me some slack around the wrists.

Damn! My shoe came off! More bad luck. No. Wait. I can slip my foot out. I can feel it coming loose. Some slack. Come on. Give me some slack at the wrists.

No. It won't work. My legs are tied separately from my chest and arms. I'm screwed. I can't break free in time before the ocean drowns me.

Frank gave one more attempt at crying out. Maybe someone could hear him.

"HELP!" he cried over and over.

Out in the ocean, too far to be heard, sailboats passed. Power boats buzzed by, too quick and too far to see or hear him.

He was doomed and he knew it.

The knowledge of one's impending, inevitable death is a terrible thing to confront. Panic sets in. The mind races and enhances the action. He ranted at himself...control. Keep control. There has to be a way out.

From behind him came a chill wind. He sensed something unusual, but couldn't define it. He turned, as best he could, towards the beach area. There was a misty shape standing on the beach. The strange apparition hovered above the beach, not quite touching the sand. The shape was obviously identifiable as female.

The surrounding veil of mist cleared and facial features became distinct.

The eyes were bright and seemed to possess a brilliant light, which shone from them. Then...Frank realized the vision before him had no eyes. It seemed that a light blazed through the two holes in her face where eyes had been.

And then she was gone; dissolved in the slight wind and was no more.

What the hell was that, Frank wondered. And suddenly he knew. He knew in that instant that all the misgivings he held about the medium were mistaken. Laura was right. He knew he had just seen the spirit of Vera Lancaster.

* * *

After Jenny Douglas hit Frank Whitney with the wrench, Johnnie Limbo wiped his bloody face and shoved her down the stairs into the cabin. He snapped the lock shut, closing her in.

"Stay in there," he shouted, "until I finish this guy."

She heard the motor kick over and felt the boat swerve into motion. Johnnie is going out to sea. He'll kill Frank. Drop him over the side. Oh, God, she thought, what have I done?

But soon the motor stopped and the anchor dropped. Where were they, she wondered? Had they gone far enough from shore not be seen?

Jenny looked out the cabin window. Surprisingly, the Lancaster house on the hill was in full view. They had drawn closer to land. Below, at the shoreline, a small white cabin cruiser was tied up at the Lancaster Island dock. She heard activity on the deck above her and within minutes the inflatable rubber craft buzzed into motion and sped by the window heading towards land.

There were two men on the dock waiting for Johnnie Limbo to arrive. She recognized Elymas but the other was a stranger. They unloaded Frank Whitney, who was bound with rope and appeared to be still unconscious. The boat docked at the ramp and the men talked for a moment. Then two went into the water, bringing the still unconscious Frank Whitney with them as Elymas watched. The men carefully tied Frank to a piling. Within minutes they were done. Then they got out of the water and went their separate ways.

While the unidentified man drove off, Johnnie hopped in the rubber craft and came back towards the sailboat. Elymas remained on the landing, staring directly at her. It seemed as if he saw through the hull of the vessel and was able to probe her vision. Jesus, she thought, how creepy can you get? The diabolical bastards; they were going to let Frank drown while he was tied to the dock.

Johnnie Limbo boarded the sailboat and unlocked the hatch.

"What's happening?" Jenny asked. "What was all that on the dock?"

"None of your damn business," Johnnie said as he entered the cabin. "Now get undressed. I'm horny."

"What'll I do with this bottle of brandy?" Jenny asked, holding the unopened bottle in front of her.

"Open it. I'm thirsty," said Johnnie.

As he stepped past her Jenny swung the bottle with both hands at Johnnie's head. She caught him behind the right ear with her entire body behind a forceful wallop that knocked him to the floor. But he was not out. He began to get up when she delivered the second shot that rendered him lifeless.

Was Johnny Limbo dead? She bent over his body to see if she had killed him. She didn't see his left arm move slowly toward her. She sensed movement and pulled away. The arm dropped back and Limbo was unconscious but alive, barely.

Whacking guys is getting to be a habit with me, she thought.

She quickly jumped into the inflatable motor craft tied at the stern, got it started, and steered towards shore.

* * *

Frank Whitney could not believe his eyes. A sailboat—it looked like the one Jenny Douglas had climbed aboard earlier today—was anchored about as close as it could get to the rocky shore. Its keel prevented it from getting into even more shallow water. It was a few hundred yards from where he was tied. In a few minutes an inflatable rubber powerboat came into view. The small craft drove directly towards the dock to which he was lashed. It bounced along on the shallow waves, growing larger in his view. There was a figure at the motor steering the craft but he could not make out the features.

Closer and closer it came. Finally, the pilot's face was large enough to identify. He couldn't believe what he saw. Jenny Douglas was steering the boat.

Damn! he thought, as the waves lapped at his chin, now what?

The powerboat drove past him at the foremost piling, stopped as Jenny got out and lashed the boat to the dock. She sped down the ramp close to where Frank was tied

"Thank God!" she exclaimed. "I'm in time!"

She took off her shoes and dove into the water. She surfaced in front of Frank and treaded water.

"How are you holding up?" she asked him.

"Jenny," Frank said. "What the hell is going on?"

"I'm sorry for what happened Frank," she said. "I'll get you out of this."

Jenny held a steak knife, lifted from the kitchen on Elymas' boat, in her right hand as she tread water. She dove down and within a few minutes and a few dives his legs were free. Frank thought about Jenny and Laura while Jenny worked on setting him loose. The girls were both champion swimmers and in high school were on swim teams. She came up for air again after three dives.

"Hang on, Frank," she panted. "Hang on!"

In a few minutes she was hacking at the bonds on his arms that would have sealed his fate.

Chapter 38

In a vision Laura saw Frank lashed to a piling on a dock, struggling to get free. She recognized the disaster about to happen. The tide was slowly coming in and would soon drown him. In her mind she screamed, knowing she was powerless to help and was only witnessing a vision of his dilemma. Was this happening now? Was Frank in danger at the moment she saw him? How did her eyes see what was not in front of her? Of course, she thought, they are Vera Lancaster's eyes.

She awoke with a start, coming out of her stupor, disturbed by voices coming through the obscurity of her mind. Male voices, arguing? Challenging each other? She couldn't determine who was talking. Frank! No. Not Frank.

Where was she?

Her body moved, responding to commands from her brain. She was lying flat on a cold, hard bed. No, not a bed. It was a hard wood surface. A floor. Where was she? What was she doing here? She moved her arms under her body and lifted herself. Was she still in Vera Lancaster's house? Yes, of course. She remembered now. The demon had bent her mind to his will. She remembered the pain. And then, suddenly, he had relinquished his hold on her.

Frank. What of Frank? Where was he? Was he in immediate danger of drowning? The vision she had seen eclipsed all other thoughts. The scene returned in an instant. Frank was alive. But he was in desperate trouble. She was sure of it. She must find him immediately.

She got to her feet. In the darkness she began to see shapes. She knew immediately where she was; in Vera's temple behind her alter. She staggered toward the figures. There were two men, vaguely outlined, standing a distance of about a dozen feet from the alabaster altar.

One of the men snapped on a flashlight and swung it in her direction. The beam settled on another form not far from her to her right. When she turned, as a natural reaction, she stifled a scream. The light revealed a third man dressed in black. Elymas? She

243

stumbled forward into the room as Elymas, who had assumed Carl Spendler's facial features, recognized her movement and turned to her.

"Well, what have we got here?" his voice snarled. "Could it be Laura Whitney emerging from a shell?"

She was puzzled. The man in black was speaking to her. Who was he? His face and body were flooded with the light from the flashlight. Then she recognized him.

"You are...Carl Spendler...aren't you?" she managed to say.

"Certainly, as you say," the voice of Elymas answered frivolously.

Suddenly a new voice from the source of the flashlight beam echoed in the room.

"Don't listen to him, Mrs. Whitney! Over here. I am Spendler!"

Laura held her hand over her eyes to shield them from the glare of the flashlight. Spendler turned the light on his face. Laura recognized him. But who was the other man with Spendler's face?

"Don't listen to him," Spendler repeated. "He is Elymas, the fiend. Come here to me."

Of course, she thought. The first man was garbed entirely in black, exactly as she remembered Elymas. "Yes," Laura said to the man holding the flashlight. "I understand. You are Spendler."

She got her balance and walked shakily towards Carl Spendler and Gerry Stuart.

"Yes," she said confidently. "I know it is you."

The demon was infuriated.

"Stop!" Elymas shouted. "You are mine! You may not leave!"

Laura was obstinate. "You cannot stop me!" she retorted. "I am going to my husband."

"You are mine," the demon said. "I will take your eyes if you go with Spendler!"

Laura was aghast. This creature was making claim to God's domain.

"Then take them, you bastard!" she cried out. "Nothing is more important to me than the life of my husband. Take my damned eyes and be done with it once and for all! I will pluck them out for you. I can live without them!"

She turned and hurried toward the two men. Gerry Stuart had regained control and was standing erect next to Spendler. When

Laura reached them Spendler put his right arm around her shoulders and brought her to him. She sighed and welcomed his strength.

"Now it is three of you, is it?" Elymas said. "It fits. Barnabas, Paul and the 'thorn in his side'. Just like your flawed scriptures. It deters me not. I will defeat all. Three humans or a thousand cannot thwart the will of Elymas."

"And what is your will?" Gerry Stuart asked.

"You know well, priest. It is to defeat sanctity. As it must be."

"You will fail!" Gerry Stuart retorted. He turned to Spendler and said softly "Carl, the scriptures state that the sorcerer, Elymas, was a messenger who was used to spread the word of Satan throughout the world. He preyed on weakness. Paul's 'thorn in the side' was the affliction he bore with the devil always being with him. The truth that Paul used to defeat Elymas was exactly what this demon thought was his own strength. He believed Paul could be defeated because he was weak. But it was this fact that was effective against the demon. Weakness was the very thing that delivered the power of God. God recognized Paul's weakness and Elymas was rendered blind because God was on the side of the meek. Our weapon against him is to defy."

"What should we do, Gerry?" Spendler asked.

"Turn your back on him and walk right out," Gerry answered. "Treat him as powerless and unimportant. Deny him. He grows strong by preying on weakness."

"Will you continue to defy me, Spendler, knowing the consequences?" Elymas demanded.

Gerry Stuart took a deep breath and, in the loudest voice he could muster, he roared, "There are no consequences! There is nothing you can do to stop us. We deny you. You are a figment of the imagination. You are the tree falling in the forest. You exist because we allow you to exist. You are nothing but the embodiment of fear. Without fear you have nothing. No control. You don't matter! You are irrelevant! Return to hell where you belong!"

"Damn you, priest," bellowed Elymas. "You know too much. But you underestimate me. Beware!"

The trio turned away from the demon and moved toward the sliding entrance doors. Elymas raised his right hand and pointed at them. Suddenly the doors slammed shut with a nerve-shattering whack. As he prepared to wreak havoc, he stopped instantly. His eyes grew wide as his head turned to the distraction that had appeared to his right. A figure had suddenly appeared in the room. It was a glowing, angelic woman who floated as if on wings across the space between Elymas and the group at the door who had turned back to face the demon.

"What is it?" Laura asked Spendler. "What's happened?"

"I don't know," Spendler said. "But it looks like he's spooked."

It was then that Laura saw Vera Lancaster's spirit.

"It's her. Vera Lancaster. She's here," Laura said.

"Where?" asked Gerry Stuart. "I don't see her."

"Nor I," said Spendler.

"Believe me," Laura reiterated. "She's here."

Elymas cringed and backed away from the group, fading into the dark shadows on the other side of the tabernacle. His voice rattled in the dark. "The first hand is yours, ghost hunter. This may be 'check' but it is not 'checkmate.' I grant you, Spendler, we will meet again."

* * *

Carl Spendler and Gerry Stuart successfully marched out of Vera Lancaster's house. They were astonished that the ploy they used might have worked. But Laura knew it was Vera Lancaster's appearance that had put Elymas down. Spendler and the priest turned their backs on him and walked away, dismissing him as so much driftwood, taking Laura Whitney with them.

Outside the building Spendler turned to Gerry Stuart and said, "What the hell was that all about?"

"Come quickly," Laura urged. "We've got to find Frank. He's in trouble. I know it. Below, on the dock."

Laura scurried past the two men, down the long flight of steps leading to the dock. Spendler and Gerry Stuart followed her. They got to the dock simultaneously, all three converging on the desperate situation at hand with an exhausted Jenny Douglas diving to free Frank Whitney.

As soon as Laura saw Frank's dilemma she dove into the water besides her friend. She emerged almost in direct contact with Jenny.

"Jenny," she beamed, "where did you come from?"

"Oh, Laura, thank God you're here." Jenny hugged her friend in the water. "I'm exhausted," she said.

The water was already over Frank's mouth. He stretched his neck out at far as he could to gulp air. He had begun to drown.

Laura took the knife from Jenny and dove underwater behind him. She hacked through the ropes around his chest while Jenny worked on those binding his hands. Someone hit the water beside the women as they came up for air. Gerry Stuart had jumped into the water in front of Frank Whitney. He held Frank's head out of the water as he gasped for air.

"Hurry," Gerry Stuart cried. "I can't hold him out of the water much longer."

Jenny was having trouble getting the ropes untied around Frank's hands. Finally Laura gulped air, submerged and cut him free.

Laura broke the surface. "He's free!" she cried, gasping for air. "Pull him up!"

The three struggled and dragged him to the landing ramp. Gerry tried desperately to revive Frank who was beginning to show signs of revival. Once inside the house Frank was on his feet and breathing normally.

He surveyed the people surrounding him. "What the hell! Sure looks like a party to me," he said, smiling.

Chapter 39

At their colonial house in Northcove, Long Island, Ralph Douglas and his two children waited impatiently in the doorway. Jenny had called from Maine that she was alive and well and coming home.

After suffering through the dreadful morning hours a taxicab finally arrived at the driveway and Jenny stepped out, no baggage in hand. The children and Ralph Douglas rushed to her, wrapped her with overdue affection and embraces.

A return to normalcy and the promise of happiness renewed their lives. Arms around each other, they entered the house and snapped the front door shut against the assault of evil.

* * *

One week later, in New York City, Frank and Laura attempted to revive the routine of their interrupted life. Both breathed deep sighs of relief and pressed on. Laura went back to the life she loved while Frank resumed work at the ad agency. He hoped Laura was finished with her obsession. She apparently turned her back on what had transpired.

All seemed normal...for the time being.

* * *

Frank showered and threw on a bathrobe. It was nine PM on a Monday night in New York City and just in time for a football game on TV. Laura was having a late dinner and meeting in town with Charles Collins, the new owner of TheArtGallery where her work was still exhibited. He sat in the dark room, his mind pondering the episode in Maine. He wondered how the results of the confrontation with the madman, Elymas, would play out in the long run. He believed there was more to come and it was not going to be pleasant. He had at least succeeded in getting Laura away from that woman's house. She was his beloved Laura again. Now the prospect remained of what to do with the old house. Sell it? Rent it?

He heard a sound from outside the front door. He raised his head and glanced in that direction. It was a soft noise, like someone tinkering with the lock. Was Laura home already? He got up, lowered the TV sound and listened.

"Laura," he called out, expecting the door to open and reveal his wife. "Is that you?"

No answer. "Laura!" Louder.

Still no response.

"God damn it!" he swore. Someone had made noise on the other side of the door. He definitely heard movement. There was someone in the hallway.

The door was closed and locked, but under the seam at the floor, a dark fog-like mist drifted in. He felt a jolt of momentary panic. A fire!

Frank closed his robe and moved forward. Got to get out of here, he thought. Don't want to be trapped in a fire. What to do? Fling the door open and burst through the flames? No. That merely invites the fire into the apartment. He had heard that if you wet towels and stuff the along the seam at the base of the door it would help curtail the flames until help arrived. He started for the bathroom.

Suddenly the door burst open with a fury. It swung wide and collided loudly with the foyer wall.

The mist was dark, almost black. It spread through the doorway into the apartment. In the body of the mist, a shape began to form. It was a man draped in black. The fog surrounded and clung to him. The face was familiar. It became clear.

"What the hell!" Frank exclaimed. "What is going on here?"

He recognized Elymas immediately.

"Goddamn! You again? I thought we'd rid ourselves of you."

The figure moved into the room, bringing the mist along with such force that Frank could hear its movement. A chill swept through Frank's body as he realized just who and what this madman was.

"Your time has come," Elymas spoke in grim finality.

"Fuck you!" Frank exclaimed. The face of the demon was a cruel, fierce glare, masked in a grotesque distortion, which defiled reason.

"You think of yourself as a fighter, a boxer," Elymas said. "How do you think you'd match up against me?"

Frank whipped the robe off and flung it across the room.

"You're toast, you bastard," he said calmly.

The fog dissipated until it had completely vanished. Frank stepped closer to Elymas with his guard up. Elymas held up his left hand, palm outward, and halted Frank's approach. He then removed his jacket and shirt, revealing the suddenly sculpted muscular body of a heavyweight boxer; nothing at all like the appearance he presented a moment ago.

Frank raised his clenched fists and struck out at the figure before him, tossing thumping shots that would have felled a normal man in an instant. It was as if his fists fell on air.

The demon fighter struck a one-two combination landing with ferocious force on Frank's chest that threw him across the room. He smashed into a wall, hitting with such force that he shattered the plaster surface.

"Come on, boxer," Elymas taunted, "get up. I thought you could fight."

Frank gasped for air as he got to his feet. What the hell! Frank thought. What's happening here? I never expected this. Got to be careful. First get my wind back. Got to outbox this bastard. Think of him as just another opponent. You fought better than him. Then fight. Dodge. Weave. Jab.

Elymas charged, throwing a powerhouse blow at Frank's chest. Frank dodged by moving to his right and chopped a right cross to Elymas' cheek.

The demon squared off again, facing Frank at a distance this time. "Let us continue," he said. "This time I will not underestimate you."

He let Frank take the lead as a double left jab ripped his right eye. Elymas lifted his right hand to rub the eye and in that instant Frank delivered a right cross that drove his opponent back. Elymas stumbled, almost tripping over a chair.

Surprise brought a grin to the demon's face. "Well, what do you know," he said. "The mortal can fight. But now it is time to pay the piper, so to say."

The demon moved on Frank with sudden blinding speed and strength that it became impossible to retaliate before he was struck repeatedly. It seemed as if he were a child sparring with the greatest heavyweight champion of all time. In minutes his face was a mash of battered tissue. Blood clogged his eyes and it was impossible to see. He was hit so many times he was unconscious before his body landed prostrate on the hardwood floor.

Elymas looked down scornfully at the fallen victim. "You live by the sword, you die by the sword," he said mockingly.

He donned his shirt, carefully adjusted his tie and jacket and left apartment.

* * *

In a New York hospital Frank Whitney lay in a coma. His body functions were normal but he remained comatose. It was as if some power controlled his body and trapped his mind in a void.

Laura spent every moment at Frank's bedside clutching his hand, brushing his brow and whispering in his ear. The swelling in his bruised face had subsided considerably in the days he lay in coma but the stitches had an unworldly appearance.

Laura had faith that he would fully recover. She prayed to God every day that his brain had not been damaged. Only righteousness seemed the proper route to counteract this force that kept him in oblivion.

And yet nothing came of the prayers. Frank remained in a coma. Prayer to an uninterested God seemed useless. God did nothing. The advanced technology of modern medicine could do nothing. What could she do?

She sat in the hospital room staring at Frank's lifeless body. She rested her brow on the heel of her hand, her fingers digging into her hair, and cursed aloud.

"Damn you, Elymas. Damn you for all eternity," she cried. "I know you did this. May you suffer forever."

Her head sunk into her hands and she sobbed freely. When she gained control of her emotions she thought that if the demon put Frank in this condition he probably was the source to end it. Put an end to him, then. How?

Vera Lancaster had been the catalyst to summon the creature into existence. His presence was of her doing; the medium, the dead medium. Was she the answer? Was the cause of this dilemma also the solution? If God will not answer my prayers maybe the dead will.

* * *

In New York Father Gerry Stuart heard the last of the confessions for the evening. It was close to nine PM when he was done. He left the confessional and glanced around. He could see no one in the church. As far as he was concerned confessions were finished for the evening.

He walked to the altar and genuflected before the host. It was then he heard the massive oak door in the front of the church creak open. When he turned he saw a lone dark figure standing in the archway at the front of the church. A late confessor, he thought.

"Are you here for confession?" he called out. "I'm just finished for the day." He motioned toward the confessional booth he had just left.

The figure didn't answer. There was something familiar there. It was difficult to make out the face in the subdued light at thirty yards. Yet...

Mother of God!

It was Elymas! Surely it was!

"What do you want in the house of God?" Gerry cried out, his voice echoing in the huge space. "You don't belong here."

In the dim light Gerry saw the glaring red eyes, which seemed twice their normal size. Suddenly the voice rang out in deep, reverberating resonance, cracking the silence like a slice of lightning.

"The hell you say, priest!" replied Elymas. "What do you know of it?"

"I know that you are the symbol of evil," Gerry Stuart insisted. "I know you are a demon of hell. I know you are an anathema in the house of God!"

"You really are a child, priest," Elymas snapped. "You know nothing. You and your horde do not get it, do you? Perhaps you never will. Let me put it to you bluntly so you will understand, once and forever. There is no hell. And no heaven. God, The Master, rules all. Good and evil reign equally."

Gerry was aghast.

"You lie!" he cried. "God rewards the good in mankind with Heaven. Hell punishes the evil. There is life after death. Damn you! You lie!"

"No, priest. I do not lie. There is but one Master, over all. He, Who created good, dually created evil and endowed mankind with both. If there exists the promulgation of good in mankind there must equally be the same for evil. It is the nature of the human creature. One force exists, parallel to the other. And beyond...for you there is no beyond. Only a beginning and an end. Do I make myself clear?"

"God damn you!" Gerry raised his eyes to the ceiling searching for an answer. "Why do you lie? What do you want of me?" he screamed.

"I am here, priest," Elymas roared, "to finish what you started."

"What in hell..." Gerry blurted out.

"Did you and Spendler think it was finished because you deemed to walk away?" Elymas roared. "It ends at my discretion. Play with fire and you will get burned."

The demon raised his right arm and pointed upward. Behind Gerry, hung a life-size, plain wooden cross without the Christ figure. It was suspended by cable from the cathedral ceiling ten feet above the altar and was located directly at the center of the main aisle.

A sudden driving gale force of wind lifted Gerry from the floor, catapulting him in the air, hurling him against the hard surface of the suspended cross. His back and outstretched arms were pinned against the surface of the cross by an overwhelming force that kept him immobile.

Then came the unimaginable. Horrendous iron spikes slammed into each of his wrists fracturing flesh and bone and impelling him to the cross. The pain was repeated as more spikes drove through both feet. The final damning skewer crashed into his chest, bursting his heart.

Father Gerry Stuart had been crucified.

Elymas lowered his right hand, turned and walked from the church.

"Did I just hear the fat lady sing?" muttered the lover of clichés.

253

Mike Walsh

* * *

It was not over. Spendler knew he would have to face Elymas again in the future and destroy the demon conclusively; drive him back to hell where he belonged.

But Spendler didn't expect the confrontation so soon.

He caught a cab cross-town to St. Luke's Church to confer with Gerry Stuart and was surprised to see a large crowd of pedestrians gathered around the church. As he approached the entrance, two police cars and an ambulance blocked the way. He approached a police officer in the street.

"What's going on?" he asked.

"Move on," the officer informed him.

"I'm here to see a friend. A priest," Spendler said, his voice ringing with apprehension. "Can I get through?"

"Just a minute," the officer said. He motioned to a man in civilian clothes. The man left the personnel he was with and came to Spendler.

"This man wants to see a priest in the church," the uniformed officer said.

"I'm Detective Malloy," the plainclothes officer said. "Who are you looking for?"

"I'm a friend of Father Stuart," Spendler said. "Gerry Stuart. What's happened here?" There was a fearful suspicion in his voice that implied that something was seriously wrong.

The detective rubbed his chin pensively. "What is your name, sir?"

"Carl Spendler. Tell me what's happened?"

"I've got bad news for you, Mr. Spendler. Father Stuart is dead."

"Dead?" Spendler was stunned. His legs trembled as he quickly felt faint.

"He's apparently been murdered," the detective said. "But it's the damndest, most bizarre crime I've ever seen. No one can explain how it happened."

"May I see him?" Spendler asked.

Detective Malloy escorted Spendler into the church. "This isn't a pleasant sight," he said. "You'd better brace yourself." He pointed to the huge cross above the altar. Firemen were in the

254

process of setting up ladders to get Gerry Stuart's body down from its location. The dripping blood from the lifeless body stained the altar below.

"Mother of God!" Spendler exclaimed. "How did this happen?"

"That's what we'd like to know," Detective Malloy said.

Spendler stared at the pathetic figure nailed to the cross. His eyes welled with tears. Poor Gerry, he thought. The bastard, Elymas, got him.

"How do you explain something as strange as this?" Detective Malloy asked.

"You don't," Spendler said simply. But he actually did know how to explain Gerry's bizarre death. He knew for sure.

* * *

When she heard of Gerry Stuart's death Laura knew immediately who had murdered him. In her remorse, as she sat by Frank's bedside, she now believed all the deadly incidents in the past year were caused by Elymas.

Why did Elymas destroy people involved in my life but never me? She wondered. The list was long, always people close to me. Was he trying to harm me by ridding me of all protection; and for what ultimate reason? To isolate me, to shatter my mental stability? Why not just kill me?

Was he simply afraid of me? Could that be it? Why was he afraid of me? He was about to attack all three; Spendler, Father Stuart and me, at Vera Lancaster's house, but he stopped. Why?

The reason suddenly become overwhelmingly obvious...Vera Lancaster's spirit had made an appearance. She protected me. Was he afraid of her spirit? Was it from heaven, filled with goodness, in contradiction to the essence of Elymas?

This monster must be destroyed, she thought. But how? She could not accomplish such a task alone. She needed all the help she could muster. She started by calling Carl Spendler.

"Mr. Spendler," she declared. "Elymas did this to Father Stuart, didn't he?"

"Yes, I believe it had to be him," Spendler replied. "Who else would have killed Gerry in such a fiendish manner? It was the demon's doing. I'm certain."

"Oh God," Laura said, her voice teeming with emotion. "My husband lies in a hospital on the edge of death in a coma and this monster put him there. And I believe he's keeping him there. He must be stopped."

Spendler was uncertain of what to say. Only a few weeks had passed since he and Gerry Stuart had returned to New York. Frank was hanging on the edge of life while Gerry Stuart was murdered.

"I'm not sure how to fight him," Laura said. "But I feel the only approach left to me is supernatural."

"What do you mean?"

"We can't beat him on a personal, physical level," she said. "I propose an attempt to beckon the spirit of Vera Lancaster to help us."

"You're serious, aren't you?"

"Certainly. I believe he fears her. I think that through her we can destroy this devil's hold on us. She has visited me before. She has been trying to reach me all through this ordeal."

"If he fears her why would he respond to her?" Spendler said.

"I don't know," Laura answered. "I believe it might work. Why did he show up in Maine while Frank and I were there? Perhaps he is enamored of his own ability; caught up in his ego. Perhaps, by us going back there he might think we are challenging him and dismissing his power. Something along the line of what happened already. Perhaps he might come because we have, in essence, hurled down the gauntlet."

Spendler pondered the concept for a moment, then said, "I'm willing to help you any way I can. If you think this might work, let's give it a shot."

"Thank you," Laura said. "Will you join me in a séance, Mr. Spendler?"

"A séance?" Spendler sounded doubtful again.

"Yes. I believe we can eliminate the demon through the same manner that brought him to us. And by summoning Vera Lancaster we may have in her the catalyst to drive him away once and for all."

"Well, if nothing else, it's worth a try."

"I can't see any other way to fight him except through spiritualism," Laura said with finality.

Chapter 40

Now for the next step, Laura thought. With Carl Spendler beside me I stand a fighting chance. The name she had on a notepad in front of her was Martha Fuller. She dialed her.

"Martha Fuller?" Laura asked of the woman on the other end of the line.

"Yes."

"This is Laura Whitney. I am at Vera Lancaster's house," she reminded her.

"Yes, of course," Martha Fuller said. "What can I do for you?"

Laura explained again the series of events at Lancaster Island including the appearance of Elymas. She gave the reason she and Carl Spendler had returned.

"And who is this person, this Elymas?" Martha Fuller asked, a slight tremor in her voice. Did she already know him? Laura thought.

"I believe he is an evil spirit," Laura said. "You told me Vera might have reached a spirit at the last séance. I believe it may have been this demon Elymas."

Martha Fuller was silent for a long moment. That silence told Laura more than a full explanation might have. "Mrs. Whitney," Martha finally said, cautiously, in a hushed voice, as if someone else might hear—Laura imagined her checking over her shoulder to make sure there were no eavesdroppers—"at Vera's last séance there was some strange occurrence; a presence, a vision. I don't know what to call it. But I never told anyone. Poor Susan Gray. She collapsed into her own sheltered world and never spoke about what happened. But there was some mystical happening and the appearance of some kind of energy. I can still see it to this day."

"Can you describe it?" Laura asked.

"It wasn't a person. It was a mist in the air. I had seen this kind of phenomenon before. Ectoplasm, that type of thing. But this was different. It circled Vera's body and lifted her in the air. It formed itself into a substance, almost a body, and it hovered above us."

"Did it identify itself to you?"

257

"No. Not a word. But how could I forget? All hell broke loose. Susan was smashed into the wall. Chairs and table flew around the room. I often wondered and worried what had happened back then. What all of that really meant. What killed Vera? They said it was a heart attack. But something caused the attack. Trauma. And look at poor Susan. What happened to her? Is it possible...?"

"Yes," Laura responded. "I think that was Elymas's entry, his window to actuality. And I think this 'being' attached itself to Vera. And I, somehow, through my eyes perhaps, became connected to it."

"Who is Elymas? I haven't heard that name."

"I believe he or it is an evil entity. I believe he was somehow brought forth into Vera Lancaster's reality through that séance. I believe he is an evil entity and he alone caused her death."

"Then you must be in danger as well," Martha replied.

"I have accepted that," Laura acknowledged. "At first I was completely baffled by the strange occurrences in my life. Now I think I understand more of what has happened. I've come to believe the demon does not seek to destroy me."

"Why? What causes you to believe that?" asked Martha.

"In Vera's journal I discovered a passage, which stated that some spirits attach themselves to their conjurers. Perhaps that is what has happened to me. I think he might fear Vera's spirit through me. I suspect that her pure spirit is the antithesis of the evil he represents. But he seems bent on destroying people who are involved in my life."

"Why? What causes you to believe that?" asked Martha.

"I don't know. I've found no explanation that is rational. He has been destroying too many decent people. I must stop him. I must fight him. Perhaps drive him back from where he came. But I need help. If I can get a few people to help me I think we might succeed."

"What do you hope to accomplish?" Martha Fuller asked.

"I think we can reverse the result Vera achieved and demolish this villainous spirit," Laura stated. "Close the book on him the same way it was opened. I want to conduct a séance. I need anyone who worked with Vera, who knows the ritual. I want to rid the world of this monster and I think we can do it together. I am asking you to help me, Mrs. Fuller. I expect danger where Elymas is concerned. I won't deceive you. There have been a number of deaths that might be connected to this being. I want you to consider before responding."

"Of course I'll join you in your quest, Mrs. Whitney," Martha Fuller said enthusiastically without hesitation. "Vera would want me to help and I could not deny her."

* * *

Martha Fuller was enthralled with the idea of assisting Laura Whitney in a séance, whatever her motives. The idea that there was even the remote possibility that the spirit of her beloved Vera Lancaster could be reached thrilled her beyond comprehension. She was eager to get on with the process.

Bert Fuller came into the room. He smiled at her.

"What's cooking?" he said. "I understand you're going to help that Whitney woman in a séance to reach Vera Lancaster's ghost. I'd like to be a fly on the wall to witness that."

"How did you know about the séance?" she asked. "I never told you about it."

"Oh, I overheard it somehow," came the answer with a grin.

There was something odd about Bert since he came back, thought Martha. Although he swore he loved her and saw "the error of his ways," he just didn't seem sincere. Nonetheless, she accepted him whatever the reason. But she couldn't put her finger on the difference she felt. Whenever he got close to her and she looked into his eyes, there was a strange feeling of being with a person she did not know, whose thoughts were not as they once were. Had he changed so much during his brief departure?

"You don't need a fourth party at the séance, do you?" Bert asked.

"No, Bert. We do not," Martha said. "You were never interested before. Why the sudden change?"

"Oh, I don't know. If you can't beat them, join them, I always say."

Martha was genuinely puzzled by the quip. "Why did you use such terminology?" she asked. "Do you want to beat us?"

"Lighten up," Bert said. "It's a cliché. Everyone uses clichés, don't they?"

Martha turned away from his stare. Something was stirring within her, telling her Bert had seriously been changed by some collision in his psyche. She had been uneasy around him since his return but she now found it difficult to face him. Whatever had happened to him was disturbing to her.

He placed his hands roughly on both her shoulders and spun her around to face him. A sneer cracked his face. His expression was almost maniacal.

"What the hell is going on here?" she exclaimed, her body shaking with fear.

"It's time for you to meet my lord and master," said Bert Fuller. He stepped aside and Elymas stood before her. His black piercing eyes burning through her, leaving her weak.

"Good God!" Martha exclaimed. "Who are you?"

"Certainly not the name you just invoked," said Elymas. He moved swiftly, smothering Martha Fuller in a ferocious engulfing embrace that overwhelmingly absorbed her entirety.

* * *

Laura and Carl Spendler arrived in Seen By Chance in the evening and settled at the motel in town. Laura called Martha Fuller immediately upon their arrival.

"When can we start?" Martha asked Laura.

"I would like to start right away," Laura said. "But I think we should put in a little time smoothing out the rough spots. Do you know the ritual?"

"Yes, but I need a little brushing up, though," Martha answered, her eagerness obvious.

"By the way," Laura said. "I've got another person for the séance. His name is Carl Spendler."

"The parapsychologist?"

"Yes," Laura was startled that Martha Fuller had heard of Spendler. "You know who he is?" she asked, genuine surprise registering in her voice.

"Certainly. I've read some of his works. Vera spoke highly of him. He should be just the element we need to make it work. That makes three of us. A little weak but we should be alright."

"Where can we meet?" Laura asked.

"At my place," Martha Fuller said.

On the trip there, Laura spoke to Spendler. "I just hope this attempt works."

"We don't have many choices. This sounds best. The murdering brute must be stopped," Spendler asserted.

When they arrived at Martha Fuller's the woman ushered them inside and sat them in the living room.

"Do you think we can really summon Vera's spirit?" Martha asked as she brought them sandwiches.

"I have faith in her," Laura replied. "I think her spirit has been searching for me. She is trying to communicate. I believe she wants to be a catalyst to fight this fiend. I need to point her in the right direction. Together I think we will have enough energy to make this happen."

Martha Fuller smiled. "What if he is stronger than her and is able to defeat Vera?" she said.

Laura's curiosity was piqued. "What was she like, Martha?" she asked.

"How do you mean?"

"As a person. I read her diary," Laura had placed the journal that she had brought on the edge of the dining room table. She referred to it with a flick of her right hand. Martha Fuller's eyes followed the motion and stayed on the volume for an inordinate time. She did not touch it or attempt to pick it up.

"I know she had a lost love," Laura continued. "She was into black magic. I know she was psychic. But you knew her on a personal level."

"Not so. I never really knew her on a personal level," Martha Fuller vowed. "She was a very private person."

Laura was puzzled. "She never opened up to you, as close as you were?" she asked, thinking it strikingly odd that Martha, who grew up with Vera since childhood, did not know her friend personally. It didn't ring true. Laura compared her lifelong friendship with Jenny Douglas that was intimate enough for each to be privy to their most cherished secrets. "In her diary she remarked that you were her confidant. I would have thought..."

"Odd thing about Vera," Martha Fuller abruptly interrupted. "She kept her personal life very secretive. She talked about the spiritual world, about her clients, her upcoming experiments; but

Mike Walsh

not at all about her own life. You're one up on me. I never read her diary. But now that you have it here I would love to read it."

Again Laura thought this an oddity. The book was sitting on a shelf in the old house on Lancaster Island for anyone to take and read. If Martha Fuller wanted to read it she could have at any time.

"All right then," Spendler interjected. "From what you know of her what do you think our chances are?"

"In doing what, exactly?" Martha Fuller said.

"In winning," Spendler said, curbing his cynicism. He believed Martha Fuller was too innocuous to be useful. "You know, good guys against bad guys,"

"I believe we will prevail. After all, 'might is right'," she said, adding a cliché.

"By the way," Laura said as an adjunct to their conversation. "Where is your husband? Perhaps he would like to help us at the séance."

Martha Fuller laughed. "That rat! He ran off and left me months ago. He hated Vera Lancaster."

"But we saw him here only two weeks ago. You introduced him...Bert, you called him," Laura said. "We met him."

"Sure, he came crawling back," Martha Fuller said, fidgeting. "But he's not the same man he once was. No doubt about it."

* * *

Elymas was not visible in Vera Lancaster's house or anywhere on the grounds. The apprehension of facing the demon was allayed by his absence. The party moved through the house quickly and set up a table in the temple to accommodate their ritual.

Sunset enveloped the building like a great shroud and darkness whispered its foreboding presence. A white cloth was laid over the table. Around the room the group placed white candles in five-foot-high bronze candlesticks; material garnered from a storeroom in the basement of the house. They were ready to begin.

The three joined hands. Martha joined with Laura, she with Spendler, he completing the circle with Martha Fuller. Laura repeated over and over words the medium had scripted in her journal, imploring her to make her presence known. Laura intoned the name of God, Christ the Savior, and the spirit of Vera

262

Lancaster in that order, in the name of all that is holy and sacred.

Then, suddenly, Martha Fuller's hand broke from Laura's. Martha moved, knocking her chair backwards with a clatter. She stood up, fully erect, her arms outstretched. She clutched her head with both hands. Laura and Spendler recoiled in horror. Their hands parted and both stood gaping at the shocking occurrence before their eyes.

Then she began to physically change shape. Something adverse was taking place within Martha Fuller's body. She groaned and squirmed, as if in agony. She clutched her head with both hands to crush the unwelcome occurrence.

Laura and Spendler recoiled in horror. Their hands parted and both stood gaping at the metamorphosis occurring before their eyes.

In an instant Martha Fuller was no longer standing at the table. She leaped into the air above their heads. There, hung suspended in midair, was a misshapen, exaggerated portrait of unspeakable deformity. Nothing visible held her in this position. Her body had completely changed and had shed its clothing. Her form had grown larger.

Now the face was a grotesque mask, combining the features of humanity with the sharply defined characteristics of a cabalistic beast. The physiognomy was a misshapen, exaggerated portrait of unspeakable deformity. The eyes were hollow and glaring, making the creature before them seem soulless. The body was huge, the shoulders rounded and massive, covered with scale-like skin colored a deep gray. The hands and feet appeared to be huge gnarled claws. Stunted wings sprouted from the hunched back.

Suddenly the demon left his position and crawled around the walls of the room, defying gravity many feet above the floor.

"It's Elymas!" Carl Spendler shouted. "He's tricked us! It's not Martha Fuller! We are seeing him in his true form."

The demon lowered itself to the table. The fierce red eyes blazed. It reached out and slammed both hands down hard on the table. The long, red, pointed tongue darted from its mouth. A rasping voice bellowed in deep resonant tones from the bowels of hell.

"Ready to join Father Gerry, Spendler?"

Spendler rose to his feet. "Damn you!" he bravely cried. "You killed Gerry, you bastard!"

The demon laughed, "You can't stop me, Spendler. Why bother?"

Laura felt helpless. Had she failed? Could no one stop this diabolical fiend, she thought. His power is greater than ours. We are defeated and at his mercy. Why had we even tried? She thought of Frank in the hospital in New York. All is lost.

Then, suddenly, above them, highlighted by the candles, a cloud of white spectral mist formed and swirled in a corkscrew gyration, swiftly becoming substance. Hovering in the air, it took human shape; a woman, her hands outstretched before her, the palms upturned, beckoning. And Laura saw...

She knew...it was Vera Lancaster.

Her spirit appeared in full form. The face became defined. The ghost was angelic, dazzling in the light. Her countenance was unmistakable. A piercing, radiant light shone from the two hollowed-out cavities where once her eyes had been. The heavenly form moved swiftly. Her arms reached forward and enclosed Laura in embrace. The immaculate spirit flowed around Laura. Within seconds it dissolved and assimilated into her body, leaving behind, for a brief instant, a brilliant glow that lit the room.

Laura experienced a surge of energy flow through her arms and into her body. She was astonished. It was like an electric jolt. It had the sensation of a magnificent rapture that flooded her entire being, a concentrated center, an overall tingling of nerves. And then she felt, in her brain, a potent eruption of power that seized and took control of her movements. She was subjugated to the dominating force now within her.

Laura reached out and pointed both hands at the demon. From those precious fingers emanated an unseen force that rocked him.

Elymas recoiled. His massive body convulsed, twisting in obvious discomfort as he tried to escape the torment he felt. The celestial power plunged deeper into the grotesque body of the demon. Elymas cried out in agony, his arms and claws tearing his chest...to no avail. His efforts were no more effective than slashing at the air around him.

As the power of Vera Lancaster's spirit fully engulfed his body, the demon screamed, a blood-chilling wail that rocked the room. He slashed about the room ripping at his body, his long, apelike arms flailing wildly. He crashed into the tall candlesticks, knocking some against the white drapery. In an instant the flames gorged on the flammable silk and ravaged the hundred-year-old walls.

The demon was choking on the energy emanating from Laura. In his terror he backed into the spreading flames, still clutching his throat, trying in vain to stifle the panic he felt.

His massive body twisted in a wild pirouette and he was wrapped in falling, fiery drapery. He became ravaged by quickly spreading fire. Instantly, the entire mass of what was once the arrogant, defiant beast was engrossed in flames.

And suddenly, he was gone, leaving in its place, the charred corpse of Martha Fuller.

"Let's get the hell out of here!" Spendler yelled, grabbing Laura's arm. "This place is going to burn." He felt a sudden ebullience at the touch of her arm and glanced at her face. There was a glow to her that hadn't been there before. Could what he had witnessed be true? Had she absorbed the spirit of the dead medium and been granted an energy, a sense of the Elysian Fields? And then, as quickly, it was gone, over with.

Laura reached out and clutched Vera Lancaster's journal in her hands and tucked it under her arm.

Keeping low to the floor they scrambled to the doors as the flames raged behind them. Laura turned and glanced back.

Out of the wreckage the distinctive, ethereal mist that was the spirit of Vera Lancaster floated in the air amidst the raging fire. Her vaporous substance swirled into an angelic female shape and rose out of the flames. It glided upward, holding out both arms to Laura and vanished as mysteriously as it had come.

"What the hell happened back there?" Spendler said in a state of near shock.

"I don't know," Laura said. "I think she destroyed him. Vera Lancaster saved us."

"Where did Elymas go?" Spendler said.

"God only knows. Back to Hell I hope, where he belongs" was Laura's solemn answer.

* * *

265

Mike Walsh

Johnny Limbo watched the screeching fire engines roaring across the bridge to Lancaster Island. He sat at a bar in the center of town recovering from his still hurting head. The best medicine he found wasa few double bourbons.

"What the hell is going on?" he asked the bartender.

A patron who had just sat down next to him offered, "Big fire. The old Lancaster place. You know, the one on the island where that weird dame died."

"No shit!" Limbo exclaimed, smiling.

"Yeh," the patron said. "It's the truth. Say, why are you smiling?" he asked Limbo.

He turned to the patron. "I wasn't smiling," he said haughtily. "I was fucking laughing."

He got to his car, turned it over and headed out of town, back to civilization as he knew it.

Would he follow me, he thought. Would he run me down? Should I stay and face his wrath? He thought a moment longer and decided he would take his chances on his own, like he had all his life. Better off to be rid of him...but would it be like getting that monkey off my back once and for all?

Chapter 41

Frank Whitney still lay in a comatose state in a hospital bed. Laura sat by his bedside. She reached over and kissed his brow. A tear dropped from her eye and settled on his cheek.

She gently brushed away the teardrop and sat back in her chair. The passing minutes seemed like torturous hours as she continued her sojourn. She dozed, her head drooping forward, leaning upon arms that rested on Frank's legs.

And then, suddenly, the return of that magic moment she felt at Vera Lancaster's house occurred again. A surge of dynamism raged through her body. She became aglow internally with a force that was impossible to contain. She felt it once and now it was here again. Vera had blessed her and given her this gift, this strength that would not be denied.

She laid both hands on Frank's cheeks and held his face before her. She gently kissed one closed eye and then the other. A tear dropped from her eye and settled gently on his forehead.

"I love you dearly, my darling. Please come back to me," she said softly.

After a moment one of Frank's eyelids flinched and slowly opened. Then the other followed.

"Damn...I'm...thirsty," Frank uttered through thick tongue and dry lips, his voice weak and strained. "What round is it?"

Laura was startled by the raspy sound of his voice, that penetrated her fuzzy mind. She snapped upright from the chair and smothered him with her embrace and kisses.

"Frank," she whispered, her voice crackling with emotion. "Thank God, you're awake."

He answered weakly, "Laura...where am I?"

She lowered her head on his chest and sighed softly. "You're back, Frank. You've returned to me."

* * *

It was a hot, sunny morning in September as Carl Spendler ran through Central Park in New York City. He was on the tarmac heading south. He had just passed Sixty Seventh Street. It was Saturday and the wide thoroughfare was closed to vehicular traffic except for horse drawn carriages and pedestrians. People passed him in both directions. Some jogged, others zipped by on roller blades or bicycles. It was quite active for ten AM.

There were people all along the walkway that paralleled the boulevard, some sitting, some reading newspapers, others enjoying coffee, some merely observing the view.

For a fleeting instant Spendler thought he recognized someone. For a moment his heart leaped. It was a man dressed in black, leaning against a tree. When he looked again the figure was gone. His imagination? Was it...? Could it be...?

Damn...there he was!

Elymas stood on a slight hill abutting the tarmac road, leaning against the trunk of a tree. As Spendler ran past him the demon lifted his right arm and pointed a slender finger at the parapsychologist.

"Now...!" the demon said simply, knowing Spendler couldn't hear him.

Spendler saw him. Yes. It was Elymas who was pointing directly at him.

"Goddamn!" Spendler swore, stopping in his tracks. He turned and faced the demon.

Suddenly, he was no longer on solid ground.

The tarmac beneath him dissolved...from solid matter to liquid. Spendler sank into a churning pool of water. He sunk in over his head and was suddenly treading water. He broke to the surface, gasping for air. There were waves, like powerful white water rapids, slapped at his body, tossing about.

He was suddenly fighting for his life.

Again he broke the surface and took air into his starved lungs. He saw people all around him still moving on solid ground, all oblivious to his plight.

The turbulent water pulled him under. He struggled to survive. His right arm jutted out before him as he reached upward toward lifesaving air. His projected arm reached out and landed on a solid surface. Spendler strained, lifting his body with his right arm until he was able to get the other arm to the surface. Then he employed all the strength he could muster and pulled himself up out of the water. He felled gasping to the hard tarmac surface.

Passersby stopped and gaped at the strange scene before them. A man had apparently slipped on a small mysterious puddle of water and had fallen to the rock-hard surface of the boulevard. Although there was no water to be seen anywhere other than the small puddle he was creating by his dripping clothing, he was totally soaked.

Spendler got to his feet as a small group of people gathered around him. He looked to the trees where he thought he had seen Elymas. And there he was, standing by the tree. The demon in black raised his right hand to his brow, tipped it to Spendler and said, loud enough to be heard, one word..."POOF!"

He smiled and disappeared into the trees.

An illusion; a trick of the mind?

* * *

Although he must return to the abyss, to the dark world, he knew there would be another time, another day of light. There had been so many lives, so many times. There would be another.

Elymas did not hate the dark. He belonged to it. He resigned himself to the inevitability that he could spend eternity without the light. There would always be the prospect that he would be granted over the centuries to come, to bring evil once more into the light.

Oh well, he, the lover of clichés, thought...winning isn't everything...when at first you don't succeed...a bird in the hand...good things come to those...all that glitters...those who choose to run away will live to fight another day...

THE END

Elymas, the demon,
continues his onslaught of death in
SLAIN
the next novel in the *Trilogy of Evil*